THE NEW SPICE BOX

THE NEW SPICE BOX
CANADIAN JEWISH WRITING · VOLUME I

EDITED BY RUTH PANOFSKY

NEW JEWISH PRESS

FIRST EDITION

Copyright © 2017 The New Jewish Press

Introduction copyright © 2017 Ruth Panofsky
Permission acknowledgements for each section begin on page 251.

This edition published in 2017 by
New Jewish Press
Anne Tanenbaum Centre for Jewish Studies
University of Toronto
170 St. George Street, Room 218
Toronto, Ontario M5R 2M8
www.newjewishpress.ca

Cover and book design by Mark Goldstein

LIBRARY AND ARCHIVES CANADA CATALOGUING IN PUBLICATION

The new spice box: Canadian Jewish writing. Volume 1 / edited by Ruth Panofsky.

Includes bibliographical references.
Issued also in electronic format.
ISBN 978-1-988326-02-3 (softcover).—ISBN 978-1-988326-03-0 (HTML)

1. Canadian literature (English)—Jewish authors. 2. Canadian literature (English)—21st century. 3. Jews—Canada—Literary collections. I. Panofsky, Ruth, editor

PS8235.J4N49 2017   C810.8'08924   C2017-901148-0
                                                  C2017-901149-9

MIX
Paper from
responsible sources
FSC® C004191

PRINTED IN CANADA

CONTENTS

Editor's Introduction   vii

PART ONE: VOICE

Helen Weinzweig, "My Mother's Luck"   3
Shulamis Yelin, "Shekspir Was Jewis"   17
Sharon Nelson, "The Liberation"   23
S. Weilbach, "The Linoleum-Floored Room"   25
Libby Scheier, "Cut Flowers"   41
Seymour Mayne, "The Story of My Aunt's Comforter"   45
Ron Charach, "One Laughing Uncle"   51
Matt Cohen, "Trotsky's First Confessions"   53
David Solway, "Acid Blues"   67
J. J. Steinfeld, "The Idea of Assassination, Toronto, 1973"   69
Karen Shenfeld, "Theatre Doctor"   83
Karen Shenfeld, "My Father's Hands Spoke in Yiddish"   85
Kenneth Sherman, "Who Knows You Here?"   87

PART TWO: PLACE

David Solway, "After the Flood"   99
Nora Gold, "Yosepha"   101

Ronna Bloom, "Personal Effects"   115

Chava Rosenfarb, "Bergen Belsen Diary, 1945"   121

Goldie Morgentaler, "My Mother's Very Special Relationship"   137

Ron Charach, "The Only Man in the World His Size"   143

Judith Kalman, "The County of Birches"   147

Robyn Sarah, "After the Storm"   163

Gabriella Goliger, "Maladies of the Inner Ear"   165

Sharon Nelson, "On Tasting Any Fruit for the First Time in the Season"   179

Susan Glickman, "Between God and Evil"   181

Eva Hoffman, "Exile"   183

Malca Litovitz, "Provincial Olive"   189

Elana Wolff, "Snow Bolls"   191

Naïm Kattan, "Cities of Birth"   193

PART THREE: PRACTICE

Malca Litovitz, "The Welcoming"   203

Merle Nudelman, "The Sabbath Queen"   205

Ronna Bloom, "Yom Kippur, 1998"   207

Janis Rapoport, "Pesach 5735"   209

Gina Roitman, "Pesach en Provence"   211

Merle Nudelman, "The Finding"   217

Janis Rapoport, "From This Time Forth and Forever"   223

Libby Scheier, "Elat Chayyim"   225

Rhea Tregebov, "Some Notes on the Story of Esther"   227

Robyn Sarah, "Vidiu"   233

Susan Glickman, "(The) Others"   235

Elana Wolff, "Tikva"   237

Biographical Notes   239

Permissions   251

INTRODUCTION

Nearly four decades have passed since Lester & Orpen Dennys issued *The Spice Box: An Anthology of Jewish Canadian Writing* under its historic imprint in 1981. At the time, few such anthologies existed and *The Spice Box*, edited by Gerri Sinclair and Morris Wolfe, was hailed as a landmark collection. Among other works, it included English translations of Yiddish verse by J. I. Segal and Rokhl Korn, poems by A. M. Klein, Irving Layton, and Miriam Waddington, and prose by Ted Allan, Adele Wiseman, and Mordecai Richler, authors widely recognized for having brought Jewish writing to the fore in Canada. *The Spice Box* was instrumental in delineating the field of Canadian Jewish writing and soon became an estimable title for Lester & Orpen Dennys.

In 2015, when the Anne Tanenbaum Centre for Jewish Studies founded the New Jewish Press, co-publishers Malcolm Lester and Andrea Knight conceived *The New Spice Box*: an anthology that would pay homage to its predecessor—long out of print—that would bring together distinctive contemporary voices and serve as an enduring record for future readers and writers.

As Rebecca Margolis noted in her 2015 overview of the subject, the "question of what constitutes Canadian Jewish literature" (444) has never been fully addressed.[1] Historically, Jewish writing lacked the Canadian equivalents of New York intellectuals Lionel Trilling, Alfred Kazin, Leslie Fiedler, and Irving Howe as interpretive guides, and it faced the further challenges of a dispersed population over a vast geography and a small reading public. Scholarly interest has intensified since the mid-twentieth century, resulting in monographs that study the work of key writers, as well as biographies of poets A. M. Klein, Irving Layton, and Leonard Cohen, and novelist Mordecai Richler.[2] The broader contours of Canadian Jewish literature, however, still await investigation. Perhaps a more comprehensive probing of literary output will emerge out of the recent rise of Canadian Jewish Studies as an academic discipline.

For the writer, it has never been easy to articulate how it feels to be either Canadian or Jewish, identities often regarded as marginal by the wider world. Further, any notion of Canadian Jewish identity—individual and collective, personal and cultural—has forever been rooted in transnational and transcultural experience. It is fitting, then, that critic Norman Ravvin reads Canadian Jewish literature as a "tradition characterized by disjuncture" (616)[3] in breaking away from the locations, cultures, and religious practices of a largely European past *and* remaining separate from the anglophone, francophone, and allophone constituencies of the Canadian present.

All literature of the Jewish diaspora—that of Britain and the United States, Australia, as well as Canada—emerged from the disruptive experiences of exile, immigration, and settlement. Thus, it is understandable that contemporary writers are especially attuned to global shifts that continue to affect demographics and politics, cultures and economies. These new variations in writerly perspective generate even more challenging questions, such as those framed by Margolis herself: "What makes literature Jewish and Canadian? Is it enough for a writer to be of Jewish and Canadian origins or to have a Jewish identity and at one point to have called Canada home? Does a writer need to be writing on Jewish themes and in a Canadian setting?" (Margolis 444).

Rather than proffer answers to these exceedingly slippery questions, I prefer instead to embrace their open-endedness and to show, through this anthology, that there are, indeed, innumerable ways in which literature is both Jewish and Canadian in orientation, multiple ways in which writers identify as Jewish and Canadian, and countless ways in which Jewish Canadian experience is written into literature. In the pages that follow, readers will find original and varied responses to the intersectional complexities of cultural and national identity that ground this project.

Since each anthology has its own focus and unique parameters, my first task as editor of *The New Spice Box* was to develop a suitable approach to a singular project. The methodologies adopted by previous anthologizers of Canadian Jewish Literature—Miriam Waddington, Norman Ravvin, and Michael Greenstein, for example[4]—served as useful reference, but the dual responsibility of making editorial choices and establishing a rationale for this specific enterprise was mine alone. Much of the effort informing such work took place behind the scenes: in first surveying the field, then reading, interpreting, and selecting material, and finally assembling a collection. In the end, if that labour remains largely invisible to the reader, then I will have succeeded in melding praxis and presentation.

To produce this selection of Canadian Jewish writing, I read widely and deeply across the genres of poetry, short fiction, and creative nonfiction published from 1980 onward. I also attended to earlier work that did not find its way into the first iteration of *The Spice Box*. Eventually, I amassed so much excellent material that it became clear one volume could not properly capture the range and calibre of work I had chosen to represent contemporary Canadian Jewish writing. Happily, the publishers agreed and we settled on the publication of an extensive, two-volume edition. Thus, presented here is volume one of *The New Spice Box*, with volume two to follow.

This expansive anthology gave rise to particular challenges, however. Throughout the project I grappled with two essential questions: how to organize diverse materials across two individual but linked volumes, and where to divide the volumes. I sought to resolve these difficulties by adhering to a set of editorial principles, clear but flexible, that directed my work on this collection. A desire to uncover the twin touchstones of original expression and writerly craft, and to balance the representation of genres, styles, and authorial perspectives, underwrote my editorial deliberations.

In selecting material for this project I was guided first by its title, with its emphasis on newness. *The New Spice Box* showcases work that is fresh and relevant, profound and lasting—problematic as it may be to assign such literary merit. Although much of the writing is recent, some of it is historic, such as that of Shulamis Yelin and Chava Rosenfarb, for example, whose prose appears in volume one. In addition, this anthology does not replicate content included in *The Spice Box*, but it does feature new stories by Helen Weinzweig, Matt Cohen, and Seymour Mayne, writers represented in the 1981 collection.

Although both volumes of *The New Spice Box* reproduce extracts from several works of creative non-fiction, I have refrained from including excerpts from novels. The decision to omit excerpts—I do not believe they best represent an author's work—means that novelists, such as Lilian Nattel and Nancy Richler, for instance, are absent from this anthology. Also missing are others who treat Jewish subject matter but, for a variety of reasons, choose not to self-identify as Jewish writers. Only two prose works appear in English translation. In this volume, Chava Rosenfarb's "Bergen Belsen Diary, 1945" was originally published in Yiddish in 1948, and Naïm Kattan's tale "Cities of Birth," published in English in 2005, was conceived in French. The date of first journal or book publication always follows each selection.

Birthdates are a practical means of structuring an otherwise sprawling anthology that spans generations. Thus, volume one includes work by authors born between 1913 and 1961, while volume two presents the work of authors born between 1946 and 1986. A wish to produce two volumes of near-equal length accounts for the overlap in birthdates.

Diversity of literary expression is born of the many places Jews originate. Volume one features work about the Holocaust by writers who immigrated to Canada from Europe, specifically Germany, Hungary, Italy, and Poland. Naïm Kattan, who was born in Baghdad and educated in Paris, eventually settled in Montreal and worked in Ottawa at the Canada Council for the Arts for nearly twenty-five years. A number of authors were born in the United States—in Baltimore and Brooklyn, for example. Locally born writers hail from northern Quebec, Hamilton, Kingston, and Saskatoon, in addition to Montreal, Toronto, and Winnipeg, the traditional centres of Jewish life in Canada. In volume two, the geographical borders expand even farther to include authors born in Latvia, Scotland, and Israel, as well as Calgary.

Invariably, place of residence, like place of origin, animates an author's work. Jewish writers have always known the rural and urban spaces of Canada, and the authors represented in volume one are no exception. They write from one end of the country to the other: from Charlottetown, Prince Edward Island, Saint-Colomban, Quebec, and Gananoque, Ontario to Lethbridge, Alberta and Vancouver, British Columbia. Krakow-born Eva Hoffman spent her adolescence in Vancouver, resided for many years in New York, and now lives and writes in London, England. In volume two, writers are spread further west in Canada, from Calgary to Coquitlam, Victoria, and farther to Gabriola Island. Others reside over the New York border, in Brooklyn, Clinton, and Plattsburgh.

Across this anthology, all writers—no matter where they were born or raised, have lived or travelled—identify as Jewish, either through cultural or/and religious affiliation, and have direct links to Canada. In their work, they address Jewish subjects—some do so more obliquely than others—by treating historic events, probing their cultural inheritance, scrutinizing gender roles and sexuality, observing or critiquing religious custom. In many instances, their writing is explicitly Canadian in either setting or focus; in others, it is far less so.

The features of "difference and change" (Ravvin 616) that define Canadian Jewish writing, as observed by Ravvin, are borne out by this collection. Here, subject matter, literary perspective, and style range widely to reflect the variation and ingenuity that have come to characterize Jewish writing in Canada. Individual pieces, for example, recall youthful memories of reading Shakespeare in Yiddish translation, picture a father's emphatic hands at the moment of death, conjure the spectre of Leon Trotsky, and evoke the haunting past of a Berlin childhood and youth. Narrators include a favourite nephew of a loving aunt, a newly liberated survivor in the throes of grief, a perpetual exile who imaginatively traverses the cities of Baghdad, Paris, and Montreal, and a child of survivors who hosts a seder in Provence. Stylistically, the writing is mixed: comic and tragic, realistic and imagistic, expressionistic and surreal. In an attempt to stay true to its eclecticism—which Margolis celebrates as the "new diversity of voices and the struggle for new identities" (445)—and divergent moral attitudes, poetry, short stories, and creative non-fiction appear together under the thematic headings of voice, place, and practice that shape this collection.

Part one focuses on voice, which refers broadly to the artistic foregrounding of language and idiom to establish identity. Although each piece in this anthology appears in English, the language is often inflected by the lilt and syntax of Yiddish. The effect is to summon a formative Eastern European past that either will not or cannot be relinquished on Canadian soil. For so many writers in this collection, Jewish identity becomes visceral and corporeal through the expressive and embodied use of the English language.

Enter Lily, the indomitable protagonist of Helen Weinzweig's story "My Mother's Luck," and her unremitting tale of hardship. Lily manages to survive a miserable childhood, youth, and marriage in Poland. Driven by will, impelled by a sense of justice, and graced with an innate intelligence, she eventually divorces her husband and immigrates to Canada. Eschewing further subservience to men, she becomes a single mother to her daughter, Esther, whom she raises under hardscrabble conditions in Toronto's Kensington Market neighbourhood. Lily is an unapologetic, embattled figure with a desire for freedom and a determination to thrive. Her inimitable voice presides over the whole of this volume: a collection of prose and poetry that reconstructs the historic past as it moves fitfully toward a present and future located, however uneasily, in the urban centres and rural spaces of Canada.

In part two, the governing idea of place is used conceptually and acquires multiple meanings. Literally, place denotes geography. Adapting to the environment of Canada can confer a sense of continuity and stability through connection with the past, appreciation for the present, and belief in the future. Lack of adjustment, however, may lead to a heightened sense of disruption and isolation. Figuratively, place also refers variously to historic events and cultural memory, to the lived experience of immigration and settlement, to persistent feelings of exile and marginalization.

This collection, like *The Spice Box* of 1981, necessarily invokes current ideas about nation and culture to further its larger project of locating the spatial and ideological parameters of contemporary Canadian Jewish writing. Many authors included in the earlier anthology, for example, were influenced by the prevailing view of national and cultural identities as determinately confluent. In contrast, writers in *The New Spice Box* often explore their cultural inheritance by referencing an historic past generally not rooted in Canada.

For Eva Hoffman, for example, Vancouver of the 1950s is the physical and metaphorical site of her "primal scream" of "birth into the New World." Vancouver does not feel welcoming to the dejected adolescent, who forcibly accompanies her survivor parents from Krakow, Poland to Canada's west coast. Like so many immigrants, Hoffman's parents seek freedom from oppression and new opportunities for themselves and their two daughters. Hoffman, however, was content in Krakow and is unsettled by the newness of Vancouver. She abhors its bland food and lack of culture, dearth of old buildings, suburban homes surrounded by pristine gardens, and backdrop of forbidding mountains. More significantly, Vancouver neither sparks nor encourages her intellect. She leaves as soon as she can, escaping to Texas on a university scholarship.

Hoffman's hostility toward Vancouver renders the city as a liminal frontier that is still being settled. Here, though she feels ungrounded, her aspirations for the future are nonetheless kindled and nurtured in the unscripted cityscape, where anything is possible for the newcomer. Thus, in preparing Hoffman for her inevitable departure, Vancouver proves to be an invaluable stop on her trajectory to becoming a future writer and intellectual.

Hoffman's view of Canada as too new a country to ever become home to the cultivated European Jew may be extreme, although some of her discomfort is spread across this collection. Even as a much maligned, temporary location, however, the country holds out the promise of freedom—a promise that consistently undergirds all excruciating and exhilarating experiences of Canada found in this anthology. Thus, today's Jewish writing inscribes a Canadian territory that may lack coherence—it is at once a place of loathing and fear, repose and safety—but is always richly imagined.

The works included in part three, entitled practice, emphasize ritual and/or tradition. At the core of this section is prayer, both as ceremony and idea. Here, the Sabbath is observed as the holiest day of the week, while Passover, which commemorates an historic passage to freedom, is celebrated as a holiday that continues to give structure and meaning to Jewish life. Several poems educe the pain of losing a loved one and the comfort that comes from observing the rituals of lamentation: in reciting the mourner's kaddish—the prayer for the dead—and sitting shiva—the week-long mourning period following the death of an immediate family member. In praising the spirit of love, the beauty of nature, and the redemptive power of poetry, and hoping for the well-being of children, other poems read as secular prayers.

"Some Notes on the Story of Esther," Rhea Tregebov's essay in which she describes her coming of age as a Jewish female writer, reads as a personal manifesto. Here, Tregebov admits that she once produced a performance piece, which juxtaposed her own verse with the images and words of her spouse's elderly Russian Jewish grandmother, to counter "the feeling of being invisible." In fact, once she recognized that she had been denying her core identity, Tregebov determined to make visible, through her writing, her "Western [Canadian] roots, my un-bourgeois, left-wing background, my Jewishness"—in other words, her self. This act of publicly unveiling one's authentic self through writing is itself akin to Jewish prayer: a communal offering that is deeply felt and profoundly personal.

As readers will undoubtedly note, many pieces traverse the classifications of voice, place, and practice that shape this anthology. In fact, the headings are intended as readerly guides through a collection that shows contemporary Canadian Jewish writing to be reflective—as it looks back on the past and reads it anew—and open—as it partakes fully of the present moment and casts outward to the future, to further investigation of the ever-evolving Canadian and Jewish identities. For if there is one thing shared among the assembled authors, it is their sense of freedom to write as Jews. That most regard their freedom as a right affirms the degree to which they are also Canadian.

∞

I wish to acknowledge the support of my publishers Andrea Knight and Malcolm Lester, whose vision for this project matched my own. I also owe a special thanks to the indefatigable Kathryn Stagg for invaluable research assistance.

WORKS CITED

Margolis, Rebecca. "Across the Border: Canadian Jewish Writing." *The Cambridge History of American Jewish Literature*. Ed. Hana Wirth-Nesher. Cambridge: Cambridge University Press, 2015. 432–46.

Ravvin, Norman. "You Say You've OD'd on Leonard Cohen: Canadian Jewish Writing and the Mainstream." *The Oxford Handbook of Canadian Literature*. Ed. Cynthia Sugars. New York: Oxford University Press, 2016. 602–18.

NOTES

1 See Rebecca Margolis, "Across the Border: Canadian Jewish Writing," in *The Cambridge History of American Jewish Literature*, ed. Hana Wirth-Nesher (Cambridge: Cambridge University Press, 2015), 432–46.

2 See, for example, Michael Greenstein, *Third Solitudes: Tradition and Discontinuity in Jewish-Canadian Literature* (Montreal/Kingston: McGill-Queen's University Press, 1989); Andrew Stubbs, *Myth, Origins, Magic: A Study of Form in Eli Mandel's Writing* (Winnipeg: Turnstone Press, 1993); Norman Ravvin, *A House of Words: Jewish Writing, Identity and Memory* (Montreal/Kingston: McGill-Queen's University Press, 1997); Ruth Panofsky, *The Force of Vocation: The Literary Career of Adele Wiseman* (Winnipeg: University of Manitoba Press, 2006); Zailig Pollock, *A. M. Klein: The Story of the Poet* (Toronto: University of Toronto Press, 1994); Elspeth Cameron, *Irving Layton: A Portrait* (Toronto: Stoddart, 1985); Ira B. Nadel, *Various Positions: A Life of Leonard Cohen* (Toronto: Random House of Canada, 1996); and Charles Foran, *Mordecai: The Life and Times* (Toronto: Knopf Canada, 2010).

3 See Norman Ravvin, "You Say You've OD'd on Leonard Cohen: Canadian Jewish Writing and the Mainstream," in *The Oxford Handbook of Canadian Literature*, ed. Cynthia Sugars (New York: Oxford University Press, 2016), 602–18.

4 See Miriam Waddington, ed., *Canadian Jewish Short Stories* (Toronto: Oxford University Press, 1990); Norman Ravvin, ed., *Not Quite Mainstream: Canadian Jewish Short Stories* (Calgary: Red Deer Press, 2001); and Michael Greenstein, ed., *Contemporary Jewish Writing in Canada: An Anthology*, Jewish Writing in the Contemporary World (Lincoln: University of Nebraska Press, 2004).

PART I · VOICE

Helen Weinzweig, "My Mother's Luck"

July 6, 1931

I have decided, my mother said, to go with you to New York to see you off. Your boat sails a week from tomorrow. In a week you will be gone; who knows if we will ever see each other again. No, no, stop it. I can't stand anyone slobbering over me. *Now* what are you crying for? I thought you wanted to go to your father. I'm only trying to do what's best for you. You should be happy, going to Europe, to Germany, travelling in style, like a tourist. Not the way we came to this country, eh? Steerage, like cattle. Everything on that boat smelled and tasted of oily ropes. Hardly what you would call a pleasure trip. But then, how would I recognize pleasure—how would I know what there is in this world that gives happiness—when I have been working since I was nine years old. My feet, my poor feet. I can't remember when my feet didn't hurt. Get me the white basin, no, the deep one, from under the sink. And the kettle: the water should be hot enough. Take a chair, sit down. No, I'll fill it myself. We will have a talk while I'm soaking my feet. I suppose we should have a talk before you go. I know, I know; you don't have to remind me; can I help it, the long hours; you think I like to work so hard? It's not only you I have no time for: I don't have time to breathe, to live. I said, sit down! What do you care about your silly girlfriends?

They'll find someone else to waste their time with. Jennie? Write her a letter. Ah, that feels better. My poor feet. I'm looking forward to sitting on the train. They told me it takes fourteen hours from Toronto to New York. Just think, I will be off my feet for a whole day.

Why do you look so miserable? I just don't understand you: first you drive me crazy to go to your father and now you sit like at a funeral. Tell you what: in New York we will have a little party before your boat sails. We'll go to a big, fancy restaurant. Sam and me and you. Yes. You heard right. Sam. Are you deaf or don't you understand Yiddish any more? I said, Sam is coming with us. You might as well know: he is moving in with me next week. Your room. No use leaving it empty. There you go again, telling me what I should do. No one tells me what to do. I will stay alone until the Messiah comes, rather than live with another woman. I despise women: they are false and jealous. With a man you know where you're at: you either get along or you don't. They are not hypocrites like women. Marry Sam? What for? To give satisfaction to the old *yentes*, the gossips? I will never marry again: three times was plenty. Get a little hot water from the kettle. Ah, that's better. Now turn low the gas.

So, tell me, have you got your underwear and stockings clean for the trip? Your shoes need a good polish. You don't need everything new. Let your father buy you something, I've supported you for sixteen years, that's long enough. God knows as He is my witness I can do no more. That's what I told your teacher when she came to see me in the winter. She looked around the flat as if fish was rotting under her nose. I couldn't wait for her to leave, that dried up old maid. I told her, I'm an ignorant woman, I'll let you educated people figure out what to do with my daughter. Just one thing you should remember, Esther, it was your idea, not mine, that you should get in touch with your father. Whatever happens, you will not be able to blame me. Of course, you can come back if you want. You have a return ticket. You can thank Sam for that. He said I should let you make up your own mind if you want to live with your father. You don't deserve Sam's consideration. The way you treat him: not talking to him when he greets you on his Sunday visits. He—what? Watch that tongue of yours. I can still give you a good licking if I have to. The smell of sweat is the smell of honest work. I don't like it either, but I've had enough from the educated ones, like your father, who know everything except how to raise a sweat. They all talked a lot, but I could never find out what they wanted from me. I cooked and cleaned and went to work. I tried to please the customers all day and then I was supposed to please them at night.

Like that talmudist, Avrom, you remember him—well, perhaps you were too young. One night I came home from work, tired and hungry, and there he was, exactly where I had left him at eight o'clock in the morning, at the kitchen table. In twelve hours nothing had changed, except there were more books and more dirty plates on the table. — And where, I asked him, am I supposed to eat? He didn't even look up. He raised a white hand. —What means the hand in the air? You think maybe this is Poland and you are the privileged scholar, the permanent guest at my table? In America everybody works who wants to eat. With my arm, like with a broom, I swept clear the table. I waited he should say something, maybe he would realize and say he was sorry he forgot about me, but all he did was look at me like he didn't know who I was. Then he bent down and picked up the books one by one, so slow you would think every book weighed a ton. His face got red like his hair, he was breathing so noisy I thought he was going to bust. Just the books, not the dishes, he picked up. He went into the bedroom and closed the door. All I asked was a little consideration, and for that he didn't talk to me for a week.

So what's the difference to me whether they know enough to take a bath. Sam will learn. He needs a nice home. He's a good man, he works hard, a presser in a factory. So maybe he will be tired at night. And he can pay his own way to New York. A working man has at least his union to see he gets a decent wage. What protection has a scholar got? He leans on the whole world and the world pushes him away. Not that I care about money. I am decent with a man, not taking from him every cent, like their greedy wives. Last week Sam handed me his sealed pay envelope. —Here, he said, take out for New York. Buy yourself a nice coat. Naturally, I wouldn't take his money. So long as he pays the rent, a little for the food, it will be enough. If I was to take his money, next thing he will be telling me what I should do. You can be sure the minute he tries to boss me, out he goes, like the others.

Your stepfather, the first one, made that mistake. Max. Tall, the best-looking man I ever knew. He worked all night in a bakery and came home seven o'clock in the morning smelling like fresh bread. You two got along well. He made you lunch every day and filled your pockets with bagels for your class. Every Saturday he took you to the show. Remember? When I came home from the store Saturday night, which was his night off, he was ready to step out. I could only soak my tired feet. One day he got a raise. —Lily, he said, you can stop work. Sell the store. Stay home and look after Esther and me. I said, —and suppose you lost your job, what will become of us in this Depression? And suppose your boss gives your job to his brother who came last night from Poland? Max thought we should take a chance. —Maybe someday I will have my own bakery, he said, I want you should stay home like a normal wife. He was not very intelligent: he couldn't get it into his head we would have no security without my beauty parlor. After that, Max was not the same. He talked to me as if I was his servant. —You, he would call me, instead of my name; you, don't make me nothing to eat. I have a bad stomach. —See a doctor. —A doctor won't help. I choke on your meat. He came and went in his work clothes, so that there was flour dust on the furniture. I even paid for the lawyer to get the divorce, just to get rid of him.

What are you sitting like a lump for? Get me a little hot water in the basin. Careful, slow; do you want to burn me! You are such a *shlima-zel!* Wipe it up. Are you blind as well? There, over there, by the stove. Ah, that feels good. I hope you will have it easier than me. Maybe your father can give you the education your teacher said you should have. All I have from life is sore feet. My poor feet, look how calloused and shapeless they have become. Once I had such fine hands and feet. The ankles, they used to be so thin. When I was young they said I had the hands and feet of an aristocrat. If you're really so smart as they say you are, you won't have to slave like me. You should have a life like the aristocrats in Europe used to have before the Revolution. I hope you will have a name everyone respects. What a life those fine ladies of Europe used to have: they got married and lived free as birds. Like George Sand or Madame de Stael. Surprised you, eh? I know more than you think. In the papers I recognize names sometimes I first hear in Zurich: Freud, Einstein, Picasso. What's the matter? See, I did learn something from your father. He may tell you I was stupid, he used to tell me I was an ignorant ghetto girl.

Your father taught me to read and write in German. He tried to educate me. So did Isaac. I could always tell there was going to be trouble when they said—Lily, try and understand.... And then I'd get a lecture. You would think that after your father I would not again be trapped by fine words. Yet I could not resist a man with a soft voice and clean fingernails. They gave me such fine compliments: how my eyes are the colour of violets; my skin so fair and delicate; how charming my smile; and they quote poetry to add to the feeling. I jump at fine words like a child at candy. Each time I think, this time it will be different, but every man is your father all over again, in a fresh disguise. Talk. Talk. How could they talk. If it wasn't anarchism, it was socialism; if it wasn't atheism, it was religious fanaticism; if it wasn't Moses, it was Marx. Sometimes I wanted to talk, too. Things weren't that easy for me, and I wanted to tell someone about my troubles. They listened for a minute and got a funny look on the face like I remember from the idiot in my village. Once I said to Isaac —That awful Mrs. Silberman. Three bottles of dye I had to use on her hair, it's so thick and long. Naturally, I charged her extra. You should have heard her scream blue murder over the fifty cents. —Where you live up the hill, I told her, they would charge you double. I don't make profit on the dye. I called her a cheapskate. Anyway, it was her husband's money not her own she was fighting over. She

called me a low-class low-life. I told her never to come back. Isaac didn't
say I did right to throw her out. He explained to me about the capitalist class, and I said, —Don't give me the manifesto. You didn't see her
ugly expression, I told him. And he said —Her actions were governed
by the class struggle: she is the exploiter and you are the exploited. It
was nothing against you personally, Lily. —But I'm the one she tried to
cheat; I'm the one she cursed, may she rot in hell. —That's an ignorant
approach to a classical social problem, Isaac explained —now, Lily, try
and understand.... Still, Isaac and me got along the best. He had consideration. He used to read to me while I was cooking late at night for
the next day. On Sundays, we did the laundry together. He couldn't
find a job, so he helped me what he could. I found little things for him
to do, so he wouldn't feel useless. In the winter he carried out the ashes
from the furnace from the store. He fixed the chairs and painted behind the shampoo sink. He was very artistic, the way he fixed up the
windows with pictures and coloured paper. He made all my signs, like
the "Specials" for the permanents. I was satisfied. Good or bad, nothing lasts forever.

Isaac decided to go into business for himself. Nobody can say I
stopped him. I gave him the money to buy a stock of dry goods to ped-
dle on credit. He knew a lot of languages, but that didn't put money in
his pocket. He spoke Russian, the customers cried in Russian; he talked
in Ukrainian, they wept in Ukrainian; he sold towels in Yiddish, they
dried their eyes on his towels. They prayed for help on his carpets; they
lay sick between his sheets. How could he take their last cent, he asked
me. So he gave everything away. Then he wanted more money for new
stock. —I'm not the welfare department, I told him. The way he let people make a sucker out of him, I lost my respect. Then why did I marry
him? God knows I didn't want to get married again: twice was enough.
The government ordered me to get married.

Oh don't look so innocent. You think I don't know how all that
court business started? It was you. You, with your long face and wet
eyes, whining at other people's doors, like a dog, as if I didn't feed you

right. I can imagine—Come in, come, Esther, sit down and have a piece
of cake and tell me all about that terrible mother of yours. Women!
Slaves, that's what they are, every one of them; yet if another woman tries to live her own life, they scream blue murder. I can see them,
spending their empty nights talking about me, how I live with a man,
not married. The Children's Aid wouldn't tell who snitched on me.
Miss Graham, the social worker, was very nice, but she wouldn't say
either. —I don't like to do this, she said, having to investigate reports
from neighbours. Your daughter is thirteen years old and is paying a
price in the community because her mother lives in sin. I said, —I am a
decent, hard-working woman. See, my rooms are clean, look, my icebox is full with fruit and milk, Esther is dressed clean, she never miss-
es a day of school. A marriage licence does not make a better wife or
mother. She agreed with me, but there was nothing she could do. I had
to marry Isaac or they would take away my daughter. I said, —This is
a free country, I'll do what I want. So they summonsed me to Family
Court. —Your daughter, the judge said, needs a proper home. I told
him, —Judge, Esther has a good home. She has a piano in her room and
I pay for lessons. You should hear how nice she plays. —That is not the
issue: it is a question of morality. —Judge, I said, I know all about mor-
als and marriage. And what I don't know, the customers tell me. You
should hear the stories. Is it moral, I asked him, for a woman to have
to sleep with a man she hates? Is it moral for a man to have to support
a woman whose face he can't look at? —Come, come, he said, these
are not questions for this court to answer. We are here to administer
the law. If you do not marry the man you are living with, we will take
the child and place her with a decent family. Go fight city hall. So we
took out the licence and got married. I have bad luck. Isaac decided to
write a book on the trade union movement in the textile industry. He
stopped peddling: he stopped helping me. He talked of nothing but
the masses: ate and slept the masses. So I sent him to the masses: let
them look after him. Just shows how much the law knows what's best.

Love? Of course I loved him. For what other reason would I bother with a man if I didn't love him! I have bad luck, that's all. I attract weak men. Each time I think, aha, this one is different. It always begins with the compliments; it always ends with the silence. After he has been made comfortable in my bed, his underwear in my drawer, his favourite food in the icebox, he settles down. I rush home from the store, thinking he is waiting for me. But no. He doesn't look up from the paper. He sits. I ask, —Do you want fish or herring for an appetizer? He says to the paper, —It doesn't matter. We eat. He sits. All I ask is a little consideration for all I do for them. Maybe once a week I would like to have a change. I wouldn't mind to pay for a show. I'm not ashamed to go up to the cashier and buy two tickets. Most women would make a fuss about that, but not me—I'm a good sport. I'm not one of your bourgeois women. That was your father's favourite word. Bourgeois. He said the bourgeois woman sold her soul for *kinder, kuchen,* and *kirche.* See, I even remember a little German. That means—oh, excuse me! You know what the words mean—I forgot you are the clever one....

Hand me the towel. No, the one I use for the feet, the torn one. You're like a stranger around here, having to be told everything. I'll make a cup of tea. You can stay up a little later tonight: I feel like talking. No, sit. I'll make the tea, then you won't get in my way. What do you want with the tea—a piece of honey cake, maybe?

You and your father will get along, you're both so clever. Words, he had words for everything. No matter what the trouble was, he talked his way out of it. If there was no money for meat, he became a vegetarian, talking all the time how healthy fruits and nuts are; if he couldn't pay the rent, he spent hours complimenting the landlady on her beauty and charm, although she was fat and hairy; if I thought I was pregnant again, he talked about the joys of motherhood. When I cried day and night what would become of us, he talked the hospital into doing an abortion. But mouth work brings no food to the table. How was I to know that, young and inexperienced as I was? When I got married, I wasn't much older than you are now. I was barely seventeen when your father came home to Radom on a visit from the university in Zurich. It was before the war, in 1911. I was only a child when he fell in love with me. Yet, it can hardly be said I was ever a child: I was put to work at nine, gluing paper bags. At fourteen, I was apprenticed to a wigmaker. Every day, as I bent over the wooden form of a head, my boss would stand and stroke my hair, saying when I marry and have my hair shorn, he would give me a *sheitel* for a wedding present if I promise to sell him my hair for the wigs. My hair was beautiful, thick and silky, and a lovely auburn shade. I lasted three months, because his wife got jealous and dragged me back to my father by my silky hair. My father decided I must have done something wrong and beat me with his leather belt. What was there for me to look forward to, except more work, more misery, and, if I was lucky, marriage to a butcher's son, with red hands? So you can imagine when your father began to court me, how could I resist? He had such fine manners, such an educated way of saying things, such soft hands, he was a man different from anyone I had ever met. He recited poetry by Goethe and Rilke, which he translated for me. He called me *"Blume,"* which means flower, from a poem that starts, *"Du bist wie eine Blume."* He didn't want a dowry: I wouldn't have to cut my hair. He was a modern man: his views caused a scandal. Your father wasn't much to look at—short and pale and poor teeth. You know that small plaster statue of Beethoven on my dresser? The one you hate to dust? That belonged to him. He imagined he looked like Beethoven—he had the same high, broad forehead and that angry look. Still, to me his pale, shaven face was very attractive compared to the bearded men of the town. So we were married by a rabbi and I went back with him to Switzerland. Four years later, just before you were born, we were married in the city hall in Zurich so you would be legal on the records.

Let me see, how old is he now? I'm thirty-eight, so he must be forty-eight. The *landsleit* say he never married again. I bet he never thought he'd ever see his daughter again. He won't be able to deny you: you're the spitting image. Pale like him. Same forehead, and the same red spots across when you get nervous. I'd give anything to be there when

you're both reading and pulling at your hair behind the right ear. You
certainly are your father's daughter. Even the way you sneaked around,
not telling me, writing to Poland, until you got his address in Munich. I
should have known you were up to something: you had the same look
of a thief as him when he went to his meetings.

Those meetings! An anarchist he was yet. The meetings were in
our small room. Every other word was "Revolution." Not just the Russian revolution, but art revolution, religious revolution, sex revolution.
They were nearly all young men and women from the university, students like your father. Since he was a good deal older than the rest, he
was the leader. They yelled a lot. At first I was frightened by the argu-
ments, until I realized that these intellectuals didn't have anything to
do with the things they fought about. It wasn't real people they knew,
just names; it wasn't what they themselves did that caused so much
disagreement—it was what other people somewhere else were doing.
Where I come from, I was used to real trouble, like sickness and starvation and the threat of pogroms. So I didn't pay too much attention
until the night we all had a big argument about Nora. First I should
tell you about the young women who came to these meetings. They
thought themselves the equal of the men, and the men treated them
like comrades. Not like in Poland, where every morning of their lives,
men thank God for not having been born a woman. In Zurich, the
young ladies wore dark mannish suits, had their hair shingled, and
smoked cigarettes. Beside them, I felt like a sack of potatoes.

This play, *A Doll's House*, shocked everybody. Before you were born,
your father sometimes took me to a play. For that, he found money. He
called the theatre food for the soul. All such money-wasters he called
his spiritual nourishment. I went anyway, because it was nice to sit in a
big warm theatre, in a soft seat, and watch the actors. Remind your father about the night we saw *A Doll's House*. About ten of us came back
to our room and talked until three in the morning about Nora. For the
first time, I was able to join in. I was the only one who sympathized
with the husband—he gave her everything, treated her like a little doll,

loved her like a pet. This is bad? So they have a little argument, so she says she must leave him and the children. Leave the children! Did you ever hear such a thing! —The servants know how to run the house better than I do, she tells her husband. —Servants! I said to myself, there's your answer—she had it too good. If she had to struggle like me for a piece of bread, she would have overlooked her husband's little fit. She should have cooked him a nice supper, given him a few compliments, and it would have all been *schmired* over, made smooth. Of course, I don't feel like that now, but that's what I thought the night I saw the play. The men agreed with me: it was stupid to leave a good life, even a bourgeois life, to slave for someone else as a seamstress. The women were disappointed in their comrades: couldn't these revolutionaries see that Nora was being exploited by her husband...? The men argued that she was responsible for bringing up her children and should not have left them to the mercy of servants: that motherhood was sacred in all societies. The women said Nora was an intelligent, sensitive human being and was right to refuse to be treated like a possession, like a piece of furniture. Nora had to leave to keep her dignity and her pride. Exactly, the men said, dignity and pride are bourgeois luxuries. In the new society... Back and forth the rest of the night.

All the next day, I could think of nothing but what Nora did. It never occurred to me that a woman leaves a man except if he beats her. From that time on, I began to change. I shingled my hair, I started to sit in the cafés and smoke. When I got pregnant again, I refused to go for an abortion. Four in three years was enough. I don't know why your father, with all his education, didn't know how to take care I shouldn't get in the family way. So you were born. Your father had to leave university and be a clerk in a shoe store. He hated the job: he hated me. You cried a lot. Nothing in your father's books explained why you cried so much. Then your father talked me into going back to work. They were glad to have me back at the beauty parlor. I was a good marceller. It was better to work than be stuck in a little room all day.

And the anarchist meetings started again. While everybody was making plans to blow up the world, I was busy running down the hall to the toilet to vomit. I was pregnant. Well, look who's back they said at the clinic, sign here, Lily. I hope you will have it easier than me. Your father should send you to college. Maybe being educated will help, although sometimes I wonder. I met educated women who never knew what to do with themselves. Once, I remember, I asked one of my customers, *Frau* Milner was her name, —And how was the march yesterday for getting the vote for women? —It was called off, I couldn't lead the march to the city hall, she said, I got my period, only it was a miscarriage and I was hemorrhaging and couldn't get out of bed. —So you think the world is going to stand still until we stop bleeding?

What finally happened? What do you mean, finally? Things don't happen all at once. You want a drama like in a play, a big fight, with one person wrong, one person right...? Nothing like that. I came back from the warm, clean hospital, where they were so kind to me, they looked after me like a child, I came back to a cold room, and dirty sheets, and our six dishes and two pots sticky with food. There wasn't a penny for the gas and I couldn't heat your milk. You cried, your father yelled he couldn't study. After going to university for four years, I couldn't understand why he still needed to study. I had to get up six in the morning to take you to the crèche at one end of the city and go to work at the other end. You wouldn't stop screaming, and I spanked you, and your father said I was stupid to take out my bad feelings on an innocent child. I sat down, beaten. In that moment I knew I was going to leave. There is a second, no longer than the blink of an eye, when husband and wife turn into strangers. They could pass in the street and not know each other. That's what happened that night.

How did we get here? A good question, but a long story. We've talked enough; I'm tired. What's the difference now? Well, all right. You can tell your father how I did it: I want him to know I was not so stupid. He never knew I was getting a divorce until it was all over and I was out of the country. One of my customers was a very beautiful girl. She had long hair which I used to dye a beautiful shade of red, then I marcelled it in deep lovely waves from top to bottom. She came every Monday morning, and every week she would show me new presents from her lover. She was the mistress of a famous judge in Zurich. Her secret was safe with me: our worlds were miles apart.

One day, instead of going to work, I took you and went to the Court House. You were four years old; the war was over. I wasn't sleeping with your father because I was afraid of getting pregnant; and he wasn't sleeping at home much. At the Court House I bothered a lot of people where is Judge Sutermeister; I found out where he was judging. You were very good that morning while we sat outside on a bench, waiting. People smiled at us and asked you your name, and found things in their purses or briefcases to give you—pencils, paper, bonbons, a small mirror. About twelve o'clock, when the doors opened and people came out, I stood in the doorway and watched where the judge went. He left through a door at the back. I went in with you, through the same door. He was sitting at a big desk, writing. Oh, he was an elegant gentleman, with grey hair. He looked very stern at me, and I almost ran away. I didn't wait for him to speak. I stood by his desk and told him my troubles, right away I said I wanted him to get me a divorce, and that I knew all about him and *Fräulein* Olga. He got up, he was so tall, and made such a big scene, like he was on stage; he was going to have me arrested. But I stood there, holding on to you and the desk. —And what will become of her if I go to jail? And what will happen to your career and your sweetheart if your wife finds out her money buys rings and pearls for your mistress? For the next six months, I kept on like usual. *Fräulein* Olga was the messenger for me and the judge. She didn't mind. She said it gave her something to do, asking me lawyer's questions, writing down my answers, bringing me papers to sign. One Monday morning, *Fräulein* Olga came with a large brown envelope holding my divorce papers. Inside also was a train ticket and some money. The judge wanted me to start a new life in America. I agreed. I remembered I had a cousin in Toronto. *Fräulein* Olga was very sad. —Who will do my hair? And she cried.

Two days later, I left our room with you. This time, we went straight to the train in Hamburg. We stayed near the station overnight. I bought underwear for us, a new sweater for me, and a nice little red coat for you. We took the boat for New York. A sailor gave you a navy blue sailor hat with the name of the boat, *George Washington*, in gold on a ribbon around the hat. You wore it day and night, on Ellis Island, on the train to Toronto. It looked nice with the blond curls. I could go on and on. The things that happened, what I went through.... It's one o'clock already! Let's go to bed. First, wash the cups. Wash them, I said. I can't stand a mess in the kitchen. Remember, never leave dirty dishes around. Show your father I brought you up right. Which reminds me: did you buy rolls like I told you? Good. Sam likes a fresh roll with lox for Sunday. Just think, in a week you will be on the ocean.... Go already. I'll turn out the light....

1989

Shulamis Yelin, "Shekspir Was Jewis"

The road home from Strathearn School seemed longer than usual that dull November afternoon. It was already after four o'clock and Mamma would be worried. But not half so worried as when I would have told her what had happened in school that afternoon.

No need to ask if Mamma was at home. Mamma had to rest a lot and we had to be good children and not aggravate her.

As I turned the doorknob I heard her voice.

"So late you're from school?"

"I had to help the teacher correct spelling books." Mamma and I considered this an honour.

"Nice," said Mamma. "You going to Shule now?"

"Yes, Mamma. But first I have to do my homework for Lerern Sherr."

"First eat something," Mamma offered. "The bread man brought fresh kimmel bread. Don't forget to shake up the milk or you'll take off all the cream."

"Don't worry, Mamma. I'll do it."

I entered the dining room and laid my books on the massive oak table. I was not at ease.

It was hard to stay after school with such turmoil in my heart, even to help the teacher. Now I had to hurry or I'd be late.

As I bit into the great buttered oval of crusty bread fragrant with Mamma's luscious plum jam, I was tense. Surely I couldn't break this news to Mamma. If only it had happened in the morning. Then I could have discussed it at noon with Papa when he came home for lunch; but it had happened in the afternoon, and he worked late every night in his tailor shop on Main Street.

The sideboard facing me held the secret of my distress. It was made of polished oak, like the round table and high-backed leatherseated chairs, its lower section a china cabinet with brass-knobbed leaded glass doors. Instead of holding our new set of porcelain dishes, our china cabinet held books. Papa, a self-taught man, loved books, and just as Mamma saved her pennies to pay Mr. Popper, the peddlar, fifty cents a week until the china was paid for, Papa spent his pin money on books. The books stood in two rows, one behind the other, in their colourful cloth bindings, some singly, others in sets of two or more. The newest acquisitions always had the place of honour up front.

"Books are teachers," Papa said, "and you have to give them a place of honour in your home."

Thus it was that I first became acquainted with the names of Tolstoy, Pushkin, Chekhov, Dostoievsky, and with our own Yiddish classicists: Mendele, Peretz, Sholem Aleichem, and—Shekspir.

The gold letters on the red cloth binding announced proudly in Yiddish: *Shylock—Der Koif man fun Venedig.* (Shylock, the Merchant of Venice) *fun Villiam Shekspir.* How was I to know that Shakespeare wasn't a Jew? Had I ever heard his name anywhere else than at home or in any language other than Yiddish?

So, when our Grade Four teacher had told us that afternoon in the English public school that she was going to read us "a tale from Shakespeare," I raised my hand.

"Please, Miss, we have him at home in the china cabinet."

"In the china cabinet?" she had repeated in amazement, her lovely British accent trailing into the halls of Strathearn School. "What?—I mean whom?"

"Shekspir!" I announced proudly.

"Do your parents read English?" she asked with interest.

"They don't have to. Shekspir writes in Yiddish. He's Jewish so he writes in Yiddish."

וויליאם שעקספּיער

William Shakespeare (or as the Yiddish under the picture says it: Villiam Shekspir)—the frontispiece from the all Yiddish edition of *Shakespeare's Famous Works* (3rd reprint) published by Druckerman in New York, 1912

Miss Cranshaw was aghast.

"Who told you this?" she asked.

"Nobody." I was mistress of the situation. "My father buys his books. We keep him in our new china cabinet where we keep all the books."

"In Yiddish?" Miss Cranshaw asked again. "You're sure it's Shakespeare?"

"Sure I'm sure! The book is about Shylock, a Jew who...."

"Of course!" Miss Cranshaw was relieved. "Shakespeare did write a book about a Jew called Shylock. But Shakespeare was an Englishman—perhaps the greatest Englishman who ever lived. And he wrote in English, more than three hundred years ago, in beautiful poetry. In English!"

The first page of the *Merchant of Venice* from the author's copy of *Shakespeare's Famous Works* (New York: Druckerman, 1912)

The children laughed. All but three of the thirty-six were Jews.

They became self-conscious. They laughed.

My eyes filled with tears. What was going on here? Why were they laughing? Surely they knew I was telling the truth!

"The whole book is in Yiddish!" I insisted.

"Well, Shylock was hardly a Jew to be proud of," said Miss Cranshaw coldly. "Why would your father want that book on his shelf?"

How could I break this news to Mamma? What could I tell her? If only Papa had been at home!

As I struggled with my Yiddish homework, I decided to spare her. I'd speak to my Jewish teacher. Surely she'd help me right this slander!

I ran all the way to Shule. I caught my teacher just as she was about to enter the classroom.

"Lerern Sherr," I gasped in Yiddish, "I must ask you something."

"Yes, Shulamis?" She called me by my Jewish name.

"I told my teacher in school today that Shekspir is Jewish and he writes in Yiddish...."

Lerern Sherr's pretty face suggested a smile.

"She says he is not a Jew! She says he's an Englishman and he lived more than three hundred years ago!" I trembled with indignation.

Miss Sherr put her arm around my shoulder.

"Don't cry!" she consoled me softly. "William Shakespeare *was* an Englishman." She spoke his name as it is spoken in English. "And he did write in English more than three hundred years ago."

"So why is he in our china cabinet in Yiddish?" I pleaded.

"Because Shakespeare was a great man with a great heart and a great talent," she answered gently. "He now belongs to the whole world. We read him in Yiddish because he is translated into Yiddish. And into many other languages. Because Jews and other people want to know what Shakespeare has to say."

"And Shylock—what's wrong with Shylock?" I sobbed. "She says we can't be proud of Shylock and my father shouldn't keep him on the shelf!"

"Come into the classroom, Shulamis. Come. We will talk about it in class." She ushered me through the open door.

Slowly, slowly the world spread out before me, and it would be a long time before I felt at home in the world outside my father's house.

1983

Sharon Nelson, "The Liberation"
for Sima Gelbart

We are here and we are lonely
like a winter of lost trees
like the severed hands of thieves
we have bled so much no blood is left
and we turn black with flies.

We survived:
our shaved heads
lifted
finally
to a winter sky.

I became
the oldest sister,
knew history, went
to the commandant, begged
a comb, a piece of soap.

His laughter
was raucous.
He saw
denuded head, naked bones:
What need had I
for soap or comb?

Even an animal tries
to keep itself clean.

1978

S. Weilbach, "The Linoleum-Floored Room"

When, at midnight, the *St. Louis* moved away from them and began her journey towards Hamburg, her home port, Lala was wide awake on the hard plank bed in the freighter's crowded hold. The other passengers pressed up the stair and through the hatch to watch the *St. Louis* go, and Lala went with her mother to join them. They stood on the unlit deck surrounded by the stink of engine oil, and Lala waved to the familiar, dimly seen line of stewards as they called their cheerful goodbyes across the black water. As their faces and the ship melted into silence, Lala could feel herself fading away with them. The self who remained was a seven-year-old who pressed her lips tight against fear, who walked with sober caution beside her mother's blind father, one hand poised to touch his arm when he might trip at a step or bump into a wall. This was the child who had seen the spurted blood of a suicide, who moved through her days with a hollow chest and an undiminished hunger for her missing Oma's voice.

In the dreamlike interval of the freighter's rough pitching and ploughing from the French port towards England, Lala's mind closed over much that had passed before. In her memory it is now a deep, grey, uninterrupted expanse, like a dead winter sea without waves or wind.

When they land it is morning, their first steps feel the earth sway underfoot. There are men at long wooden tables speaking foreign sounds, opening, closing trunks and cases.

Blind Opa rests his hand on her shoulder, not heavily, yet still its touch makes both her shoulders bend. And then to a train with prickling plush-covered seats, framed scenes on their compartment's walls, and houses, fields, streams moving smoothly past. Then a brown paper bag and cheese sandwiches with a peculiar vinegary sweet mayonnaise inside. Her father sits leaning into the corner, studying the sandwich, silent. Her mother divides another between herself and Opa. Sometimes the train rattles and clacks beneath them and a sooty smell blows in and out of the crack at the window-top. Near the end of their journey the window suddenly turns black, as if they have entered a cave. When they slide out of it there is a green bank almost close enough to touch. Then the grey, flat, monotonous mind-sea slips back into Lala's head and she sleeps, her sandwich uneaten.

∞

They are in one enormous room, chilly though now it's spring. The grey linoleum goes from wall to wall, marked with a murky once-yellow pattern reminding Lala of the vomit on the ship's corridor floor. One window with a thin, fly-spotted net curtain overlooks a brick wall. Between brief intervals of quiet a locomotive thunders along its length, shaking walls, curtain, the floor. Opa whispers his prayers seated on a wooden chair in the room's darkest corner. Near the window is a table covered with a once white, sour-smelling wax cloth. There are a few scratched wooden chairs. Her mother is hanging their clothes on the hooks along a wall. Several ramshackle folding-beds stand along another wall.

Someone knocks on their door and enters, bringing a warm meal in a cardboard box. Lala recognizes it is being offered with gestures of condescending pity. No conversation is possible with the English-speaking visitor, who wears a red cross on her sleeve and quickly departs again.

There is a drawer with steel cutlery and a small open cupboard with plates and mismatched cups. When they sit down to eat her father holds out his knife for her mother to see the food encrusted along its blade. Her mother gathers it all up and Lala watches her use a piece of soap, a stained dishtowel, and cold water to scrub each one. She sends Lala to fetch a clean hand towel from a suitcase in the corner with which to dry them.

Opa mutters a low-voiced blessing. By now the food is cold. Lala eats the bits of potato which taste agreeably like the ones she used to bring to their yard dog at home—sampling a few nibbles on the way. There is a thick greenish paste which her mother says must be peas, but Lala gags when she tries to swallow it. She cannot bring herself to touch the grey slice of fish with pointed bones showing here and there. No one notices because just then another train is surging past, and father glares with rage or fear, Lala cannot tell which, as the noise reverberates through the room, rattling the window glass, the cups on the shelves. She has to go to the toilet and mother shows her the small windowless stall on the landing. There is no toilet paper, only some pieces of newspaper on a nail, like in the outhouse beside the stable at home.

When she comes back she is told to finish her meal. She sits and toys with the fish, lifts a few shreds to her lips, shudders, and puts down her fork. Her father raises his voice over the oncoming noise of another train and orders her to finish what is on her plate. Lala tries, but a dry retching begins in her throat and it clenches shut. Her father tells her either to eat or get into her bed. Lala sits, head bowed over her plate.

Her mother pushes one of the beds away from the others, up close against a wall. It has sheets, a pillow, and one grey blanket. The sheet is wrinkled and unclean. Tears of misery and bitterness are trickling down Lala's face as she pulls off her clothes and climbs into the lumpy bed. The sheets feel damp. She sobs for a long time before falling asleep. But wakes again and again as the trains continue through the night.

∞

In the morning a gleam of sunlight struggles through the grimy window. Everyone is dressed and talking when someone knocks at the door. In comes a woman who can speak a little of their language, though with a strong accent. She has brought eggs, bread, butter, cheese, a bottle of milk, a pretty little tin of tea, and a pot of orange marmalade, which Lala had tasted for the first time on the *St. Louis*. There is also a box of washing powder. She gives them some copper-coloured coins, demonstrating how to use them for hot water and heat. Then she places a wad of paper money on the table and smiles at Lala. She tells them she has been sent with these things by a Jewish charity and that someone who speaks a better German will soon come to offer them advice. She smiles again at Lala and manages to convey that she wants to show her and her mother or father the way to the school she is to attend the next day.

Her mother says she must stay behind to wash some of their things with the new soap powder. Lala and her father accompany the visitor down the steep stone steps to the street. Lala is relieved that no buses or cars are rushing by, but all the brick houses are tightly crammed on both sides of the street, without even a touch of colour in a shutter or a reminder of trees on timbered faces, like on the houses at home. And all at once, as she thinks of her village, she realizes she no longer has a home anywhere.

They walk in silence. Lala understands she is supposed to learn the way and tries to count the lampposts they are passing, but there are more and more of them, and when they turn onto another street just like theirs she loses count and stops trying. Her father stares around with a worried frown; he does not hold her hand. She hopes that later the woman will take them back to their house; she does not want to walk alone with him as he is now.

The school is a low, red brick building encircled by asphalt and a high brick wall. The woman tries to explain to her father about a piece of paper Lala will have to bring to this school, but he is hardly listening. Lala forces herself to follow what is being said, though her brain teems with the hundreds of things forcing their way in. She tries hard to guess at the meanings of the English words the woman mixes in with her faltering German.

When they pass through the school doors into the hall, there is very little light and it is very quiet. They pass closed classroom doors, and Lala hears a woman speaking loudly behind one, followed at once by the sound of children's chanting voices, which suddenly stops again. They enter a room where a woman sits writing in a book behind a wide desk. Their helper seems to be explaining about Lala beginning school. The seated woman raises questioning eyebrows at her father who remains standing in the doorway. Lala can see he is afraid and, without knowing why, becomes fearful herself. But then the woman turns and smiles at Lala with a wide smile. She rises, tells them her name, and crosses to her father, extending her hand. He hesitates, then shakes it. A bell clangs urgently just beyond the door and her father's eyes snap wide in shock. The woman says something in a soothing voice, just as there are sounds of doors opening and children's footsteps walking swiftly past in the corridor. In a moment Lala can hear their voices calling and laughing in the playground beyond the window.

Her father is asked to come to the desk and write in a book. She hears him pronounce her unaccustomed full name, "Ursula," which sounds ugly to her ears, and no less strange than the language the two women are speaking to each other. When they are shown out again there are open classroom doors where she catches sight of close rows of empty desks and seats.

Their helper takes Lala's hand and they return to the street. At the next corner she stops, points to a sign on the railing, telling Lala to commit it to memory, so that she can find her way to school by herself. But its words are as mysterious as the Hebrew of their family's prayer books, much of which she has learned to pronounce, but without understanding. Lala does not know how to tell her this. Her father walks beside them enclosed in a daunting silence that discourages conversation. After turning several corners they reach a house which to Lala looks no different from the others, but here their helper stops. She starts to ask her father a question but falls silent when he does not look at her. Then she tells them goodbye, and wishes Lala a happy first day at school. She uses the name Ursula.

Lala begins to climb up the front steps, her father following silently behind. It is a little less chilly in their room because a slight warmth is drifting from the small gas stove. Sheets are draped over the backs of chairs in front of it, and daylight is coming unobstructed through the clean window, its curtain now removed. There is a sharpsweet soap powder smell and Lala sees there are things soaking in the sink. The wax cloth on the table emits its own thick, wet smell. Her mother's hair is covered tightly with her *St. Louis* scarf, and she is crouching, sweeping the floor with a handleless scrubbing brush. For a moment Lala feels relief at these signs of near-normalcy, but then she hears another train approaching fast, its thundering fills the room, and everything starts to rattle and shake as before. Even when it has receded, its memory goes on jarring the cups and plates and windowpane.

Lala has her evening meal early, so that she can go to sleep and be up in time for school the next morning. The meal of scrambled eggs and potatoes is hot, and there is warm milk in a pretty, chipped cup. Its decoration of roses with a few gold leaves Lala finds beautiful, the first lovely thing she has seen here, offering a first small hint of consolation.

It is not yet dark. The bedsheets are dry but they carry a kitchen smell of food which keeps Lala awake just as much as the din of the trains. She turns and turns but there is no escape. She calls up the pale and deep pinks of the roses on the teacup and counts them one by one, but still she cannot sleep. Then, at last the declining daylight begins to turn grey. Opa says a prayer out loud and then, through part-open lids, she sees they are eating their dinner. At its end Opa speaks a blessing before they rise. Now her mother is clearing the sink and begins to wash the dishes. Her father paces round the room. Opa is whispering his own private prayers in his chair near her bed. Lala feels a small but growing terror as she lies unsleeping, foreseeing the streets, the rows of houses, the inscrutable signs, the anonymous corners to be navigated to reach the school. And then the classroom doors, and no-one to tell her where to go in words that she can understand. Underneath her breath she begins to sob, trying not to be heard. But suddenly Opa stops his prayers. He brings his chair very close beside her, and she catches a trace of his shaving lather, and the leather smell of the prayer-thong on his arm. "Will you go to sleep, Lala, if I tell you a story?" he says very near her ear so that the oncoming train will not drown him out. When Lala nods he begins without preamble: "Once upon a time there were two children, a brother and a sister, who lived in a little house in a wood...." And though she knows this story will soon contain terrible things, and she has not been able to forget the dream of her Oma, forever lost in this very same wood, she is soothed enough to stop sobbing. And then, even before the story has reached its end, she is asleep.

∞

It is morning; sunlight lies on the wax tablecloth, and she smells hot cocoa, the sweet brown smell of the morning kitchen at home. On a plate are beige slices of bread spread with butter and marmalade. Her mother has put a cheese sandwich in a paper bag to bring to school. She has written the name of their street and their house number on a scrap of paper and put it in Lala's pocket. Her father is sitting on the edge of his made-up bed, cleaning and trimming his already clean and short nails with a little scissors from the nail set they had bought in the *St. Louis* shop.

Her mother takes longer than usual to comb Lala's wavy hair. Someone had brought a dress for her to wear to school but now they find it is too small, and trying it on has caused knots and tangles. She has to wear the same almost outgrown dress she has worn for countless days now. Her mother goes partway down the steps with her. She asks Lala if she knows the way to school, and tells her she must first go to the head teacher she had met the day before. Lala nods, praying she will somehow find the school, though not by remembering the street signs. In some other way, perhaps like their cows who knew how to get back to the stable even after having wandered far away across the fields. But she has the new fear that when she comes back at the end of the day nobody will be there. On the bottom step she hesitates. "Will father be there when I come home?" she whispers. Her mother assures her that though they are shortly going somewhere, they will be back long before the end of school. Then she begins to climb up the stairs, sending Lala a quick wave, as if nothing unusual lay ahead.

And Lala steps onto the pavement and turns left because her body says this must be the way. But as she absorbs her new situation, filled with strangers, incomprehensible foreign words, unknown places and unforeseeable demands, a dumb, dark sense of alarm builds and spreads to a trembling sensation in her belly, just below the navel. Her heart is beating hard, too, and she casts around for somewhere pleasant to put her thoughts. She cannot find it. But then suddenly two bigger girls are coming round a corner, skipping and holding hands, who surely are also going to the school. Then several more are running to join them, and now the school's brick walls appear ahead. The girls do not go inside but begin a game in the playground. They call out to each other: Elsie! Jean! Ethel! Maureen! Lala hesitates. The school's dark green double doors seem to be locked, but then she hears a bolt being drawn and one of the doors is pushed wide open from inside. Still, the girls go on playing and Lala stands paralyzed on the step, her heart beating too fast. But then more children arrive who join her there, throwing curious glances her way and whispering to each other. She knows it is about her. She longs for someone to speak to her, to tell her what she is supposed to do next, whether to wait or go inside to find the teacher with the big desk. But now a great crowd of children is arriving, a loud bell starts its clamour, and everyone is stampeding up the steps. Until suddenly the children stop and fall silent. Lala recognizes the big desk's teacher in the doorway; she is saying something in a stern voice, and the children file silently past her into the school.

She turns her gaze on Lala, who is lingering, uncertain and apprehensive partway up the steps. The teacher smiles a large-toothed smile, motions Lala inside, and says something ending with "Ursula." Lala cringes at the unfamiliar sound of the U, which is like the start of a burp. But she nods, at a loss for how to say she is not Ursula but Lala. The teacher asks her a question of which she only understands the word, "paper." It sounds so much like the German "Papier" that Lala nods again, finds the scrap of paper with her address on it, and holds it out. She takes it, glances at it, sighs, and hands it back. Then she takes Lala by the hand and brings her to a classroom with children already seated at their desks. Lala sees no other teacher there. The teacher asks the class a question. Hands shoot up and wave wildly, and all eyes stare inquisitively at Lala. The teacher calls out, "Beryl!" and a small girl with short, straight brown hair walks smiling towards them: The teacher speaks to her at some length, until Beryl solemnly says, "Yes, Miss." She takes Lala's hand and brings her to the empty desk behind her own. And Lala sits down with an overpowering sense of relief, though very close to tears. The teacher briefly addresses the class as a few last children slip into the remaining empty desks. Beryl, seated now, turns to Lala, pointing to a wooden box on her own desk, filled with bits of coloured chalk. There is a slate on which she had begun to draw. She leans close to Lala to inspect a little shelf under the desk and pulls out a slate for her. There are no chalks, however, and Beryl holds out her own, motioning Lala to take some for herself. The chalky tints are beautiful and she knows exactly what she wants to draw: a field with a rushing stream, with cows, and red and blue flowers in the grass. She is enraptured at this possibility of reinhabiting her lost home, and soon is entirely absorbed. After a few minutes Beryl leans over again and breathes a sound like "Coo!" The girl behind Lala cranes forward to see, and they whisper excitedly across her to each other. She can tell they are admiring her picture, and for a fleeting moment it seems as if there might be a place for her in this bewildering world. There is a sudden commotion as their own teacher hurriedly enters the room, and the class rises to chant a greeting. Lala quickly stumbles to her feet, head lowered to conceal her ignorant silence.

Their work begins in earnest now. Words to be learned appear on the blackboard, children read aloud from little books, and next there are rows of numbers which everyone must copy down. Lala is frozen with anxiety, but the late-arriving teacher is flustered and unaware of her problematic presence. Lala tries to look inconspicuous, studying the meaningless pages of a book from the shelf in her desk.

When a wooden crate with small bottles of cardboard-capped milk is delivered to the front of the room, the teacher chooses two children to distribute them. Lala watches everyone open theirs and begin to drink. She does the same, but the ice-cold milk is thin as water, not in the least like the thick, still-warm milk from their own cows. But she is very thirsty and drinks it all. Yet now her bladder calls for release, and no one has told her where the toilet is or if, in fact, there is one. She presses her knees together and resolves to hold it in until she gets back to their room.

A little later they all go out to the playground where everyone plays games, skips, or is clustered in groups of two or three, chattering, laughing. Lala looks round for Beryl but she has disappeared. No one approaches her or tries to speak to her. The sensation in her bladder has grown from a tiny reminder to a piercing command, against which she tightly crosses her legs and tries to shut her mind. When everyone lines up to return inside her entire concentration is bent on this effort.

Back at their desks everyone sits very still while the teacher reads aloud from a book. When she stops, the children have to answer her questions. Then they are told to tidy their desks and to stand. Now, with solemn faces everyone is singing. Lala stands with them in silence until the song reaches its last, drawn-out notes, and she realizes the class is being dismissed. She follows as everyone crowds towards the hall.

It is only as they pass through the school's outer doors and disperse onto the street that she remembers she has to find her own way home. She turns to the right and begins to walk, searching for a familiar-looking house, or iron railing, or lamppost, but they are all the same. She wavers and slows her steps, no longer sure she has chosen the right direction. Then she hears voices approaching from behind, and turns to see Beryl and another girl waving to her. They catch her up and seem to be asking where she lives. She shows them her mother's scrap of paper, and they read aloud, "Forty-four Broadhurst Gardens." With a concerned expression Beryl points to the corner ahead and they all start towards it. When they get there Beryl points to where this street meets another and mimes a turn-right gesture. Then the two girls run back the way they had come. Once there, she walks slowly, slowly, looking up at each house door. She sees the house numbers above their squares of glass and tries to match them to those on the scrap of paper. Her heart starts hammering again. What if she will not find it? But a few houses along she sees a blue enamel sign with the matching numbers. As quickly as she can she climbs the stairs to reach the longed-for toilet on the landing.

When she comes out and approaches their door she hears agitated, arguing voices—her mother's and father's—an unsettling thing which has not happened before. But then her memory recalls a long forgotten moment when her father, in irritation at her mother, had raised his voice to berate her, and Oma, who she only now realizes was *his* mother, silenced him with a quelling stare. She listens to their excited voices and then her father is shouting that this is not the time for strict dietary rules. That she should prepare the unkosher meat they have been given, that he is hungry and refuses to live on tasteless bread and cheese and scraps of stale fish. Her mother sounds beside herself and spits back how had he managed, then, in Dachau? And Lala is horror-struck at this mention of the place where the swastikaed men had taken her father. She stands stock still as her mother appeals to Opa to explain the importance of the rules they have lived by all their lives. They fall silent as he speaks a few words too low for Lala to understand. Then all is quiet again, followed by the sound of running water, the rattle of pots, and then the sudden rumble of another train.

Slowly Lala opens the door and sees her mother bent over the plate

of red meat she is cutting into small pieces. Opa is saying that in extreme circumstances it is not forbidden to eat such meat. Her mother's
back looks chastened.

When Lala pauses in the doorway her father barely glances at her,
but Opa asks, "Is that Lala?" his face turning towards the door with
his blind smile. Her mother looks round, takes in her frightened eyes
and asks her what has happened. On the very edge of tears, Lala only
shakes her head, willing herself not to cry because she knows not one
of them could comfort her if she did. They are powerless under some
terrible spell, imprisoned in this noisy, barren room, entirely ignorant
of the complicated world beyond this door, more lost even than she.
Instead, she cries very quietly that night, pressing her face into the pillow, so not even Opa will hear.

On the way to school the next morning, just before that uncertain
corner where panic might strike, she sees Beryl and another girl ahead
waiting for her. When she reaches them they walk on together, and
without having to think about it, her feet learn to remember the way.

In the interval before the first lesson they are allowed to draw again
and Lala finds that a box of chalks has materialized in her desk. Quickly she lays them out: a white, a green, a blue, a yellow, and a red, and
begins to cover her slate with blue and green waves. She struggles to
form a ship's frothy wake, gives up, and tries to draw the *St. Louis* itself.
But she finds she does not know how it might look from the outside.
Then she remembers a toy windup boat she used to play with in the
bath, and begins to make a ship with many round windows, a chimney
stack, and a flagpole. She adds a red flag but leaves out the swastika. It
is too terrible a thing to touch and might bring its dreadful influence
right into this classroom. Beryl and the other girl again lean over to admire her picture. Beryl holds out her own slate with its row of yellow
circles on green sticks. Flowers, she says, with an expression of comical
despair. Then she rubs them all out and holds out her yellow chalk for
Lala to draw them for her. Though she does not recognize the word
"flower," Lala can tell what she wants. She thinks of the dandelions,

daisies, and buttercups in the village field, and presses her teeth onto her lower lip, putting all her effort into drawing them. Then the girl in the desk behind taps her shoulder and shows her the red flowers she has drawn, pointing at some green scribbles beside them. With a grin and a shrug she whispers, "Leaves!" Then she holds out the slate and says, "Ursie, make them for me!"

Hardly believing this could be happening, Lala happily takes the slate and draws leaves round each red flower, embellishing the picture with a strip of pointy grasses below them. The girl grins again and says, "Ta!" She has a missing front tooth and all the rest are specked with brown, but her smile is wide and warm.

Later, in the playground, the two girls pull Lala into a line where children are taking turns at jumping over a row of large squares drawn on the asphalt with chalk. At its end there is a semi-circle. "That's heaven!" Beryl says, and warns her not to land on any lines. She thinks she understands. When Beryl says, "Ursie, it's your turn," she accepts the flat pebble to be thrown and retrieved, and jumps from square to square to heaven, as she has seen the others do.

The next morning on her way to school it begins to rain. The pavement bounces back the falling raindrops, and Lala shivers as her thick wet curls stick to her ears. She tries to avoid puddles without losing her fragile sense of direction and hurries on in a kind of stupor, brought on by the splashing drops, the street's gurgling drains, and the water plashing from every downspout. Then abruptly she is shocked from her trance. An elderly woman's voice is calling her name, "Lala! Lala!" She stares ahead searching for its source. Rain and puddles forgotten, she runs towards it and sees the open window and an old face looking down, calling to someone hurrying away along the street. "Laura! Laura! Don't forget!" The voice calls. The woman on the street waves a hand in acknowledgement before she vanishes round the next corner, and the window bangs shut.

Lala reaches the school drenched. The teacher tells them to remove their soaked shoes and socks and put them beside the warm pipe that

runs along the wall. There is a furtive stirring as children waggle naked feet at each other and whisper joking insults about filthy toenails.
They are allowed to draw for a little while, and Lala scrubs at her slate
to remove the remains of yesterday's picture. For a long time she gazes
at the black surface with its bloom of chalk dust, but no flower or tree
or beast, no stream or house asks to be drawn. She touches the blue
chalk to the cool slate and lets it wander till it has made a curving rising and falling line. She makes its echo just below it, and then another
and another, until almost half the slate is covered. Her hand and fore-
arm move in a slow dance, back and forth over the slate, and she sways
slightly as if rocked by remembered waves.

Beryl turns round to peer and whispers, "That's pretty. What is it?"
Lala stops to look at what she has drawn. Then her hand finds the leaf-
green chalk to make circles, like bubbles between the curving lines. A
third of the slate is still blank. She is gazing at this empty space when,
for just a split second, the old woman's calling voice flashes through her
memory, and she thinks how no one here calls her by her real name.
Then the room's busy, rustling silence is back, and she begins to form
her name over and over, as carefully as if she were drawing a flower.
And when there is a whole row of Lalas, she tries to remember if there
is an English word—any word—she now can write. She takes the bright
pink chalk and prints a whole line of ball, ball, ball, ball, ball. And
then, in the remaining space, slowly and carefully, she completes a last
row with the word, Oma. She inscribes it with all her attention on the
chalk's tip, and tries to make each O a completely perfect circle, an un-
conscious talisman of safety and protection.

∞

She can easily find her way to school and back now. Sometimes in the
mornings Beryl and one or two other girls wait for her at the corner.
Once, holding hands, they all skipped together, shrieking if one of
them jumped on a crack. And once, on the way home, Beryl showed
her a sweet shop on a nearby busy street where, with a big brown penny

and some tiny coins called farthings, she bought a little paper bag of very sweet raspberry drops which she shared with Lala.

A few days later, as Lala climbs the stairs to the linoleum-floored room, she hears raised, agitated voices. The instant she touches the door handle they fall silent, but not before she has heard her father's fraught exclamation, *"Mutter,"* and with sudden anguish knows they were talking about Oma. She enters, trying to read her parents' guarded faces. Her mother is sticking a needle into a sock she is mending, and her father is pacing the room. A train begins to announce itself through the floorboards, and Opa, who is seated on his chair in the corner, directs his sightless smile towards her. She wants desperately to know what they had been saying, but it is clear she is not supposed to have heard. That to have listened at all is to have broken the never openly declared iron rule that Oma must not be spoken of, either by her or in her hearing.

The train's thunder fills the room, then roars past with its aftermath of trembling window glass and clattering dishes. Her mother tells her she should have some bread and butter after she has washed her hands. And as the water dribbles from the tap she hears her father speak to Opa, saying a word she has not heard before: *Krieg,* war. She shuts off the water, waiting for Opa's reply, but he remains silent.

Lala asks, "What does Krieg mean?"

Her father does not stop his pacing, her mother is silent, but Opa lifts one hand to his face to touch his eyes, and says, "The Krieg was when my eyes stopped seeing." And Lala thinks he means that what he would have had to look at with seeing eyes was too terrible to bear. So she persists, asking why his eyes cannot see again now, but Opa shakes his head, tapping his fingers on his knees—his habit when he is not absorbed in praying. He seems to be weighing what he should say. But her father stops his pacing in front of Opa, who at last says, "Soon, there will be war again."

And later that evening, while sitting round the table, ready for mother to bring them the meal she has prepared, the woman from the charity who speaks a little German arrives with a letter for them from an uncle in America. Her father reads aloud that their newspapers say England will shortly be at war with Germany. As father reaches the letter's end their visitor agrees that war is only weeks away. She adds that arrangements are being made to send all of London's schoolchildren to the countryside, away from the expected bombs. The woman's quick glance at Lala tells her she, too, will be one of these children now.

And so it was. Lala, a luggage label with the name Ursula tied round her neck, and Opa's little leather suitcase in her hand, was sent away as well. Without her family now, with classmates and teachers boarding a train which carried them between green embankments, past small suburban gardens, till they came to the fields and woods of the open countryside. And then further still, in a low, green bus which brought them through the leafy, dusty, summer lanes to their unknown village homes. And to the makeshift schoolrooms in metal huts beside the village churchyard. To lodge with strangers in their narrow, crowded homes. To attend Sunday service in the ancient square-towered church, which soon will shelter them each time the siren lifts its piercing warning wail. Here they will root, to grow like alien seeds transplanted by an unexpected storm blowing them through woods and fields. Most will be happy, many run wild, a handful weep for their gritty London streets and are fetched back home, but those that stay, survive.

2011

Libby Scheier, "Cut Flowers"
for Stephen Satory and Yann Koumis

Stephen says he doesn't like cut flowers.
They die too soon.
They're too big a responsibility.
Too fragile.

My favourite student, Yann,
told me a joke today.
How many Nazis and Jews, he asks,
can you fit into a Honda?
Four Nazis and twenty Jews.
Four Nazis in the car and
twenty Jews in the ashtray.

My friend Stephen doesn't like
cut flowers, killed off
in their prime
for frivolous reasons, i.e.,
short-term interior decorating.
In the centre of the flowers

he sees the eyes of his parents
and their friends,
waiting on the long line
for soup thin as water.
The guard spills his father's soup
and he cries but the next day
he is the only one to wake up
in the men's quarters, the others
dead from the poison
placed in the soup to make room
for the fresh, new group of prisoners
arriving that day.

Yann is a sixteen-year-old Greek boy.
He hangs out with some Nazi punks
and thinks he's a Nazi.

The high-school writing workshop
discusses his joke.
He catches the most shit
from a nineteen-year-old black lesbian.
He's backed into a corner
and furious with everyone
but when I tell him I'm Jewish
he turns red, stares at me
silent and in fact shaking
and says he's sorry and that
I don't look Jewish.
We talk about some Jewish teachers
and students at school.
He didn't know anyone was Jewish
except for Sidney Feldstein who
has a big hook nose and a big Jewish name.

It's the first time we've ever seen Yann
surprised or sorry about anything.

Stephen says when you buy cut flowers
you have to cut a piece off the stem
every day and change the water
every day and in a few days
they are dead anyway.

1986

Seymour Mayne, "The Story of My Aunt's Comforter"

When Aunt Zhenia left Bialystok in 1929 she was loaded down with two large suitcases and a sizable trunk. Yet when the porters lifted it in the port of Danzig and hoisted it onto their trolleys to get it up to her berth, they exclaimed: "It's so light, lady—what are you taking to America, a bit of Polish spirit?" No doubt she gave them that gentle smile—later to be one of the lodestars of my childhood—and followed them gracefully up the gangplank.

"What's in the large but lighter case, madam," the English-speaking taxi driver asked her at Windsor Station. Her English was less than rudimentary so he gestured, pointing to the trunk, making as if he were going to lift it again. "In English, what's the word for it?" he asked. "What's inside?" She turned that soft smile to him and shrugged her shoulders. Who could understand the strange tongue, she thought. It will take me years to speak it, she figured. Again he pointed to the trunk and she motioned that she had to go to the address written out on the unfolded piece of paper she held before him. He gave in and drove her there but remained puzzled as he deposited the trunk on the front balcony of the Waverly Street duplex.

"Zhenia, you can unpack now," her landlady exclaimed one Sunday morning when she came up to visit her boarder's room, bearing a tray with hot tea and two sweet rolls her husband had just brought home from Arena Bakery. "But I am unpacked," she answered. "What's in the trunk, pearl?" asked Mrs. Snarch, not underlining her query with too much garrulous emphasis. "It's so light. When I was dusting your room before the sabbath, I went over to push it out of the way so I could get in to mop along the wall. Imagine my surprise: I expected a heavy trunk—but it was like feathers!"

"Mrs. Snarch, you are quite right—only it's not like feathers, it is feathers!" she exclaimed happily as she went looking for the key to its lock. Mrs. Snarch held herself back, curiosity growing within her by the second. After lifting the top, Aunt Zhenia put in her arms and from the fully filled trunk she pulled out a large object that glinted in a silken case, and without hesitation she hugged that comforter to her chest and face. "My pookh," she exclaimed, "my pookh for the Canadian winter!"

I can't remember exactly when I was first introduced to her comforter made of the finest fowl feathers. From early on in elementary school I used to go up to Ste. Agathe des Monts in the Laurentians to spend the December break with my aunt. She had bought and renovated a rather large house which in summer she turned into a boarding house for aging middle-class men and women who appreciated being at lake's edge and, better yet, savoured Aunt Zhenia's justly famous cooking. It was said that she never prepared the same meal twice. Boarders spread word of her warm hospitality far and wide, and invariably she would be phoned months in advance for reservations. She only took the regulars and she had enough trouble holding each couple to a maximum of two weeks. "They would have stayed until Rosh Hashanah," she would say when their cars pulled out of the driveway onto Tour de Lac which circled the lake like a necklace of gleaming summer asphalt.

But as her oldest nephew I was privileged to come and go as often as I pleased. After all, she had no children of her own, and I was the favourite. I remember weekend mornings passing by her bedroom—it was in an addition built onto the house a few years earlier. And on her bed was the pink silken comforter, resplendent like a bloated but amicable boa that settled itself so it covered the full single bed.

Little did I expect that it would be bequeathed to me years after Aunt Zhenia had died—and so unexpectedly. One night past midnight she sat up in her bed and put on the night lamp, waking her husband out of his snoring. "Max, please bring me a glass of water. I don't feel so good all of a sudden." He got into his slippers and shuffled off to the kitchen. When he got back proffering the glass, he noted she was strangely still. She had sunk back onto the pillow. She was no longer breathing.

We received the call early in the morning in Montreal. My father, who got along with my mother's family, was given the difficult task of bearing the sad news to Aunt Zhenia's only surviving full sister, Henyeh. We walked the block and a half to her run-down small room- ing house. Together we went up the wooden stairs, as I recall, and came up to the stout wooden double doors, the way they used to make them before the First World War. No sooner did we ring but Aunt Henyeh was at the door, her face contorted: "I knew it !" she cried out. "I had a bad dream last night. Zhenia's no longer with us." I never forgot that look in her eyes, nor the shudder that passed through me. My father joshed her as if to relieve the gloom: "This time you're right, Henyeh. A hundred percent right! May we be spared further sorrow." Years later I would strain at each of her words when she would phone me, expect- ing forecasts and premonitions of which no one else in the family had any inkling.

More than a score of years passed before the house was sold by Aunt Zhenia's estate, and as one of her heirs I had the choice of furniture and other belongings. My mother with much foresight reserved the pookh, or comforter, for me. And it was a happy occasion—which Aunt Zhenia would have treasured—that brought it into my possession. After all, I was going to get married, and all sides of the family began the hectic activities of providing us with all that we would need for a traditional household: dishes, cutlery, furniture—and bedding! But the first winter when we threw its silken glory upon our bed, we found it was far too warm.

"Your aunt found this comfy back in the old country where there was no central heating or insulated walls," Sandra said.

"So what are we going to do with it?" I asked my wife.

"Let's store it for now and think about it." That was Sandra's way. Just put it out of sight. Forget about it. A solution was bound to reveal itself. So it went into another trunk up in our unheated attic, and there it remained.

By the time our daughter Hava was two years old, she had completely outgrown her paraphernalia of infant blankets and coverings, so we decided to have a duvet made up for her. Doug, who ran an outdoors shop, warned us that it would be quite expensive. "Down is worth its weight in gold," he joked.

"What about the comforter in the attic?" Sandra inquired.

"What about it?" I replied.

"Let's bring it here and have Doug open it and make up a new down-filled blanket for Hava?"

The unwieldy thing made me quite clumsy as I shlepped it down from the attic.

"What's that, Daddy?"

"It's a pookh."

"A poooookh?" Hava asked, pulling one of her delightful faces.

"Yes, a great big blanket that your great-aunt brought over from Poland many many years ago."

"Was it sleeping and hiding in the attic for that long?" she added.

"Yes, and now we're going to give it a new life of its own."

It turned out that Doug could not only make Hava a duvet but he also threw in a couple of pillows drawn out of the bank of down we had deposited with him.

"Perfect," said my wife.

It just happened that I pulled my back out later that week and when Doug left the big box on our front porch, my neighbour Alessandro also rang my bell to tell me something had arrived. Slowly and painfully I went down to answer.

"You want I should take in de box?"

"Sure. But what's in it?" I wondered, forgetting momentarily that Doug was returning his commission.

"By God, this box—she is very light. What you have in it?" he asked.

"Feathers, my friend, just feathers."

"Feathers? What you need feathers? You a bird?"

"No, Alessandro. It's a new feather blanket for my daughter and a few pillows thrown in also. It was made out of a large comforter that an aunt of mine brought with her from Europe sixty years ago."

"It's a very light," Alessandro reported. "I happy to bring for you. Rest your back, neighbour."

And so as I put my head down, testing the new pillows and duvet, I could feel a special expression shape itself—Aunt Zhenia's telltale smile on my face! It was light, cheerful, ready to spread the soft spring of its warmth around to all.

2012

Ron Charach, "One Laughing Uncle"

Long after uncle Saul died, auntie Shailah boasted,
"My Sara's vorkin', my Hannah's vorkin', my Allan's vorkin' …"

Uncle Saul, by trade an electrician,
in his late-thirties grew afraid of heights,
and holed himself in his room
with all the English classics
and dozens in Yiddish, Hebrew, and Russian,
many of them humorous,
while his plump, pretty wife
trudged through snow in leaky rubber boots
door-to-door, business-to-business,
drumming up subscribers for
The Western Jewish News
to feed their three children.

Uncle, what makes an electrician fear
his heights, turns muscles into achy dough,
keeps him from driving a car,
owning a home, stripping paint
from a door?

Limping through my own late forties,
wife and children eating well
but without a taste for herring, black bread,
or prune juice in scalding water,
I look away from
his body's insurrection,
the explosive laughing at his own jokes
and beet-root shape,
his borscht-belt surrender.

2007

Matt Cohen, "Trotsky's First Confessions"

Love is like a revolution: the monotonous routine of life is smashed.
—Ivan Turgenev

Lately you hear on television that depression is a chemical condition. You are invited to imagine the victim in question, whether yourself or some famous historical figure like Napoleon or Virginia Woolf, as an empty silhouette filled with clouds of skewed molecules. For such a situation, a microgalactic misunderstanding, Sigmund Freud is of no use. Even his famous couch—let us not speak of those of his successors—was apparently the scene of quackeries and depravities best resolved by the courts. What does this say about the erotic collapse of the middle class when faced by the monstrous success of its capitalist offspring? No one knows. Inflammatory questions are no longer permitted. If you want to ask something do so politely and in terms of a survey. The answer will be a pill administered in the comfort of your own home or outpatient clinic. This pill, through processes kept secret by the drug companies, will realign your nasty neurons or supply you with those artificial hormones whose random absence need no longer ruin your life or make you a burden to your family and friends. The next day the sun rises on an entirely different person. A positive thinker whose pleasure receptors are now primed to quiver and trill with the first chirp of a bird or the feeling of toes sliding into a pair of clean socks. Experts say, for example, that under more auspicious chemical circumstances Virginia Woolf would have had the sense to reject a life built on prose without punctuation, and instead run a very successful restaurant, specializing in Bloomsburies, the fruit tart from which the melancholic literary circle eventually took its name.

Virginia Woolf, it hardly needs saying, is dead. There is something honest about being dead, just as being alive is necessarily evasive.

This necessary evasion is what makes beginning so difficult. Talk about not having a leg to stand on. It's that old stork dilemma that cracked Lenin's brain and brought us Stalin, my downfall, etc. Or perhaps it is a matter of cultural disjunction. Lately I am a fanatic on the subject because I have been preparing a little paper on Walter Benjamin—an obscure literary critic who killed himself under circumstances with which I can identify, and whose greatest ambition was to present the public with a book composed entirely of quotations. One of his own: "Quotations in my works are like robbers by the roadside who make an armed attack and relieve an idler of his convictions."

If this is going to be Benjamin's attitude I might do better returning to Virginia Woolf, who was more a case of dysfunction than disjunction. In an earlier paper, also presented to the faculty association, I attempted to lay out a sort of schema regarding problems that rhymed. It wasn't very well received. We live in an era when—despite all the new big words—ideas are less important than biography.

In fact I have "real-life" connections with Virginia Woolf. It all began many years ago. Even at the time I felt as though I were in the opening scenes of a movie. There I was, at the wheel of a rented car. Following a series of improbable events, events which do not require recounting, I was touring the south of England with a temporary companion.

As might be expected, it was a literary tour, long on quotations and short on convictions. At a certain point the highlight was a walk along the seawall that figures in a very famous spy novel. While reading the novel it had come to me I would have been useless as a British spy because I look ridiculous in damp tweeds and trench coats. Also, my father never taught me how to wear a hat. But strolling along the wall, I imagined myself not in the novel, but as the novelist himself. This was a curious sensation. Suddenly, rather than being a humble and useless intellectual of the male sex, I was promoted to being a rich and famous writer, not only a popular icon but an astute worldly man who had peered under the skirts of the Cold War and found a fortune.

Why, I asked myself, could I not do the same? As salt spray from the English Channel blew across my face, I had an image of myself pacing this wall for hours at a time, trailed by admiring secretaries taking notes while I dictated the complex Faustian story of a man who sold his soul because he didn't believe it existed. Until—perhaps at this point I would have a couple of shots of single malt—the time came, etc.

I was still half believing that I would one day return to the seawall—my Berlin Wall—to figure out the details of this masterpiece, when we came upon what seemed to be an interesting house conspicuously located on a promontory looking out to the sea. It had a sign advertising apartments to let.

We were in search of a life to believe in. Unfortunately, this is a chronic problem with me, and my temporary companions—intelligent, caring persons with both feet on the ground—always become infected by my own uncertainty. Thus begins a cycle that had already become predictable by the time of my first encounter with Virginia Woolf.

I admit, of course, that I should be able to write about my past in a more measured way. Though he had his own problems, T. S. Eliot proclaimed "maturity of language may naturally be expected to accompany maturity of mind." But who can wait? As with myself and my temporary companion, once you have bashed the brass lion against the door, it's too late to turn back.

The owner of the interesting house—a self-contented but anxious man—answered and surveyed our Canadian faces for signs of money. I had already learned that to the English our faces appear as barren New Worlds with a geography composed of television sports and credit cards. Therefore I said, "The rent is no problem." A few moments later we were in an apartment with a striking view of the sea. It had new wall-to-wall broadloom, a "kitchenette," and a frigid little bathroom with two electric heaters. The main attraction was the view. "This is where Virginia Woolf wrote *To The Lighthouse*," the proprietor announced.

We looked reverently out the window. Battered gently by waves and dappled by the sun was a lighthouse. I turned back to the owner, who nodded complacently. Once again I went to inspect the kitchenette. The stove where she baked her pies had been replaced by a hotplate.

"I love Virginia Woolf," said my companion. I knew she was seeing herself sitting at a desk looking out the window at the waves and writing the book she needed to write.

According to the dictionary at hand, "disjunction" is "the state of being disjoined." I once knew someone with this problem, my best friend. She was named Rebecca Thomas but it should have been Rebecca/Thomas.

Walter Benjamin's disjunction sprang from the fact, he believed, that he was a German Jew—two mutually exclusive realities, each closed to him because he was poisoned by the other. At one point he wanted to become, an ambition he knew was preposterous, Germany's "foremost literary critic." On the other hand he considered accepting a monthly salary to study Hebrew; although he had no interest in the subject, he was desperate for a stipend.

Apropos of my own equivalents to these problems, I once asked R/T, "Why is my life always farcical?"

Rebecca smiled sympathetically, but Thomas answered: "Don't worry, it's not a universal condition."

By writing a Ph.D. thesis on the Bloomsburies, followed by several learned articles published in worthy journals, R/T had become a professor of English literature. My occupation—"Perfect for a schizophrenic," R/T pronounced, although in my opinion she was never fully able to refute the chemical hypothesis—was the same.

Perhaps R/T should be presented in her full biographical splendour: the little squibs at the end of her articles always read: "Rebecca Thomas was born in Regina. She received her BA from the University of Alberta in Edmonton, then was a Woodrow Wilson Scholar at the University of Michigan. Her doctoral thesis, *Linguistic Recipes of the Bloomsbury Group*, was published by the University of Chicago Press." I could add that she had thick black hair, strong squarish hands, a mouth which sometimes twitched like Marcello Mastroianni trying to decide between Sophia Loren and an ice cream cone. Bright warm eyes, an elegant neck. When I first met her she also had a husband, a science fiction fanatic who drifted off into the hyperspace of computer games, then ran away to Vancouver with their babysitter.

R/T and I became friends. At first we just knew that we were people safe to talk to at those faculty parties it was best to attend for political reasons. She made the occasional remark about my "temporary companions," perhaps just to let me know she wasn't going to be one, and I observed initial attempts to find a successor for her departed husband.

We began to write each other memos. For example:

Professor Trotsky: It has come to my attention that during the past several weeks you have been avoiding self-improvement regarding your attire. Please report for lunch tomorrow at noon so that these and other failings can be discussed.

Or:

My dear Leon: You may be interested to know that I overheard your neo-revisionist tendencies being discussed over lunch at the Student Union. Apparently you have been making a fetish of wearing your ice pick. For your own sake I advise you to renounce personalist masochism in favour of collective silence.

Early on R/T (as I addressed her in memos) and I decided to attend each other's lectures for a few months and give each other "honest" appraisals of each other's classroom behaviour. This could have been professionalism at its highest, the gloomy conviction that no one else is listening, or just one of the strange ways we found to amuse each other.

More recently, we resumed the habit. It was amazing for me to hear R/T again after such a gap. It seemed to me—or perhaps the years have made me a better listener—that her own linguistic recipes had changed. She was more subtle, more complex, she spoke with assurance and conviction. The edgy unsure young woman who seemed to be describing something she sensed but couldn't quite see was now offering broadcasts from the very centre of her personal cosmology.

But although Rebecca had evolved, Thomas was unchanged. Last fall, for example, not long after the first essays had been assigned, Rebecca was just manoeuvring into position at the lectern, all wound up for a discourse on the literary-sexual politics of Virginia's relationship with her publisher-husband Leonard, when a student raised her hand. She wanted to know something about the allowable length of footnotes. Rebecca answered her question and then, as often happens when Rebecca gets distracted, Thomas stepped in.

"I was thinking," he said and looked out the window. The students, who recognized the tone of voice even if they hadn't made the diagnosis, followed Thomas's gaze. It was a day in that monochromatic zone between fall and winter. Dark grey clouds turning black in the late afternoon. Cold rain streaming from an adjoining slate roof and making the smoky grit on the windows streak down the glass.

"Suppose I were to die in Toronto. Not now, of course. Don't be alarmed. But I was thinking that somewhere out there must be the men who will dig my grave. The trees that will be sacrificed for my coffin. The mourners who will watch the coffin slide into the earth ..."

Thomas's voice became so gloomy that the students began to shift about uneasily. Not wanting to criticize directly, I sent a memo:

R/T: Excellent lecture but heavy on the melodrama. I liked the idea of your future mourners scattered across the city, unbeknownst to each other, waiting for the event of your funeral to bring them together. Even your pompous claim that your entry in "Who's Who" is just the dry run for your obituary. But the little darlings are still frightened of death. So am I. If you have a fatal illness and have been hesitating to inform me, leave a message on my machine.

When I returned to my apartment the little red light on my answering machine was flashing. "Not fatal but terminal." Rebecca's voice. Then Thomas: "Never speak of this again."

Those who wander in the literary alleyways of the past may recall a recent biography of T. S. Eliot, the poet and critic. When I was a young would-be poet, Eliot was a more than minor god. I memorized many of his poems, along with various weighty epigrams like the one cited above, and would recite them to myself—or aloud—whenever I was drunk, lonely, or otherwise sensed a void that required decoration. Perhaps that is another reason that my companions have always been temporary. But my worship went much further. Eliot, a banker then editor, was noted for his meticulous appearance and personal habits. To make my hair blond, like his, I once rubbed it with hydrogen peroxide and then spent a sunny afternoon walking the streets of Toronto. In the same vein I would part it in the middle. When I received my first teaching assistantship, I went so far as to purchase a three-piece suit and wire-rimmed frames to encase my thick lenses.

I appeared in front of my class, convinced I was the young Tom incarnate; later that morning I was told I looked like Trotsky without the beard.

To go back to the recent biography: Eliot had his own cosmetic moments, but at the time of my three-piece suit I was ignorant of the best. This happened near the end of his first marriage, a bizarre relationship which made Eliot very unhappy. Although Eliot prided himself on bearing the burden of his apparently insane wife with great fortitude, Virginia Woolf once wrote to a friend that to emphasize his silent struggle, Eliot had taken to wearing green make-up, which enhanced his unhappy ghostly pallor.

Imagine T. S. Eliot and Virginia Woolf, legendary giants whose co-lossal shadows surely extend beyond any future a professor of litera-ture could possibly imagine. There they are, in some Parnassian mo-ment of the gilded past, drinking tea and exchanging a few bons mots. Eliot's hair is perfectly parted in the middle and he speaks with built-in punctuation. Virginia Woolf is sporting a 1920s version of a long tie-dyed skirt, and drawing sketches of her lighthouse on the tablecloth. As she looks up at Eliot the sun emerges, an unexpected shaft of light illu-minates his right cheek, she sees greenish powder clinging to his pores.

I am writing this in R/T's apartment, sitting at R/T's desk. Before the movers arrive, I will have finished: meanwhile, the relevant documents are at hand. R/T's medical reports, various of her articles and research notes. From one of the files drifts a memo never sent:

Trotsky: Enough of your political diatribes! Even the beginning practitio-ner will agree that cultural impersonation is the disease of our times! I accept your invitation for late afternoon "drinks" (your use of the plural will be discussed in a separate document) on the impossible condition that you appear as your authentic self!

Why did she reject this memo? What did she send me instead? Did we ever meet, that afternoon? Certainly not our "authentic selves," whoever they might have been. Like those who so fascinated us, R/T and I were cultural transvestites; the only state to which we could claim real citizenship was that of the disjoined. Like Eliot, obviously, the American with his British banker's suit, his perfectly cut cloak of modernist free verse. "Henry James with anorexia" as R/T once termed him. Or Walter Benjamin, neither German nor Jew. His most attrac-tive option, as he saw it, was to go to Paris and become an expert on the politics of Baudelaire. Unfortunately the French were only able to read his studies of Baudelaire long after his death, a suicide brought on by the fact that the French he so admired had refused him the papers he required to escape the German police by crossing into Spain. That Benjamin, whose entire work is founded on the limitations of biography, should die for the lack of a visa is another of those events for which reasoned language fails me, though Eliot promised that "we may expect the language to approach maturity at the moment when men have a critical sense of the past, a confidence in the present, and no conscious doubt of the future." As R/T once said about the book of a valued colleague, with this kind of load the Great Wall could have been built in a week.

This year spring is slow. *April is the cruellest month.* Overnight the temperature fell below freezing and this morning there was a new thin scattering of snow on the grass. A white dusting over the cars parked along the street. When I stepped out to buy a paper I saw a bird pecking angrily at the frozen ground. It shook its head at me, fluttered to the fence, looked up to the sky to let me know he was suing God for this fracture of the bird-God weather bargain.

I had been dreaming about my own cultural disjunction, or at least about the trip between those two cultures which are supposedly mine. In the dream I was standing on deck with my grandparents, Jewish-Russian refugees who came over by boat just after the turn of the century. Their departure was not a glittering Nabokovian tragedy of lost estates and multilingual nannies. They were happy to have escaped, and they were young, dressed in black and white like their pictures. My grandmother leaned over the rail, her kerchief snapping back in the wind and her long triangular nose poking towards the Atlantic coast. Her eyes so black, the skin around them white and smooth. By the time I met her that skin had turned soft and mottled. She would look at me affectionately but also as though I were absolutely unexpected, some strange kind of pet my parents had mistakenly invented when they were alone in their room at night.

I was snuggled beside my grandmother at the rail, her arm was around me and she smelled like baking bread. She pulled me in close against her. I was in love with her. Her smell, the clean salt wind from the sea, the lush piney shoreline drawing closer.

Then she turned me around. Behind us, a squalid city filled the sky with its smoke. Suddenly we were tramping down its muddy streets. My grandmother led us into a dirty alleyway. It was filled with garbage. Old crones peered into our faces, a dog jumped at the hamper my grandmother was carrying, then sprang back when she kicked it.

We went in the back door of a rotting wood house, up narrow twisting stairs to the apartment of her grandparents. The grandparents of my grandmother. A low-ceilinged room with a dining table and a couch on which my great-great-grandfather lay. The heavy rhythm of his breathing. Drawn over him was a thick quilt. His bearded face was turned eagerly towards me, though he did not speak.

About this and other such dreams I have no one to ask. I myself am sliding through middle age—no one alive can remember my great-great-grandparents. No one can care. Let them die and be buried in their stale European breath. Their dead dreams that lived on the edge of crumbled empires whose name no one remembers.

Why mourn over these immigrants and their ancestors? They were always unwelcome wherever they went. They were always lying somewhere, sick, watching their children or grandchildren go out the door in search of some new haven, some new hope that would turn out to be false.

At certain times—in their ghettos, on their boats, walking the streets at night in their new land—they must have looked at the sky, seen that the stars had maintained their same configurations even though the land beneath their boots had changed. Glad to escape, happy to arrive, living in the midst of their self-made islands. Watching their children and their grandchildren step off those islands. Playing the fatal game of cultural impersonation that all of history had taught against. Looking as absurd in their adopted costumes as did Eliot in his green make-up and mascara.

We are in my mid-town, mid-rise, mid-price, mid-Toronto apartment. R/T is lying on the floor, her feet just sufficiently apart that she can, while wearing her high-heeled shoes, tap her toes together. "You never wanted to have children with me," she says. She is pronouncing her words carefully, which is how I know she has mixed just the right amount of Scotch into her blood.

"I would have been a terrible father."

"No. You would have been a good father."

It is amazing how reassuring I find her words. It is as though I've been given the seal of approval by the Canadian Standards Association. A fierce and necessary gratitude towards R/T sweeps across my desert soul. I slide to my knees and begin crawling towards her. The few times we've made love—not unsympathetic episodes scattered through the years—it has always been on the floor: in this apartment, once in a cabin we rented together, once in a car under circumstances that require much explanation but ended with showers to get rid of the bits of potato chips that we inadvertently ground between the carpeting and our consenting skins.

I kneel above her. She is crying. I bend to kiss the tears from her cheeks. This is a huge aberration. Between R/T and me, despite flare-ups of desire, there has never been the slightest pretence of temporary companionship. "I don't want to have an affair with you," she said when I first invited her up, lifetimes ago. "My intentions are honourable," I'd protested. "I don't believe you, and you don't understand me," she'd replied. "With me it's all or nothing and I *know* you won't understand that."

Immediately I'd imagined R/T casting me in the role of stepfather to the little brat she sometimes brought around the department, a spoiled fat-faced beribboned girl who gave me knowing and precocious sneering looks whenever she thought her mother wasn't looking.

She takes my face in her hands. "You still don't understand," she says. Although I think I do; she means we should be in a lawn-surrounded house somewhere, vibrating to the sound of running little feet. I start to withdraw but even drunk R/T is too fast for me, and soon we're rocking and rolling to our own strange beat.

Afterwards, R/T insists I come into the bathroom with her and soap her all over. This isn't the kind of intimacy I'm used to with her. I light candles for modesty's sake, make a few embarrassed jokes about hot tubs. Once R/T is actually lying in the water, and one of the candles has gone out, I regain confidence. I'm kneeling beside her, rubbing the soap up and down her body in the golden light. She's barely visible beneath the water, though her breasts float and her nipples break the surface. "Look at them," R/T says, flushing, suddenly embarrassed herself and trying to push them down. "Wait," I say, and tear some petals from the flowers she brought me and use them to make small glowing hats that bob like tiny sails on the rippling surface of the water.

When depressed, Virginia Woolf dressed in flowers. Skeptics say this strategy must have failed—she did drown herself, after all. But legends are not made of skepticism, and everyone dies in the end.

Walter Benjamin was fascinated with Kafka, whom he regarded as a fellow specialist in the problem of being someone and no one at the same time. Benjamin wrote, "On many occasions and often for strange reasons Kafka's figures clap their hands. Once the casual remark is made that these hands are 'really steam hammers.'" He also said of Kafka that "he perceived what was to come without perceiving what exists in the present." As always when he is writing about Kafka, one feels Benjamin is really writing about himself—for example, the above lines are from a letter Benjamin wrote in 1938, two years before his suicide. R/T in my bed. Not the night of the bath—that night we had the good fortune of perceiving the present without perceiving the future. But a few months later, when she was recovering from her second round of chemotherapy. The precocious sneering daughter had long since turned into a perfectly nice young woman, a graduate student with a big fellowship in biochemistry. R/T could not bear to bother her with the incessant cycles, remissions, collapses of her illness. "She already went through enough with me and her father. I'll call her when I'm dying."

Meanwhile R/T kept teaching, though it was so difficult for her to take care of herself that she eventually ended up in my apartment on a semi-permanent basis. At first it was just for a weekend—a change of beds, we joked.

That was winter. It snowed a lot, unusually, and if she was well enough I would often install R/T, covered by her favourite quilt, in my rocker-armchair by the window. With our lights out we could watch the snow beating in waves against the window. R/T would nurse a glass of sherry while I tried to drink enough Scotch to stay calm.

Often on those evenings, lights out and classical music in the background, we would pretend we were at a place we had imagined, the Modernist Cafe, where we would see Eliot, Woolf, Benjamin, and Kafka sitting at their table, drinking drinks we would invent for them, making terrible puns we also supplied.

At the end of such a visit, when R/T had gone into her pre-midnight doze, I would walk over to her place and get her the various files and books she had requested. Of course she was always about to be well enough to move back. Twice a week I would change the milk in her refrigerator, replace the loaf of bread, take the rotten fruit from the bowl on her table and replenish it with bright fat oranges and gleaming red apples.

In the worst weather R/T would wear her coat while she was teaching. As always she insisted on delivering her lectures standing up. Thomas hardly ever appeared; when he did it was in response to a particularly hopeless question and he would snap back something brittle and bitter. Then Rebecca would shake her head and smile, as though this eruption were a gastric accident best ignored.

After her lectures, I would drive her home. Sweaty and shaking, entirely drained, she would let me help her from the car and upstairs to bed. Sometimes it would be hours before she could speak again.

At my insistence Julia started coming to visit us. "You're like an old couple," she said one night when I was seeing her to the door. And she gave that old knowing smile—this time without the sneer—but how could I explain to her?

Beginning is difficult, ending has its own problems. Something about Rebecca, her mannish Thomas-like hands, the way, when she drank, she used her eyebrows for punctuation.

I would sleep on the couch and when I came in to see R/T in the morning her eyes would be bigger. This was in April, the cruellest month. Her students were used to me and it seemed the most natural thing in the world when one day, instead of taking my usual seat at the back, I moved up to the front. After I had finished the lecture R/T had prepared the week before, I told them the story of the lighthouse and said that if any one of them should ever go there, they might think about R/T. I might have liked to say something about the unconsidered perils of companionship, the temporary nature of things, the way we feel, you and I, when the evening is spread out against the sky, but I didn't. I read them my last memo and the reply R/T had left for me on my answering machine.

For a few moments there was silence. The sky was blue, the windows open; then you could hear the sounds of spades biting into the raw earth, the slow uncertain shuffle of mourners gathering to remember.

1994

David Solway, "Acid Blues"

I didn't see flames I didn't see visions
I didn't see gold candelabra
hanging from the ceiling
I didn't see enamelled cherubim
I didn't see my ancestors combing their beards
I didn't speak with King Solomon in person
I didn't meet his 980 concubines dancing the hora
(I didn't see the paint peeling off their flesh
I didn't see the flesh peeling off their bones)
I didn't see castles in my thumbnail maps in my fingerprints
I didn't see Mandrake and Lothar
doing card tricks for the multitudes
I didn't see Jesus bending over campfires boiling coffee
I didn't see jewelled lights invading the sky
I didn't see the phoenix rise from an ashtray
I didn't see the bloody signature of time
in whirling incense sticks
I didn't see flowers blossom like grenades
I didn't hear the music of the spheres
And I didn't see God sitting in booths
though I canvassed all the restaurants

1971

J. J. Steinfeld, "The Idea of Assassination, Toronto 1973"

1

February 1990

Cold and snowy out there today, but I like being snowbound in my old farmhouse. I find seclusion good for thinking and writing. This is a real snowstorm, not like the ones we used to get in Toronto. Toronto, where I grew up, went to school, married, divorced ... part of memory, notes in journals and diaries. Now I live alone and have a fairly quiet rural existence far from any city. I do all right, writing articles about self-sufficiency and spiritual renewal for Canadian and American publications. The occasional political essay, too, using different pseudonyms depending if I'm writing for the Left or Right-leaning magazines that use my work. But my heart isn't in that chameleon journalism anymore, good as I was at it. Except for the odd bout of depression, my life is fairly intact. Unfortunately, another bout began yesterday after I snowshoed into town for supplies and heard two old men in the store talking about Jews and their ways ... their lies ... Jews this and Jews that. I didn't know what to do, but I almost grabbed one of the old bastards by the neck. There isn't a Jew within a hundred miles of here, but that doesn't seem to stop anything. One of the old guys pulled out a little pamphlet about a Jewish conspiracy—I can't figure out where the fuck he got it when we can't even get *The Globe and Mail* out here—and showed it to his crony. I started to tell the two old men about Larry but I stopped; they weren't interested. Whenever I hear or read about someone preaching hate against Jews or claiming that the Holocaust didn't happen, I try to imagine what Larry would have done if the hateful person had said those things to his face. I do my best to imagine Larry at twenty-two, seventeen years ago, and Larry today, at thirty-nine like me, had he lived to 1990. I've had years to come to terms with the early death of my friend Larry, the only close Jewish friend I ever had, and his memory does not dull for me with the passing of time. Neither do those two winter weeks in 1973 when Larry was planning to kill a neo-Nazi right in a university classroom in Toronto. Back then we were both going to be brilliant political science professors who would set the academic world on its head. Back then we believed that the world was ours to change, to improve, to make fairer....

2

February 1973

... The lights in the classroom flickered, a momentary disruption during a winter snowstorm. Our professor made a brief joke about the instability of the universe, and then told the class that a vote would be the best way to resolve the issue that had occupied the first ten minutes of valuable class time with unpleasant arguing.

"The vote is seven to two, good.... I will get in touch with him," the professor said after he had finished counting the upraised hands. Larry and I were the only two to vote against inviting a neo-Nazi to speak to our graduate seminar.

"There are flaws in participatory democracy," Larry declared to the class, crumpling a sheet of paper he had ripped from his notebook. During the first ten minutes of our seminar he had been working on a drawing of an overweight Hitler making love to a most displeased cow, and did not want the professor to see this drawing. In previous weeks the professor had made unflattering comments about some of Larry's political doodles. Larry had real artistic talent. But in those days he had his heart set on being a scholar, writing about the history of totalitarianism. He was upset by the vote. We both were.

"Don't you find the prospect exciting?" the professor asked Larry. "You'll be able to debate a neo-Nazi in a civilized setting ... in our classroom."

"You don't debate poisonous minds, you eliminate them," Larry said with conviction. Larry was gnawing on the end of his pen, his jaws working high-speed, yet his verdict had been delivered resolutely. My friend's forceful words generated a renewed discussion among the other graduate students.

"You're not compelled to attend," the professor told his student. The professor was attempting to ease the tension in the room, to regain control of his class.

Larry stopped his pen-gnawing and announced loudly, "I'll show up...."

Our political science professor, a thin man in his mid-forties, endeavoured to have one guest "expert" a month for our graduate seminar on "Violence and the State in the Twentieth Century." It was both Larry's and my favourite class, for reasons that had to do with the reading material and discussions, not our professor. The previous month the professor had invited one of the organizers of the Marxist-Leninist party in the province; the month before that it had been an authority on terrorism and subversion.

"One has a duty to remove malignancies, if that removal can benefit the state and its citizens politically," Larry said, mimicking our professor's earlier words. Larry rarely allowed a statement or argument to pass without unearthing a principle or larger issue. He always made me feel that life was important, that even as graduate students we were part of something worth engaging in with passion and commitment.

"Not in a democracy. I was clear on that point," the professor corrected his argumentative student. Larry grunted his grudging agreement.

"That brings us right back to today's topic: Assassination as a political tool," the professor went on. "For the time being, let us approach assassination as a political reality, ignoring any moral implications."

Larry scolded the professor by saying that ignoring moral implications was reducing our discussion to nothing better than simple-minded cocktail-party chatter, but the professor merely continued as if Larry had coughed inadvertently and not condemned him sarcastically: "What I want to discuss, is how assassination affects history, government, and society.... A good starting point would be specific assassins and the assassinated." The professor went to the blackboard and drew two lines which divided the board into thirds. In block letters he labelled the top of each section: ASSASSINATED ... ASSASSIN ... COUNTRY.

"Let us see what kind of list we can compile," he said in the cheerful and enthusiastic tone he used, attempting to make his seminars fun, regardless of the weight of the topic under discussion. It was a tone that irritated Larry, and he could mimic it perfectly.

I tried to liven things up by asking if we should include failed attempts, and Larry said that the very attempt, even if it fails, prods the machinery of state to react. I always sat next to Larry and we often debated in class over points large or small, much to the delight of our classmates.

"For the sake of time, we'll leave the near-misses off this list," the professor said, and ended our conversation.

Before the seminar was over the list on the blackboard was up to twenty-eight assassinated, less than a third with the corresponding assassin's name. With each name, though, the class grew more excited and animated: Julius Caesar, Archduke Ferdinand, Mahatma Gandhi, Trotsky, four American presidents, Martin Luther King, D'Arcy McGee, Malcolm X, Czar Nicholas II ... we had some list. Larry submitted only one name to the list: George Lincoln Rockwell, the former leader of the American Nazi Party. Throughout the class Larry's mood vacillated between frivolous wisecracking and severe rebukes of his classmates and professor, and it was evident that our professor had to suppress the urge several times to ask his best student to leave. The class went five minutes past schedule before the professor told us good-naturedly to get lost and look up more of the assassinated, find a hundred if we could.

"Time to get our caffeine fix," I urged Larry as we left the classroom, the lights starting to flicker again. Outside, it was snowing and miserably cold, Toronto in February, but Larry was calm, almost serene. There was no indication that he had been agitated a few minutes before.

He told me in an even, sedate voice that hinted more of vision or augury than anger, "I'm going to kill that damn hate-spouting creep if he comes to our seminar."

"Don't be ridiculous," I said, thinking that Larry was on another flight of fancy. Larry frequently had schemes and plans to change the world; he was forever fiddling mentally with a world that he felt was unfair. My friend had espoused socialism long before I had, and pursued it earnestly; my involvement with socialism was lukewarm at best, even though during my university days I never missed an opportunity to call myself a socialist. In another time and place, I'm sure that Larry would have been a revolutionary, but we were in Toronto in 1973. Usually I admired my friend's intensity and passion, but that afternoon there was something in his manner and mood swings that unsettled me.

"He's a Nazi," Larry said.

"More a crackpot anachronism. It will be good sport picking apart his minuscule brain," I told my friend.

Larry stopped abruptly and stared at me. He was getting more than a little peeved at me when he said, "A goddamn Nazi is coming to speak in a graduate seminar. Can't you appreciate the absurdity of that?" Larry flung his arms apart, as though to embrace all the absurdity the world could disgorge in the middle of a cold afternoon in the slow-beating heart of a university campus.

I conceded that I couldn't think of anything more absurd, but he kept at me anyway: "I can't expect to make society perfect, I'm realistic enough not to delude myself, but I can kill the Nazi—a political act, a little warning to the goosesteppers in our midst."

"That's not how people will see it, Larry," I tried to tell him, and he told me something I hadn't known before.

"My father was teaching a summer-school course on Chaucer in the States when George Lincoln Rockwell was killed in August of 1967. In celebration my father went out and got drunk. I was sixteen then but boy do I remember that day. My incredibly sober father had never gotten drunk before in his life."

"One of his own Nazis wasted Rockwell, you said that yourself, Larry," I reminded my friend.

"A minor detail," he argued back. "Does it matter which American actually dropped the bomb on Hiroshima? The impact and repercussions are all that's relevant.... If I see that asshole in our seminar there will be one less Nazi crawling around ... proof that someone learns from history."

"There goes your academic career," I said with an uneasy smile, following my warning with a deep-voiced "boom."

"Big fucking deal," he told me. Larry could cross the line between the eloquent and the crass effortlessly.

"It's not worth it. You'd be locked away from our sheltering academic womb.... What about your thesis?" I said, deciding it was prudent to humour Larry and also to appeal to his common sense. We were both well along in our thesis research, and we were having an informal race to see who would finish his master's thesis first; Larry was winning at the time.

"Did you listen to all that bullshit today?" my friend hollered at me, and he was only warming up. "And the week before? And the fucking week before that? I'm sick of cheap words. History is full of people who act and we wind up sitting on our asses dissecting their actions."

"It's not that easy to assassinate someone. Not everyone is cut out to be a killer," I argued with a rationality I considered unassailable.

"I got lots of motivation," he told me. "I've been reading books on the Holocaust for as long as I can remember ... I watched my mother quietly go mad."

After that last statement by Larry we continued to walk across the campus, but in silence, the campus afternoon uneventful, without threat, some remote landscape *after* a savage storm. Larry rarely talked about his European mother, only his Canadian father, the acclaimed Chaucerian scholar, and I was afraid to ask questions about his mother who had been in a Nazi concentration camp as a young woman. I was uneasy while we were walking and stopped before we reached our coffee-shop destination.

"Hell, Larry, Toronto isn't exactly Sarajevo," I told my friend, figuring that I had gotten off a good and irrefutable line.

"Any place can be Sarajevo!" he shouted at me with so much intensity that I bent my head defensively.

"Are you serious about killing that man?" I asked, looking again at my friend.

"If the bastard shows up, you'll find out," Larry said to me, and then we entered our customary spot for post-seminar discussions, me perplexed and concerned and not wanting to leave my friend alone.

3

"He has consented to speak to us," the professor said after everyone was seated for our next seminar. "His only proviso," the professor added with careful precision, "is that no one tape-record him. Fair enough?"

I, like the others in class, turned towards Larry for his reaction. Larry smiled at the curious group, appearing to enjoy the uncertainty he was creating; next he jotted down a few notes and began another one of his political doodles.

Larry, usually talkative and lively in class, was subdued during most of the seminar we had on anarchism. He made a five-minute presentation on some obscure German anarchist, reading his paper without looking at the others or me, yet he was more distant than absorbed. Larry answered questions about that German anarchist as if relating tidbits of gossip about a controversial movie star. The class was most interested in the German anarchist's steadfast belief in free love and his opposition to formal marriage. I also gave a short presentation that afternoon but I can't even remember the name of the anarchist I discussed.

"What are you going to use, an ice pick or a stick of dynamite?" I asked Larry as we were making our usual after-class trip for coffee. During the last week I had often thought about Larry's threat to kill the Nazi who would be speaking to our graduate seminar.

"A gun. It's the simplest. I don't want to blow up the whole class trying to get one asshole," Larry said, and patted confidently a pocket of his heavy overcoat.

"Don't pull a gun out here, Larry," I teased. "Students panic easily."

"I do have a gun. I had it all through that orderly and sanitized discussion on anarchism." There was a short silence and Larry added, "It's loaded, all loaded."

"Keep the gun in your pocket. Better yet, get rid of it," I said. I was humouring Larry and beginning to enjoy myself. The conversation had become a diversion for me, playful banter making the possible reality of blood or death difficult to accept.

"Throw the gun in here, Larry. Help keep Toronto immaculate," I joked as I ran up to a garbage container and kicked it once.

"No!" Larry yelled. The word seemed to detonate of its own accord.

Suddenly I felt that Larry had not been kidding. The one word, the simple harsh syllable, guaranteed the truth. Unconsciously I reached for Larry's coat pocket, the blind heroism of a soldier caught in swirling battle. He slapped at my outstretched arm, but I didn't recoil or complain. My attention was fixed on my friend's beautiful eyes. I thought of the malcontents and fanatics who had stepped into the role of assassin and I wanted to see their eyes, to make sure that Larry was not their spiritual brother.

Then, rubbing my arm as much for dramatic effect as out of pain, I said, "You just can't kill someone, even if he is an evil bastard."

"I'm tired of all the bullshit," Larry said, and looked around cautiously. A few seconds later he reached inside his overcoat pocket and told me, "I'll give you a peek at my instrument for changing history."

To me it was now incontestable that there was a gun in my friend's overcoat pocket. Incontestable and frightening, but I didn't want to appear frightened.

Larry removed the gun and held it boldly at me, butt first. He acted as if he were offering a reluctant disciple a holy relic. Although there was no one nearby, I was certain that hundreds of armed police officers would surround us at any moment.

"It's a German Luger," he told me, and I stepped back from him, not wanting to be near the weapon.

"I love irony and poetic justice," my friend said, and then put the gun away.

"Think before you do anything, Larry. We can work together against this brainless Nazi jerk in other ways and have a bigger effect," I said.

"My decision is irrevocable...."

I didn't know how to dissuade or stop Larry. I was worried about the direction my friend's thinking and talk had taken, but I knew that thought and action could be miles apart. I was pondering what was happening to my friend the way someone might consider the motives of a complex character in a poorly constructed mystery novel. We were in graduate school in Toronto, after all. I thought of the assassinations of the Kennedys and Martin Luther King; I thought of assassins like Lee Harvey Oswald and Sirhan Sirhan; I thought of Pierre Laporte ... the FLQ; I thought about a movie I had seen on television several months before about the assassination of a long-ago monarch. Larry did not seem to fit into these thoughts, yet he had a gun and acted obsessed with the *idea* of assassination.

But I wasn't just worrying about Larry. Standing there and thinking about the gun, I couldn't free myself from the concern that I would be inextricably tied in with Larry, that everything about my friend would be investigated if he tried to kill the Nazi in class, successful or not. The RCMP would dig and dig, and find out how many times a month my friend crapped; they would search out everyone, I was positive, with the remotest connection to Larry. People would talk of a conspiracy. I would lose my Canada Council fellowship; I would never get a teaching job. Christ, I thought, I wasn't even a Jew like Larry.

"Come over to my apartment this evening. We can talk and plan strategy," I tried to tempt Larry. I don't think I would have lost any sleep over a Nazi's death, but Larry couldn't be the one to kill him. It would ruin my friend's life, I feared, and maybe my own.

"I'm going to the library later," Larry said without emotion. "I want to finish up my research for a paper due next week...."

I felt overwhelmingly relieved to hear that, and I smiled at my friend. Someone who would talk of completing a school assignment would not jeopardize everything with an irrational act. The more I thought about my friend, the more preposterous the idea of an assassination attempt became. There was no treachery or coldness in Larry's eyes. My friend was a gentle and sensitive twenty-two-year-old whose only crimes seemed to be excessive idealism and an over-fertile imagination.

"I want to get as much done as possible before I kill the Nazi," Larry declared firmly, the words of a man who hated the damn annoyance of loose ends, and I became scared as hell.

4

I was in a confused and tense state all that week, but Larry was cool as could be. He wouldn't talk about what he was going to do anymore.

We had a few beers before our seminar and I was no closer to understanding my friend or his motives. Larry was in particularly jubilant spirits and I began to believe the threat was a hoax. The Luger had been real, but maybe Larry didn't have it with him this week. He had been noncommittal about the Luger at the bar, drinking his beers with an abandon that indicated only carefreeness to me. I had three beers that afternoon and felt very lightheaded.

Even as we walked to class Larry was vague about his plans. It was snowing again, and I suggested that we make a snowman of Hitler and take snowball target practice, but Larry told me I was being silly. The Nazi was already in the classroom when Larry and I entered. Larry was dressed in a stylish three-piece suit. He had never worn a suit and tie to a seminar before, and I interpreted this as further proof that my friend was not going to do anything drastic. "Heckle the bastard, give it to him good, Larry," I whispered. Larry told me to do the heckling, he had other things on his mind. He looked away from me and said sadly, "I wore this suit to my mother's funeral."

The guest speaker sat at the head of our rectangular seminar table, next to the political science professor, and the two of them chatted amiably. Our professor was wearing a camel's-hair blazer, as was his custom whenever there was a guest speaker. The guest wore a thick V-neck sweater with a colourful checkered design in the wool, dark tie, and light-grey slacks. What people were wearing, for some reason, seemed important to me that afternoon.

I couldn't take my eyes off the guest speaker, but Larry barely glanced at him. My friend was busy writing in his notebook, not doodling this time. It disturbed me that the Nazi was so plain-looking; on the street I would have mistaken him for a middle-aged office worker, if I noticed him at all. Perhaps, I thought, this was not the Nazi, but a harmless academic replacement who was going to lecture eruditely about neo-Nazis in Toronto.

When the ninth graduate student arrived, the professor began his introduction. For all his neutral, uncritical remarks, our professor could have been introducing some little-known politician who was going to tell us how it felt to live in obscurity.

The Nazi thanked the professor, stood up, and moved to a place near the centre of the blackboard. He immediately picked up a small piece of chalk but didn't make an attempt to write anything, instead squeezing the little white chunk while he spoke. The man talked about the social ills that were plaguing Metropolitan Toronto. Students interrupted with questions and he answered them without difficulty. After several minutes of listening to the Nazi, I realized that the man had not yet mentioned the word "Jew" or referred to Hitler. I kept expecting a Nazi salute or a loud "Heil Hitler."

Before the Nazi had finished speaking, Larry pulled out his Luger. I shouted "Don't do it!" and everyone in the room turned towards me, not Larry. Larry aimed his gun at the guest speaker's head but quickly lifted his hand and shot once into the ceiling. The guest speaker, shuddering at the noise, emitted a shrill scream that was louder than the blast from the Luger. Larry slammed the gun down on the seminar table, his hands trembling as though he had done something horrible. He looked at the guest speaker and uttered one non-earthshattering word: "Asshole."

I was completely confused but I picked up the gun, I don't know if it was to keep it from Larry or merely a frightened reflex. I wanted at that moment to know what a Jew would feel. I looked at Larry's eyes, detected what I thought was deep anguish, and realized that the Nazi was an insult to everyone. I shot the gun into the ceiling also, and momentarily thought of shooting in the direction of the Nazi. By then our guest speaker was crouching in a corner, trying to hide, and the other students and the professor were on the floor. I shot into the ceiling once more, for good measure.

Then Larry got up from the seminar table and walked to the door. The students and our professor were still on the floor. My friend turned and said softly to me, "I wanted to kill him, I really did," before he left the classroom.

5
(*February 1990*)

I saw Larry only once after that last seminar. He appeared to be very sad, but did manage to joke that Emma Goldman would have been very disappointed in him for not hitting his target. He moved out of the country before his case was resolved. I was placed on a year's probation by a soft-hearted judge, suspended from the university for ten months by school authorities, and returned to finish my master's thesis in 1974. By then I had lost interest in pursuing an academic career. I can't say for sure that single episode in the graduate seminar changed me, but I certainly looked at life differently after that.

After spending most of the rest of the 1970s and a good part of the 1980s at a series of journalism jobs, I moved far from Toronto and into my old farmhouse nearly three years ago. Larry, I found out from his father, was killed in 1979, in a car crash, an accident without any sense … but it was in Israel, whatever that is worth to the soul of my friend….

For all I've gone through in the last seventeen years, I still don't know any better now how to handle the haters and hate literature; but I bet Larry would have, had he lived. Next time I go back into town for supplies, I will tell those two old men about Larry, whether they want to listen or not.

1991

Karen Shenfeld, "Theatre Doctor"

My Zayda knew,
the show must go on.

He was their top banana—
Ann, Georgia, Marjorie, Sally,
Gypsy, too,

The Great Girls who
gave the boys the business.

"The burlesque house again?"
Bubby asked dismayed,
suspecting foul play.
Zayda gave his lemon tea
a final sip, brushed moon-
cookie crumbs from flecked
moustaches, exited on cue,
toting his black leather bag
like a prop.

Inured to the charms of
feminine flesh,
he swam backstage,
with nary a sidelong glance,
the palest blush,
through schools of chorus girls,
soubrettes, shedding spangles,
the dust of stars.

He cured their ailments,
great and small:
painted Gypsy's tender throat;
corseted The Tiger Girl's lower lumbar;
daubed mercurochrome upon Sally's breast
(her wound, accidental—
an ostrich feather's errant quill).

I heard it said it was he
who bandaged the wings of Zorita's doves,
the bloodied nose of Rose La Rose.

Admitted to private chambers,
he witnessed transformations,
the polishing of nature's gifts.
What more was he privy to?
Spats with boyfriends, managers?
Secret longings, fears?

Of this I cannot tell.
He was silenced by an ancient oath,
the discretion of a temperate soul.

1999

Karen Shenfeld, "My Father's Hands Spoke in Yiddish"

My father's hands spoke in Yiddish,
the *ganze megillah* of curses,
complaints.

Ever in motion,
they argued with themselves.

Gai kochen aufen yam! my father's
hands said. Go shit in the sea!

In the *mamaloshen,*
they spoke their last, impatient words,
rose palms up from the narrow bed—

Nu? Shoyn!
All right already!

then fell like bricks.

Their final kvetch
bemusing the angel of death.

2010

Kenneth Sherman, "Who Knows You Here?"

I have often tried to imagine my paternal grandfather in the village of Lipsk, Poland, in the year 1904 as he prepared to depart for the New World. I used to look at the photographs in *A World Vanished* and in *Remnant: The Last Jews of Poland* to help me imagine his village of dilapidated shacks and dirt roads. I do not know if Lipsk contained a *yeshiva*—a house of learning—redolent of cigarettes and yellowing manuscripts, where old men pressed palms ponderously to foreheads and where young boys—wisps of earlocks creeping out from beneath their black hats—studied at a long table. If there was such a table my grandfather was not seated there. He began his apprenticeship as a tailor at a young age, perhaps because his family needed the extra income, or it may have been that he wanted to find a way out of a place that he described as impoverished, squalid, oppressed, and oppressive. He never read The *Wisdom of the Fathers,* but he was streetwise. And daring. You would have to be, setting out for a New World by yourself at the age of fifteen.

It took him a little over one year to work his way across Europe as an itinerant tailor, travelling through Germany, Holland, and France, arriving finally in England where he bought steerage to Canada. When he arrived in Toronto in 1905 he was sixteen years old and an experienced tailor. At that time, the city's garment industry was largely undeveloped, especially the Jewish garment industry. Initially unable to find work as a tailor, he spent his first Canadian winter employed by the city's Works Department doing the most Canadian thing of all— shovelling snow. The sidewalks on Yonge Street were wooden then. I can picture horse buns steaming in snow, auburn moustaches, plaid scarves, paper notes worth twenty-five cents bearing King Edward's bearded profile.

In the spring he landed his first job as a tailor and worked in several sweatshops until he found a more secure position at the large clothing manufacturer, Hoberlin's. As it turned out, his absence from the *yeshiva* did not impede his success in the New World. In fact, his early apprenticeship as a tailor—the time he spent at the cutting table instead of the study table—was to his advantage. Though a large proportion of East European Jews would work in the garment industry, only a fraction of them were actually skilled tailors. What attracted the other 90 percent was the fact that it was the only industry where earnings were directly related to individual effort and initiative. This was called "piece work." The more pockets, linings, belts, or vests a worker turned out, the more he or she was paid. People with little experience could be taught to do some portion of the garment. Only a few could measure, cut, fit, and sew together an entire suit.

Many immigrants would work only for Jewish companies where they would have the high holidays free for religious observance. Some chose to work independently, as peddlers, so that, even though the earnings were meagre, they could keep their own hours and have Saturday off for observance of the Sabbath. Taking a job at a gentile firm, my grandfather made his decision early on to leave a portion of his heritage behind. Attending synagogue was not important to him. He was clearly bent on succeeding and quickly understood the importance of hard work and "flexibility." For twelve years he worked at Hoberlin's. He eventually saved enough money to open a tailor shop on Spadina Avenue. A few years later he moved his business to College, just west of Bathurst.

As a child, I had a chance to see my grandfather practically every day since we lived in the apartment above his shop. He was a man of medium height with black hair and a dark complexion that set off his Baltic blue eyes. His ears were overly large. As a child, I likened them to an elephant's, but years later I heard a woman describe them as Clark Gable ears. He liked the occasional drink and kept a bottle of Seagram and Sons whisky behind a bolt of cloth in the back of the store. "It's good for the blood and the balls," he told me when I was older. He had a reluctant smile and his brow was often furrowed as if he were interrogating life. Most of the time he seemed too preoccupied to notice me, but once in a while he would bend down and squeeze my cheek, or pat me on the head, give a short laugh and then walk away. As I grew older, I read into these gestures both affection and something just short of condescension: "You're lucky to be born here," he seemed to be saying. "But what can you really know about the hard knocks of life?" He'd lived through the Depression and lost much of his European family in the Second World War. I was born in the benign and tranquil Canada of 1950. I had been spared, it seemed, the terrors of history. He was probably thankful for that and at the same time convinced that as a result, I would be soft, naive. Perhaps he didn't know that I could read that history in his face, in the shifting intonation of his voice when he expressed anxieties, anger, or jubilation.

Like many other immigrants of his time, my grandfather started out as a socialist and remained sympathetic to workers throughout his life. But he never involved himself with politics in any practical way. He mistrusted orthodoxies, both political and religious. He railed against injustice whether it was of the right or of the left. If he was against anything, it was what Chesterton had called "a certain expression on the human face." He was a realist. Though he did not unconditionally buy the North American notion of the "good life," he did want to celebrate his experience in the New Land. After all, his Hebrew name, Simcha, means "celebration." He believed in hard work and was certain that without the flow of money, there would be only social disruption and

powerful resentments—Poland all over again. He was, above everything else, a hard-working craftsman and took a great deal of pride in
his work. A few months ago, in the change room of the YMCA, I was
introduced to an elderly gentleman who had known my grandfather.
"He made a very fine suit," the man told me. I have heard this from
others over the years and the comment always sets him apart in my
mind from the mass of businessmen and speculators.

He was not a reader. Though he came from a people that revered
Scripture and was himself a *Kohen*—that is, a descendent from a line
of priests—he had defied his culture's imperative and never learned to
read or write. He loved going to the movies. On Saturdays, when he
was in his sixties and the business was mostly in the hands of his sons,
he would instruct my father: "Drive me to the pictures. I *vant* to see *cul-
boys.*" I've often wondered what he saw in Hollywood Westerns. On the
Sabbath, when other men of his generation were walking home after a
morning in synagogue, my grandfather was sitting in a darkened theatre watching a magically lit screen. Those movie houses of yesteryear
were temples. Grand, spacious, they had majestic names like the Impe-
rial, the Capitol, the Palace. The patrons sat in plush seats. There were
seashell light fixtures mounted on the walls and out of each one there
rose a plaster-relief Venus.

My grandfather must have identified with the parables being acted out on the giant screen. The heroic loner rescues a good but belea-
guered man and his beautiful daughter from a sinister railroad tycoon
and the henchmen in black hats. As an immigrant who had done fairly
well after years of hard work and suffering, he must have seen in himself both the victim and the hero of those Westerns. And like the tight-
lipped protagonists of those films, my grandfather was taciturn, severe-
ly laconic. He liked to cite the Arab saying: "A word is like a stone. Once
cast, it cannot be taken back." A man so cautious with speech must
have loved the sparse drawl of Randolph Scott or John Wayne.

As for the gangster figure in Hollywood films—these he knew first-
hand. He had a number of relations who were involved in the under-

world. Some of their names sounded as if they came straight out of Damon Runyon's 1932 short story collection, *Guys and Dolls:* Louis the Lush, Harry the Hunchback, the Kay brothers. They were serious criminals, with close ties to Detroit's Purple Gang. A week after my grandfather opened his first tailor shop, thieves broke in and stole most of the cloth. They evidently were not aware whom they had picked on. My grandfather's gangster relatives put the word out on the street that the merchandise must be brought back—or else. Two days later it was returned, no questions asked.

As a boy, I was proud that some of my relatives had been underworld figures. Though I now feel no such pride, I marvel at the metamorphic possibilities offered by life in the New World. These men, whose fathers had been law-abiding shoemakers or carpenters, rabbis or cantors, took illegal bets, threatened men who had defaulted on their "loans," set failing businesses ablaze, and spoke with the gruff intonation of George Raft. Some of their children, in turn, would become professors, surgeons, and social workers. Certainly the major principles governing North American life in this century are motion and mutability. We have heard much about the rapidity of technological change, but less about the radical transformations of individuals from one generation to the next. It may well be that our search for roots, for some linkage to the past, is a way of counteracting these dizzying changes of identity.

And yet most people's family history does not go back very far. Detailed knowledge of one's European lineage—names, dates, who married whom—is the prerogative of the wealthy and powerful. The names and characteristics of those who lived before my great-grandfather are lost forever. I can locate only their sentimental stereotypes in Yiddish tales and stories. The Russian poet Osip Mandelstam did not bemoan this hiatus. As far as he was concerned, "An intellectual needs no memory—it is enough for him to tell of the books he has read, and his biography is done." This is essentially true. Families, however, persist in conjuring romantic anecdotes about those relatives that they do remember. Thus, an uncle once told me that Louis the Lush had beaten up two policemen who had come into his bookie shop to trash the place. They only managed to tear the phone off the wall before Louis took care of them. According to my uncle, Louis had driven the head of one of the policemen through the hole left by the missing phone. This strikes me as a scene out of a movie. But if people who are part of a minority feel powerless, the image of the rebel gangster will help dispel that feeling. I recall as a boy seeing Louis at a family wedding and being disappointed that he did not fit my image of a gangster. Granted, he was tall with slicked-back hair and a Ronald Colman moustache, but the moustache was the only glamorous thing about him. Beneath his tired, bloodhound eyes were heavy bags. He was slightly bent and shuffled with the weariness of a man who could no longer be surprised.

My father told me that during the Depression, Louis's mother, a widow, used to manufacture alcohol in her house. It was sold in clear, unlabelled bottles from various places, including my grandfather's store. Worried about the money she made from this and other illegal traffic, she kept her profits along with her jewellery buried in her backyard garden, never telling a soul of the exact location. When she died suddenly of a stroke, her family went into a state of panic. By moonlight and flashlight Louis and his brothers dug holes in the backyard, and carefully replaced the earth so that the neighbours would not become suspicious. The gangsters had become pirates. I can see their ghostly images working spades and shovels; I can hear their whispered curses, for the treasure was never found. Evidently, the mother had not trusted her own family. Perhaps she had mentioned burying the money in the backyard only to throw them off the track. Perhaps it is hidden under the hardwood floor or behind some wall of that house. Perhaps it is in some investment plan under a pseudonym, never to be claimed, compounding toward infinity, while all the characters that initially collected it have long since perished.

In the 1930s, while this was going on in North America, a major catastrophe was in the making across the ocean. I remember as a small boy sitting in my Aunt Doris's dining room in the mid 1950s, looking with her through the back pages of her photograph album. The photographs taken in Toronto were for the most part spontaneous. Some had wisecracking comments written on them. My father with his eyes rolled up—"Count Dracula strikes again." My mother and two of her sisters, each lifting a leg, as though they're in a chorus line, —"Broadway Babes." But there were portraits I did not recognize. These were photos from Europe, most of them taken in a studio, the subjects, posed, formal, stiff. "Who is that?" I would ask, and my aunt's one word response, "Dead" would be accompanied by a disheartening silence. And then as if offering an explanation she would add two words. "The war." Once she pointed out a woman who looked strikingly like my grandfather. "Your grandfather's sister," she sighed.

I was five or six at the time. It would be several years before I was to discover that "the war" was a euphemism for something much more dreadful than a bomb falling on a house, for that is how I imagined a woman would die in a war since women were not on the battlefield. And yet I did feel something was being hidden from me since there were other photographs of elderly people and small children who had died in "the war." Had they all been in the same house when the bomb fell? It was not until I was ten, and saw a documentary on the annihilation of Europe's Jews, that I began to understand what had happened. My mother wondered aloud whether I should be allowed to watch the black and white images unfolding on the television screen. My father responded, "Let him watch. He should know."

In 1936 my grandfather, who had been in Canada for thirty years, brought his father over from Poland. It was hoped that the old man would take to the New World and send for his wife, but it was not to be. According to my father, my great-grandfather walked out to the corner of College and Euclid, stared at the traffic, and uttered one word—the Yiddish for "zombies." He was a devout Jew, and with that one word, he pronounced his unequivocal judgment of North American culture. It is reported that he spent the next three weeks in a state of taciturn disgruntlement, until a ship carried him back to Europe. Unfortunately, that single utterance not only described his feelings about the soulless materialism of North American society; it also sealed his fate. Three years later war broke out in Europe and a year after that my great-grandfather and great-grandmother were shot dead by members of an *Einsatzgruppe*. I am named after my greatgrandfather. We share the Hebrew name Yacheel, which means "God lives." Considering what happened to him and to the millions of other innocent victims of the twentieth century, one could pronounce the name with an ironic smirk. On the other hand, one might call it out as a defiant affirmation. In any event, a name does carry some import, especially when it is handed to one out of the whirlwind of historical calamity.

Every family tells stories that assume, with time, the proportion of myth. Their purpose may be to pose questions that continue to perplex, especially if the stories are ongoing, if we are living out traces of them. My great-grandfather rejected North America and that rejection led to his death. But we cannot dismiss his choice as foolish. In fact his story is repeated because it presents us with a classic contrast between the Old World and the New, between spirituality and materialism, piety and pragmatism, tradition and liberalism. He saw the billboards and automobiles of a modern city with the intuitive eyes of a visitor who happened to be a deeply spiritual man. He called North Americans "zombies"—the walking dead. Allen Ginsberg, disturbed by the zombies he saw two decades after my great-grandfather's visit, wrote: "What sphinx of cement and aluminum bashed open their skulls and ate up their brains and imagination?" That is from his long poem *Howl*, whose biblical fervour would have appealed to my murdered namesake.

My grandfather succeeded in the New World because he did not spend much time looking back. His survival skills were finely honed. He built a successful business, helped his children buy their homes, their cottages. He helped support his less successful brother who had emigrated later with his wife and child. But what had he given up? Only a few years ago an incident occurred that highlighted the classic tension between my grandfather and great-grandfather's directions. My father, driven I believe by nostalgia, wanted to show the apartment above the family tailor shop to my brother and me. The tenant had moved out and it was temporarily vacant. Although I had few concrete memories, I was moved by the thought that I had spent the first five years of my life there. My brother on the other hand—at the time, a real estate speculator—pulled a tape measure from his pocket and began measuring the apartment. He was thinking aloud about renovating it and renting it for a higher price. This was not simply because I had once lived there and he had not. We are two different types and I wondered at the time if he was following my grandfather, while I, stepping back into a wonderment and reverence for the past, was following my great-grandfather.

Of course, people are really not so one-dimensional. Each of us tends to intuit many possible choices and directions. I recall walking with my grandfather down Spadina Avenue in 1964, two years before his death. He had suffered a mild stroke and walked with a cane. Some of what were once Jewish stores were now Chinese restaurants. The Jewish community had by and large moved out of the city core. The custom-tailoring trade had begun to decline. Indoor malls were about to open where ready-made suits are lined up on racks, and streams of people move in two opposing directions, like traffic. My grandfather was telling me about a friend of his who was losing his mental faculties because the blood vessels in his brain were hardening. I responded by stating that it was too bad the process wasn't taking place in some other part of his body that would be less debilitating. My grandfather rapped me on the shin with his cane. "Do you think you get to choose?" he asked. We walked on a bit further and I began asking him about the town he came from in Poland. He told me it was so small that if a horse stood on the main street his nose would be out one end of the town and the tail out the other. He remarked on the extreme poverty. Then I asked him about Europe in general, since he had travelled across it to make his way to Canada. "Europe," he said, "is a sewer." Then he stopped walking, looked about for a moment, and asked ruefully, "But who knows you here?"

2009

PART II · PLACE

David Solway, "After the Flood"

After the flood, there was no rainbow in the sky.
The puzzled patriarch rubbed his eyes and looked again,
there was no rainbow anywhere to be seen.
There was no command, paternal and indulgent,
to be fruitful as the earth and multiply,
there was no sound anywhere to be heard
except the subversive grumbling of the animals.
He knew his master then to be whimsical and coy
and not averse to going to great lengths
to ruin a script or tweak the prompter's nose.
He wondered what to tell the waiting scribes.
After the flood, there was no rainbow in the sky.

1973

Nora Gold, "Yosepha"

1

Around her mother's swollen belly swarmed her many half brothers and sisters: All sizes and shapes, they laid their hands fearfully upon her belly, or pressed their ears to it to try and hear the life within. Rachel, an intense and private woman, was so transformed at the thought of having a child of her own, that initially she only laughed at the wonder and worry of her stepchildren, and let them lay their hands upon her.

But Rachel was a woman of many fears and dreams; and later on in the pregnancy, curled beside her husband at night, she confided her fears to him in a whisper. She told him that his children had organized against her—they all hated her baby, they wanted it to die. In many small incidents she found evidence of this: they had brought her dirty water to drink, they had pinched her stomach instead of stroking it, and lately they murmured among themselves and fell silent when she approached. At night she wept. What if they hated her baby? What if she died in childbirth, and she couldn't protect it from them? *He* would have to protect their baby.... Yaacov just kissed her temple, and stroked her hair, and even though this made her smile, a little darkness still remained in her eyes. "Do you doubt me, Rachel?" he asked her. "With all my love for you, and you doubt me?" Then the darkness vanished from her eyes, seeping somewhere inside where he couldn't see it any more, and—helpless against these fears of hers, these dreams and superstitions in which her family believed—Yaacov did the only thing he knew. He took her in his arms, wrapping her in his love, like a cloak.

For five years they had been waiting for this. For five years they'd been tending sheep on their *moshav* in southern Israel, reading and rereading the works of Herzl, Gordon; and Ahad Ha'am, and rejoicing—as one did in the early years of the State—in the honour of fulfilling the Zionist dream. But through all this, they had also been waiting. And now, with both of them past their prime, they were eager and impatient for this child. True, Yaacov already had six sons; but he did not yet have the son he wanted. With each son born, he had looked into the infant's eyes, and wondered, *Is this the one?* Would this be the one who had appeared to him in his dreams—the great leader of his people who would carry the Zionist hope forward into the next generation, and deliver them all from untold dangers and disasters? Yaacov envisioned for his people a great future, as expansive as the sea, with descendants and generations as many as the fish that fill it. And yet, with each son, he could see that this was not the one he'd been promised, the one to fulfill this destiny. Rachel knew his disappointment and secretly rejoiced. His first wife may have given him twelve children, spawned like so many fish; but *hers* would bear the star on his forehead. *My son,* she thought, *it will be* my *son....*

And the child-to-be, the prince—the comfort of their old age and the leader of his people—reached the time of his birth.

∞

At the time of its birth, the baby lay dying. When they smashed open the womb, it began to die, all around it scattered its life, its hope, the remnants of its world. It watched the broken pieces of womb and the liquid—the warm globulating stuff that had held it so secure—go cold, dry up, in this new air. In an eternity of waiting, it had prepared itself for this instant. In the months of rocking wombness, it had planned for this moment when it would emerge, show itself to its creator, and be saved from the death in this new world. The midwife's hands were soft and skilful, but the baby knew that she wasn't its mother. It would not open its eyes to her. It held itself back, fists clenched tight, until it smelled a certain smell, sensed a certain sense that said: *Mother.* The being in it, the being of its being, began to unfold. Slowly, luxuriously it opened, and its eyes opened, and it presented itself defenselessly to its mother.

"A girl," urged the wholesome midwife. "A daughter...."

For only one moment, only a fraction of a moment, Rachel looked at, and appraised, the naked being before her. Looked at, and appraised. And her lids snapped shut against her like two steel doors.

The midwife swept away, rocked against her breast, the screaming, terrified infant. "Now now, now now," she clucked as she rocked her. "Now now. Now now." Everyone, even the shepherds miles away, could hear the baby screaming in the midwife's hut well into the night. Nothing could comfort her. To the other women in the hut, the midwife, jiggling the baby, expressed her disapproval. "Can you imagine?" she said. "And such a pretty baby, too."

But no one spread the story around, and it never turned into gossip. For Rachel, that very night, from some unnamed inner bleeding, died.

∞

Yaacov never quite recovered. He retired, under some pretense or other, from public affairs. He spent more and more time alone in his work tent ("thinking," he said), and emerged only occasionally—holding his clipboard with a pencil attached by a string—to look over his sheep. Whatever he was told by his assistant, the young man who had come to help him from a neighbouring *moshav*, whatever figures or reports he was given, he nodded his head vaguely like one who's lost his sight, saying, "I see, I see," or "Yes, of course," as if he were stupid not to already have known. The eyes of his assistant grew shrewder and shrewder, and as time went on, his profits began dwindling, sheep began to get lost, and there were always excuses....

The man was suddenly old.

His children grew up around him, barefoot with their lower legs suntanned and dusty from playing jumping games outdoors and from herding sheep. The boys were back-slapping, hearty farmer's boys, which surprised him, despite the fact that this was what he had raised them to be. Like the rest of his generation, Yaacov had decried the pasty-faced scholars of the *shtetl*, and dreamed of "the new Jew"—a Whole Man, who would live not only by his mind, but by his hands, as well—and who, by the work of his hands, would redeem The Land. Yet the mind and the soul that Yaacov had taken for granted were not in his sons, and this struck horror into his heart. His girls, too, were strangers to him. They cackled in front of mirrors, grabbing ribbons from each other, and playing women games that he didn't understand, and all he could do was take himself away from them with a philosophical gaze, having patted one or another of them vaguely on the head. The boys, like animals, were always engrouped, and so were the girls—they hud-dled together, boys on one side, girls on the other, near the entrance to his tent—and so Yaacov began confusing their names. They all looked alike to him anyway, the six girls in their clothes that flapped at him like flags, and the six boys with their demands and wants and affections that came and went with the wind.

Yet he had a place for Yosepha, his skinny-legged daughter who was pale-faced and solitary as Rachel had been, and whose black eyes, with all their intensity, had answered his silent question, *Yes* before he'd asked. In the fading clarity of his mind, he thought of her neither as a girl nor a boy, but as something in between. Rachel had said, be-fore the birth, that she wanted the child to be called Yoseph, and out of respect for her memory, Yaacov had kept this name. He had added the requisite suffix "a," of course, to put it into the feminine form; but sometimes he forgot the "a," and just called her Yoseph instead. And Yosepha didn't seem to mind. She somehow seemed to understand, even without being told, the expectation and disappointment behind her name, and answered to both Yoseph and Yosepha. Yaacov confused other things, too, like Rachel's death and Yosepha's birth. These two things became utterly fused in his mind, so that after a while, Yosepha and Rachel no longer seemed to him like separate entities, but just two different bodies containing the same passionate soul. Like two different vessels carrying the same wine.

∞

But this is not why she was his chosen one. If you had asked Yaacov what was special about Yosepha—why it was her and not any of his other children—he would have spoken to you not of her soul, but of her mind. She had an eerie way of seeing right through to the essence of a thing—of a problem, or a person—in an instant separating wheat from chaff, and slicing through to the core. She did not know she was doing this. For her it was instinctive, like a rat impatiently avoiding the false leads in a maze, and going straight for the cheese. Yosepha's mind strained forward like that, toward the essence of things, as if she had no time, as if her life depended on it.

Dresses and chatter filled her with horror.

Even when she was a young child, her brothers stuck out their lower lips and frowned when she spoke, as over and over she seemed to hit, with no effort at all, exactly the answer that Yaacov was waiting for. As Yosepha grew older, she and Yaacov would sometimes engage, during the midday meal, in heady dialogues that left her brothers and sisters picking at their food and exchanging looks. Yosepha loved to read, and would recite to Yaacov from whatever she was reading—from the poet Rachel, or from Gordon on the idea of the redemption of The Land. Occasionally, too, she would tell him about something she'd read in the local agricultural bulletin, on crop rotation for example, or the latest developments in sheep farming. Once after reading there about the need for new, more modern methods, Yosepha said at the dinner table that she wanted to do something important with her life, she wanted to *contribute* somehow. She dreamed of maybe starting up a collective of all the sheep farms in the region, helping to lead them toward mechanization and modernization. Or maybe she could work with Krause and others like him who were trying to revolutionize agriculture at the national level, encouraging more scientific knowledge and technological innovation, and increasing the country's hydroelectric power. Maybe she could help them do it—help them bring about the necessary changes—so that in the coming years, Israel could compete in the regional markets (maybe even the world markets, later on). Her brothers and sisters stared at her, and then rolled their eyes at each other.

"Why aim so low?" Shimon sneered at her from across the table. "Why not become our Prime Minister, when Ben-Gurion's done his term? Or better yet, why not leader of the world?"

"Sssh, ssssh," hushed Yaacov; but to Yosepha he said, "One shouldn't speak that way. You invite ridicule and the anger of others by being boastful. Such dreams are best kept to yourself."

∞

Yosepha's brothers tried to please Yaacov the only way they knew how: by giving him gifts. They did this individually, each of them plotting alone, and sneaking into Yaacov's tent when they thought no one else was looking. For although the brothers were close, as close as brothers can be, for this they sparred separately, each willingly betraying the other. One at a time they stood before Yaacov in uncomplicated worship, longing only to serve and be loved; and stretching forth their hands, they laid their gifts—gifts of wood or cloth or stone, laboured over with love—on the table near their father. Yaacov received these offerings absent-mindedly, with vague "thank yous." He was not an unkind man, he never pushed them away; but neither did he draw them nearer. The son's disappointment and mystification, once outside the tent, turned to rage, but it was quickly swallowed and kept from the others. Stealthily, and with shame, each one rejoined the group, smoldering hate within his heart and a longing for revenge. Each of them remembered, like a myth repolished, the position of his gift on Yaacov's table, and knew that there it would sit, unstroked and uncherished, in the days to come.

The sisters vied for Yaacov's affection by trying to impress him with their beauty. They showed off their new dresses, posing this way and that, they flashed at him their various-coloured eyes, and tried to stand as close to him as they could. Each of them secretly hoped that he would rest his eyes on her, stroke her cheek, and say how pretty she'd become; but he never did. He bumbled his way back to his tent, leaving behind him a burning hum, not unlike a swarm of bees, each one longing to be queen.

Yosepha's brothers and sisters were all united by their unshared wounds, as families are often most deeply united through their secrets, and not through what is openly shared. Each of the brothers and sisters was blood of Yaacov's blood and flesh of Yaacov's flesh.

∞

Late one afternoon, when the wind was blowing and the sand flew up into the eyes and the mouth, the brothers huddled together as usual on one side of the entrance to Yaacov's tent, and the sisters huddled on the other. They were busy with their separate occupations: the brothers playing knives, becoming men; and the sisters playing primp and preen, becoming women. And around both groups, whirls of dust.

Yosepha was alone, partway between the two groups—slightly closer to her sisters, but a safe distance from them, too. She was further than all the others from the door of her father's tent, but was facing it as she knelt on a flat rock, reading a book—or trying to look as if she were reading. With each wave of laughter from her sisters, she narrowed her eyes more intensely, as if fighting off loneliness, as if telling herself: *I don't need them.* She bit her lips, and they got redder as she read.

The flap to Yaacov's tent flew open. The wind blew hard and some birds squawked in the late autumn sky. His sons and daughters stopped what they were doing, and grew silent and still, as he stood squarely, framed by the entrance to his tent.

He stood a few moments, just listening to the air and breathing it in. Then he said, "Yosepha. Where is Yosepha?"

She leapt to her feet. "Here, father!" she cried tremulously.

"Come here," he said.

She walked to him eagerly, aware of being watched, aware of the gloomy and ominous packs to her left and right: one heavy and male, like cattle, the other lighter but sharper, like pecking birds. She felt their collective hatred like a force, and her knees trembled a little as she walked between them.

When she reached Yaacov she stood before him, and he put his right hand gently on her head. He squinted first at the brothers, then at the sisters, and they watched him, their furry-haired father with his hand on Yosepha's head. She was seventeen by now, but she still looked as slender as a boy, and totally untouched by the sun that had burnt them all brown. With his left hand, Yaacov reached inside his coat, drew from it a small, beautifully bound book, and handed it to Yosepha. She looked down at it for a moment, and then stared with wonder at Yaacov.

"Your copy of Herzl," she said. "The one you brought with you from Russia."

Her father nodded. "'If you will it, it is no dream.' Do great things, Yosepha," he said. "Listen to those dreams of yours." He stood for another moment, smiling down at her. Then he took his hand from her head, and without looking at his other children, turned on his heel like a monarch, and re-entered his tent. The tent-flap dropped behind him like a slap.

Holding the book on her head with her right hand, Yosepha sauntered her way back, between brothers and sisters, to her place on the rock. The book looked like a crown in the sun.

2

Twenty-two years passed. Twenty-two years since the day that Yaacov had publicly isolated and blessed his daughter. And twenty-two years less a week since Yosepha's brothers and sisters took her with them on a trip to the Negev and abandoned her on the way home, on a dark road at nightfall. The Negev was a full day's drive from their *moshav*, and totally unpopulated except for some Bedouins from whom, every year at this time, they bought some new sheep. By the end of the second day, they'd concluded all their business and begun the trip home; but after they'd been driving for about an hour, the truck suddenly stopped, and her brothers and sisters told Yosepha to get out and walk the rest of the way. She sat there, confused, thinking they were joking; and then they grabbed her and pushed her off the back of the truck, and pried her fingers loose when she clung to it—and afterwards again when she ran after them and caught up to the truck and tried to climb back on. They laughed at her, taunting her as they drove off: "'Do great things, Yosepha!' Don't worry! Your daddy will come and save you!" Twenty-two years since Yosepha had learned what it was to be truly alone in the world, to rely upon people where necessary, but never to trust them; and to try and carve for herself whatever shape of a life her gifts and fortunes permitted her.

She spent two nights and two days alone by the side of that road, sitting, lying down, or walking, hoping that sooner or later someone would pass by—a caravan of Bedouins maybe—and pick her up. She was terrified that whole first night, trying to sleep, freezing, and alone, in a ditch; and no less frightened all the next day in the brutal heat in the middle of nowhere, without food or water. At twilight, after two days, she was so parched and hungry, cold and exhausted, that when she saw a small jeep in the distance coming up the road, she thought she was seeing a mirage. In it were a man and a woman, kibbutzniks, it turned out, from a kibbutz far up north near the Lebanese border. The woman told Yosepha that they were building the very first kibbutz in that part of the country. They and eight other pioneers ("Crazy people may be more like it," the man laughed) had started it only five and a half months before. They already had tents up, and facilities for washing and cooking, a few chickens, and the beginnings of a garden. They had to manage their water very carefully, but they were getting by. The woman gave Yosepha a drink from her canteen, and some bread, and said that she was welcome to join them, if she liked. *And why not?* thought Yosepha. She had no way to get home from where she was, and this kibbutz sounded no worse than any place else. She'd stay for a while, and make her brothers and sisters worry—they'd have to come looking for her, they'd have to climb the whole height of this country to find her. Let them have a scare. Let them think that maybe she was dead. Yosepha told the woman and the man that she'd come for a while and see. Then she fell asleep in the back seat of the jeep, being bounced over the bumpy roads like a sack of flour, or a corpse.

The kibbutz was nothing but some tents erected on an ancient hill. It was nothing but a dream. But to Yosepha it seemed fine. And when the days turned into weeks, and the weeks into months, and there was no sign of her father, or her sisters or brothers, looking for her, she thought, *To hell with them. What should I go back for?* It would be a long and difficult journey—five or six days at least—to get back home. Public transportation was almost nonexistent then—there were barely even roads yet—and of course the kibbutz couldn't lend her either its jeep or its truck for such a long time. It would mean hitching rides all the way back, once again waiting nights and days by the side of the road. *Forget it*, she decided. *If they don't care, I don't care.* She threw herself into her work on the kibbutz, and for being such a dedicated worker, she quickly won the kibbutzniks' respect. At first she did the same things as everybody else: building wooden shacks, clearing away stones, and planting a vegetable garden. But after a while they noticed that she had the wondrous ability to make anything grow, anywhere she wanted. Sometimes she dreamed it the night before, in one of her strange, multi-coloured dreams: *This plant—here, in this corner. That one—over there, by the tree.* The next day she'd plant them, against all logic, and they would grow exactly as she'd dreamed. The kibbutz encouraged her to experiment, they gave her a free hand—and her successes were so unexpected, and dramatic, so unlike what anyone else was able to accomplish at that time, that within months she had caught the attention of the government. To the Ministry of Agriculture, she was a dream come true, the land being, as it was, rocky, stubborn, and for the most part unarable. Yosepha could grow things practically in rock. She grew bright, burning poppies on an all but waterless diet; bougainvillea in desert chalk, fruit trees in weak, tired earth. There seemed to be nothing she couldn't do. The Ministry was also thirsty for a solution to the problem of Israel's water shortage, and Yosepha had exciting new ideas. By the time she had been away from home for seventeen years, she had more than half the kibbutzim in the north irrigating with her method; five years after that, she was made Assistant Deputy Minister of Agriculture; and several weeks later, consonant with one of her most vivid and disturbing dreams, drought struck the land.

∞

The drought struck hard, and nowhere so hard as in the South where, unbeknownst to Yosepha, her father's sheep grew thin and keeled over, one by one. The "crisis in the South," as it came to be called, occupied Yosepha's thoughts night and day, though it had nothing to do with her being from there, or her family. She actually remembered very little of her home or her father, other than the warmth of his body when he touched her on the head or stood near her, and the dank, sharp odour of his sheepskin tent. During the first months on the kibbutz, when he hadn't come looking for her, when it seemed that he didn't care whether she lived or died, she discovered in herself a bitterness towards him so deep that it all but eclipsed her hatred for her brothers and sisters. As time went on, she thought about them all less and less, and threw herself into her new surroundings as thoroughly as she had wiped out the old. She retained, however, a horror for dryness and dust, and a fascination with water; and these elements, though never thought about, were deep in her, and moved her through her search to irrigate with a kind of irresistible force, an almost flawless intuition.

She began to dream nightly of saving the South: watering it with one gigantic sprinkler, arching water over its parched fields like a rainbow. She dreamed of bringing the life back into the land, making it burst into bloom with new and unheard-of flowers, and colouring the desert purple and red. She infected the Prime Minister with her dream, and funds for this project poured her way. He said to her, "I will establish an institute in the South, and you will teach the farmers there to irrigate. You will fill all our deserts with life."

They flowed from all over to Yosepha's institute: herdsmen, farmers, kibbutzniks, and shepherds, all of them with that struck, panicked look in the eye of men who have watched their sheep, cattle, or field crops die—and thought, as baldly as this: *I could die, too.* Nothing less than mad desperation would have brought these men to seek help from a woman—especially one like her, as slight as a girl, pale, and unmarried.

They came to Yosepha in droves, and sat at her feet.

One day in late August, when Yosepha was just finishing her daily inspection of the Institute and preparing to lock up and go home, a man approached her. To Yosepha he looked like all the others, crude and hairy, although also handsome in a way with his rough good looks.

"Are you the director?" he asked her.

"I am."

"I beg of you to help us."

Like countless times before, Yosepha asked the man where he was from (the South, of course), what kind of a *moshav* he had, how large it was, and so on. Only after he'd told his story did she ask more personal questions. The exact location of the *moshav?* The age of the father? The number of children? And then, the name.

On seeing before her her brother Shimon, Yosepha's first reaction was an almost physical revulsion. *So this was it: This hairy being in need was now bowing before her—this being, how dare he live!* Rushing back at Yosepha like water came the terror she had felt by the side of the road, the cold, the terror, the hunger. The fear, the hatred. The fear. And Yosepha excused herself.

When she returned, she said to him, "We are very busy here, as you must realize, and very short-staffed. There is no point in teaching you alone. According to our policy, it is necessary for all those involved in our project to understand the underlying principles. Go home, and bring back with you every member of your family—all your brothers and sisters, and your father, as well. Then we can help you."

Shimon protested. His father was too old, there was too much work to be done at home, no way could everyone be spared at once. Yosepha shrugged. "I'm sorry, then," she said.

Not until several months later did Shimon return. From her window, Yosepha watched the arrival of the big, dust-covered jeep as it rattled its way up to the entrance of the Institute. Out of the jeep tumbled a man and a woman, then another man and another woman, all of them dark and dusty from the journey. Yosepha recognized them, and had to turn away.

"Give me a few minutes," she said to her secretary, "before bringing in this new group. And make some tea, please—mint is what they like."

It was starting to come back to her. She stood behind the desk in her office as if it were a shield, and buried her face in her hands. *My God! What should I do? What can I say to them?* And then: *Can I ever forgive...?*

It had cost her not to, and she knew it. It had cost her to wipe out their memory but nurture the hatred, preserve and feed her seething, nameless anger. She had hated her brothers and sisters, but she had also hated herself, she had hated being small and afraid on that road. And she hated her father, too. It was his love, after all, that had spawned their hatred; their hatred was as natural as bacteria feeding on milk in the sun. No, she could not forgive him for cursing her as he had with his blessing. She would not release the past, she would not betray the girl that she had been....

Her secretary knocked, motioned the visitors in ahead of her, then followed with a tray of tea which she set on Yosepha's desk. "That will be all," Yosepha said to her, and she left. Yosepha counted the glasses of tea: fourteen. Fourteen Duralex glasses, huddled together on the tray, like a family. No one glass could be moved without touching another.

Glancing up for only an instant, Yosepha said, "Help yourselves to tea, and have a seat," and she herself took a glass, and began drinking, still on her feet. She looked at the irrigation map on the wall to her left, and not at her visitors, as they came forward to take their tea, and sat down on the sofas in her office, sipping. They sat and she stood. The sun shone in from the window behind her, and touched the top of her head. She put down her glass, and looked up. Their eyes were watching her, every pair of eyes, and as Yosepha gazed into them, one after another, she felt herself weaken. For strength, she looked away from them to the far corner of the room, and there, suddenly, she saw her old father.

My God, she thought. *How you've aged!*

She stared at him. Then at her brothers and sisters, one by one. She couldn't speak. She just looked at them and tears ran down her face. They stared at her, astonished. Gesturing with one hand, she said, as if in explanation,

"I am Yosepha."

Her brothers and sisters all looked at each other, frightened; but not one of them said a word. At the back of the room the old man rose from his chair.

"Yosepha," he said. "Alive?! Is it possible? Is it *you?*"

Yosepha looked at his face. *He didn't know*, she thought. *He never knew what really happened.* She'd thought he *did*, she'd assumed he knew and just didn't care. He must have thought ... all these years.... They must have told him....

Never mind. It doesn't matter now.

Yosepha looked at her brothers and sisters, seated before her with bowed heads. "Don't be afraid," she said. "The past has passed. I will restore the life to your land and your flocks, and you will be rich and prosper. I will take care of you—you are my family."

And then she went over to Yaacov, staring toward her voice as though listening to a dream. She put her hands on his cheeks. And from a place so deep in her, she herself was surprised, she said to him:

"You I forgive."

1998

Ronna Bloom, "Personal Effects"

There are other people's memories in street lights
at the corner of Yonge and Dundas or under the
expressway. Other people 's memories are flicked on
passing hospitals and alleyways.
In Vancouver, the voices of teenage girls
are broadcast in the street, telling of boyfriends
and what they wanted or didn't want to do,
whispered over loudspeakers at construction sites.
A certain colour car, a certain make;
this type of pen was a weapon once,
the smell of donuts only a prelude.

Other people's memories go down hot like a swallow
forced in the mouth. Another gag another
woman remembers everything.
She sits with the policeman , the crown
attorney and the friend. The crown says
tell me what you remember and she can
recount the time on the clock as she sat in the October
car, the colour of upholstery (brown), her foot on the dash,
the man beside and the hand that came from

the back seat, its fingers holding a pen like a knife.
She has a memory for details
and the crown, also a woman, asks
why she removed her dress herself,
why would she do that?
And her memories leave
in the bodies of the police, the crown,
the friend, and herself, as they walk out the door
and go the four winds, each with their own
version, their own retelling or silence.

On Bloor Street near Holt Renfrew
there's a woman begging in a wheelchair.
Stroke melted the brain and the body followed.
Blue sweatpants, palm out. She remembers
nothing. But a woman she meets there
remembers her, remembers her for her,
remembers her once in a spring dress, springy
but she doesn't remember her back. Mouths
words and palms the change.
Now the woman walking away carries
the other's memories, like personal effects
and the wheelchair goes off, glad
of a few dollars to buy lamb chops for dinner.

Other people's memories are passed
by mouth to ear, they enter seamless
and smooth as a ripple of water,
laying itself down like a layer of earth, strata
of the mind, the rings of a tree, or the crusted
bog with its rich sediment below ready
to be cut and dried and burnt.

Another layer of memory is outside
the pool hall and another around the edge
of the pool. *It was a hot day, everyone*
was going topless, everyone. Or, *it was a summer*
night, we all got drunk and went in.
It was there at the park with the shirt
that doesn't button well, he barely
touched it, all the buttons came undone,
the jean jacket I never took off again.
They were my friends I thought
and then they were gone, or else they
were making out under the trees.
The smell of barbecue chips and silver foil
in the sun.

Other people's memories wait in line
at the Scott Mission, on good days
they are dishing up the meat.

There are memories
on the street that curves called Spadina Crescent,
a cardboard box bends around blankets
to make a paper cave that blows away
in the January snow. The man there, gone too,
afraid of dinners, says someone put a computer chip
in his brain, he was waiting in the boxes, *please come*
and get it out.

The world, he says. *No, no, not the world.*

The ink of the mind is coming through the watering can
brain , making those fantastic spirograph spirals

of colour, the orange and the blue. He is leaking.
Like watching film on fire: the whole picture dissolving
from the centre. How the film gets stuck
in the projector, the bulb gets too hot
and it doesn't move. It doesn't move
it doesn't move.

What else is there to do but guess,
a history: a piece of clothing in a bag, a neatly folded
shirt, a green baseball cap, a father,
a mother once, they were singers
or bankers, they owned a store on Barton,
they lived in the suburbs
of Montreal, they lived in Victoria.
It was hereditary, it was genetic,
it was the frozen hose against the side of the head,
it was two fingers
between the legs.
They had a house on a hill overlooking the waterworks.
There are memories in the waterworks, under
the marble floor. They are embedded there,
or flow out into the lake or
get turned into novels you can never forget.
People will tell you if you listen.
If they can.
Then every time you pass there, every single time,
you'll be haunted by something
that never happened
to you. But hearing it becomes yours
seeps into your insides marbling you
so that Yonge Street is a landmark
a cellular memory, echoing and vibrating
and flinching the body.

Other people's memories are scraping
at nerve endings, getting across
synapses, revoking the myelin sheath.
They are dissolving the muscular tissue
that holds organs in place
and the insides are going sour with agitation.

In my grandmother's attic I find her purses,
small leather rectangles, tan or black, a woven white.
Inside each is the same thing: a lifesaver, a bobby pin,
a ticket stub from the symphony at Place des Arts,
peppermints.

In my mother's house the book shelves hold the books
and the books hold the bookmarks:
A History of the Jews holds boarding passes, recipes,
lists for holiday dinners, inside *Siddhartha* how much

chopped liver, how much egg. Buried in Thomas Mann
what she made, what was eaten, *Howl* has
where we sat, who came, what was put away, what the CBC played
that day. An archeology. I don't take
what is flattened there. Just take it in.

2000

Chava Rosenfarb, "Bergen-Belsen Diary, 1945"
(Translated from Yiddish by Goldie Morgentaler)

May 6
Father, where are you?

Today, for the first time, I hold a pencil in my hand. My fingers tremble over the white sheet of paper. Where is your warm, sure hand to cover my trembling fingers and lead them again to open the sacred doors of our Yiddish aleph-bet? When I was a little girl, you guided my hand over the neat white lines. We wrote the word "Tateh" and there arose such a light from those five small letters that the word itself acquired a soul, and I saw that soul reflected in your loving smile: "Tateh."

I sit near the window. The branches of the large chestnut tree outside reach up to the second floor where we are staying. Today I can see the sky and it is of the purest blue. Perhaps it is just an ordinary blue sky with nothing remarkable about it. But I see this sky as it must have looked to the first human being when he suddenly recognized God and genuflected before the beautiful blue expanse that stretched above his head. I want to write: "How beautiful you are, blue sky," but instead I see your luminous eyes. I can feel your blessings and your dreams, your smile and your longing.

Below my window I hear a commotion. It is nothing serious. Soup is being distributed. Everybody will get a portion. People are impatient, still haunted by the anxiety of yesterday that lives on in them. Although they know that no one will go away without his portion of soup—if not at this window, he will be served at the next—but still they all try to be served first. They want to be sure of that little bowl of soup, to stir it with a spoon. There is a man standing opposite my window. He emerges from the tangled crowd holding his bowl in his hand. He does not go to his room. He does not sit down at the table. Leaning against the stone wall he gulps down the soup as fast as he can. God, how hungry he is! For years he has been hungry and for years he has been frightened. He is very thin. A heavy coat hangs from his shoulders and reaches to his ankles. Between one slurp of soup and the next he wipes his face with the sleeve of his coat. He is tired but happy. I can see his eyes dance with pleasure as they glance away from his pot to embrace everything around him, from the green grass beneath the window to the tall chestnut tree. He is so happy. What is he thinking about, this man, this Jew, this tortured emaciated Jew? Most likely, he is not thinking anything at all. Even so, I know and his limbs know and his body knows that soon he will cast off his heavy black overcoat. Soon the flesh will grow on his bones. Life has arrived!

I shut my eyes. Deliberately I put out of my mind the man standing opposite. And suddenly I see you, Father. It is you. I can see how the strength is returning to your body. You are alive. Perhaps you too are standing somewhere at this very moment with your bowl of soup, leaning against another wall. Is it possible? I ask my heart, but it trembles with uncertainty.

May 7

Wherever I look I see you. No matter what other thoughts come into my mind, you are always there. Where are you, Tateh? Will I ever be able to caress you and beg your forgiveness? I showed you so little kindness in the lost days of my feverish past. I told you very little of my innermost thoughts. You were so thirsty to know my feelings and I was so stingy in sharing them with you. Where are you now, Tateh? I want to tell you everything!

Did you hear the firing of the guns? The shots are meant to tell the world that peace has come, that the hour of freedom has arrived; those very days for which you so longed when you were shut up in the darkness of the ghetto. Have you lived to see them? The uncertainty is torturing me. My only hope is that a miracle has saved you. You were so tired after those five years in the ghetto. But then, cut off from us, how could you have survived the still more terrible atrocities of the camps? Perhaps the longing to see us again helped you to survive? Tateh, we are here. The fire is glowing, but you are missing from our joy.

May 8

It is over. Our liberation has come, but she wears a prosaic face. No one has died of joy. No one has gone mad with excitement. When we used to dream of freedom, we bathed her with our tears. We crowned her with the garlands of our smiles and dreams. Now that she is here, she looks like a beggar, and we have nothing to give her. With what desperation did we call for her in those dark days. With what power did her far-off shimmer flesh out our thin bodies? Now she is here and she beckons to us from every corner. She is right before our eyes, yet we cannot see her. She begs us: "Touch me ... enjoy me ..." But we are tired. Our past, like a hawk, circles overhead, fluttering its black wings, devouring our days with horrible memories. It poisons our nights with terror. Poor, sad Freedom! Will she ever have the strength to free us from those dark shadowy wings?

Bats circle outside the window. Their wings flutter in a ghostly dance. My unfinished ghetto poem torments my mind. It used to accompany me in the camp. With its words on my lips I used to drag myself through the snows in the early winter mornings to work. I pencilled the verses on the ceiling above my bunk. Each day a few more lines. In my mind, I hear them constantly.

Through the open window I can hear the loudspeaker announcing that today the war is officially over. Where are you, Tateh? I want to hug you. The air trembles to the distant salvos of guns. Thin clouds of smoke waft through the air. We celebrate this festive moment with a chunk of dry bread. We have nothing better.

May 10

At night when I open my eyes, I see Mother and Henia. They are wiping the sweat from my forehead and they constantly ask how I feel. We tremble over each other's wellbeing. I want to comfort them. I want to tell them that we do not need to be afraid anymore. We are free now. But how can we protect ourselves from death? No, we are still very helpless.

I have a fever. Perhaps it is a cold. Or is it, perhaps, typhus?

June 13

For four long weeks the fever boiled in my blood. It scorched my eyes and dulled my brain. From under steep mountains I saw my loved ones coming towards me. They talked to me as they used to talk in the past. They smiled at me as they used to smile in the past and pleaded for my life. They cried through my eyes and squeezed my thin, bony hands. I embraced them in the emptiness. I snuggled my hot body into their fleshless arms, pressed my swollen, living lips to their lifeless faces. I stretched my thin fingers out into the shadows of the sweaty night and thought I was caressing their hair. I felt my own burning breath scalding my face and thought that they were blowing hot air onto my cheeks. They were all there with me. I saw my friend Yakov Borenstein, just as he was on that winter day when he prepared to leave on his last journey. His eyes were burning: "Don't be sad, my friend. We will meet again …" Suddenly, my lips started to tremble. "Come with me; come with me, my dearest friend. We will go for a long walk." "I am coming, I am coming," I called back. But my other friend, Kuba Litmanovitch, took hold of my hand. "Bring me an apple …" I went with him to the cemetery. All our comrades were there. From a far-off pathway there suddenly appeared Esterl and Moniek. They were holding hands and running towards us. "Wait!" Esterl shouted. Then she laughed in my face. "So now you know that I don't have much time." Moniek lifted her into his arms and placed her in the grave, as if he were putting her to bed for the night. Then he lay down beside her.

I inched myself closer to the wall near my hospital bed and made room for them all. But they angrily pressed me even closer to the wall. Suddenly their mood changed and they became kinder. I saw the whole ghetto street full of people coming towards us in a happy festive mood. Bunim Shayevitch came too. Then I was left alone. My bed swayed like a swing at the end of a long chain that stretched from heaven to the abyss, from life to dream, from dream to death. Bunim was standing by the window of my hospital room, just as he used to stand in his home at 14 Lotniche Street, his hands in his pockets, his grey eyes squinting from behind the lenses of his glasses. He looked through the sky, through me and beyond. "I have perished," he said. He took hold of the edge of my bed and swung it round. The earth started rocking. The sky began to shake. My body was on fire with the flames of the setting sun. I took off the checkered jacket that I was wearing and used it to fan myself as I went back and forth on the swing. I did this for a long time— so long, so long, so endlessly long, until my hands detached themselves from my body, and, with my fingers still clinging to the jacket, they fell into the depths of the night. I wanted to look down, to see where the jacket had fallen and where my hands had fallen, but tears blinded my eyes. Next to me stood my father, crying. His lips were very white and glued together, yet I could hear his voice. "Daughter," he said. "I brought you some lovely broth. Boiled potatoes and carrots all mashed up into a *tsimmes*. Take it and eat. Open your mouth. Look how tasty it is and how good it smells."

The taste of something sweet and refreshing made me open my eyes. On my bed sat my mother. She whispered something. I could not make out what she was saying, but her words dripped like balm into my soul. The tears from her tired eyes cooled my burning body. At the foot of my bed stood my agonized sister. Her frightened eyes blinked a prayer at me, entreating me to live. Yes, I must live. Some blessed justice has preserved me for their sake and they for mine. I want to give this justice its due; and I want to pay it back for all the injustice that has been done to us, for our loneliness.

June 18

Nearly six weeks in hospital. I have returned to life again. My body rejoices; my soul weeps. I suspect that it was not my body but my soul that was so ill. Helpless, hopeless, I feel like someone who has spent a long time in a dark cellar and has suddenly come up to the light. I am dazzled, drunk. I squint at the light, without the strength to absorb it.

It is spring. The spring of liberation. The sun breathes life into everything. And yet, beneath its blue skies there is emptiness. The sun's rays search in vain for so many faces, so many bodies that belong to those faces. They are nowhere to be found. The rays embrace a void, except when they settle, here and there, on a few solitary, half-starved individuals.

I lead a double life. One part is thin, fragile, trembling, young, and yearning for joy. The other part is deeper and more painful, full of memory and sorrow. The first is full of shame and guilt; the second is stormy, tortured, and full of fury. The first trembles on the edge of the second, but never penetrates it. The second, however, often steals into my new young life, disturbing, destroying, poisoning the least glimmer of joy. It demands attention constantly.

June 20

I am learning to walk. Today, Mother helped me down the stairs and took me into the yard. She found an old canned goods box and sat me down on top of it. A pity that there is so much dirt everywhere. Papers litter the ground; empty boxes, broken shelves and bed frames, discarded furniture soil the fresh green of the grass. Why can nothing be clean around us? Why is there no orchestra playing music to the rhythm of my heartbeat? Why is everything and everyone so indifferent? I am learning to walk! At least the sky is decorated with a sparkling sun. I look up at the sky. We are good friends again. It is good to be alive. It is delicious, a delight. I don't want to think about anything. I want my body to acquire flesh. I want my legs to recover their strength. I want to sing. I want to roll in the grass. I want to run carefree through the fields.

Henia brought me a little sprig full of blossoms. I am lying on the bed now, as pleased with myself as a young mother who has just given birth. The sprig of blossoms stands in a small bottle on the windowsill. When I turn my head I will see it, but right now I do not have the strength. Perhaps later.

June 23

Bats fly across windows.

Their wings flutter in a dance of ghosts.

Those lines haunt me. They are from Bunim Shayevitch's poem about our fate. I can see him standing by the window of his room. Tomorrow he is going away. In the dark corners of the room there still linger the spirits of his loved ones, who are gone. Soon he too will be gone. The last of his family. He is taking a whole generation with him. Nobody will remember them. Nobody will remember him. A nameless end.

But deep in my subconscious, they live on. They wake me at night. They pounce unexpectedly when I am in the middle of a laugh that is too carefree, or enjoy a moment that is too pleasurable. But when I want to bring them back to life, to take them out from their hidden places, then the slightest touch of a warm breeze, or the caress of a golden sunray makes my limbs grow numb with pain and I am seized with a powerful longing to escape them, to forget them all.

I know that back in those days when I was to share their fate, they did not pain me. They were with me, not in fact, but in essence. Somewhere on the way we got separated; at some unknown moment they left me. I went on the road to life. Now when I think about them, when I remember them, something breaks inside me, as if it would destroy me. Then I pray that something more powerful than this pain should come to my rescue. I want to live with them. I must remember them. I pray that time not erase the details of their lives from my mind, that my memory of them remain forever fresh and ready to serve me. But I'm afraid that it will not be so. My longing will remain eternally hungry, and as time goes on, more helpless. Memory will not serve longing. It will not be possible to remember all the little things, the tiny traces of individuality, which by themselves mean very little, but when put together create individuality. What will remain will be an abstract picture, a mere approximation of what once was and now exists no longer.

June 24

Last night I had a nightmare. I woke up screaming. I dreamed that we were being chased. We ran across fields. Suddenly I lost Mother. I opened my eyes and for a long time I could not calm down. In the darkness I could make out Mother's pale face, but I could not bring myself to believe that it was really her. No, we no longer need to run anywhere. It is all over. I walk around all day as if in a fever. Every now and then a shiver passes through me without my understanding why.

June 26

What lovely days we are having! Everything is green. Blossoms fall from the trees, gathering into white carpets under every tree trunk. Those trees which have not yet shed their blossoms look like religious Jews, slowly preparing to remove their prayer shawls. But what am I saying? These are just ordinary trees losing their blossoms. It is impossible to compare them to anything else. The sense of awe belongs to those of us who observe them. We are like children. Every day we make new discoveries. The joy of awakening makes us drunk. It is good to be able to breathe, to feel, to see, to hear. It is good to be able to eat, to be able to bite into a chunk of bread. We perform this sacred ritual with wild animal joy and a sense of religious duty.

We spend entire days doing nothing, but we are not bored. A blade of grass, trodden down under heavy boots has a hard job righting itself again and must wait until the sap in its veins starts to pulse with new life. We are that trodden grass. We are preoccupied with ourselves, with straightening our bent bodies. Nothing else is as absorbing or thrilling.

I think about Poland, the country of my childhood. I long for the familiar streets of my hometown. But what will happen if there is no one there to meet me?

I can see my father's face before me. I can feel his hand caressing my cheek, the same hand which so lovingly and presciently caressed me as we travelled on the train to our final parting in Auschwitz. Tateh, the thought of your warm hand grieves me. Where are you? Where will we meet again on the many roads of this world? Where will you look for us? Where should we look for you?

June 27

I went into the forest today. It's good that they've brought us here to recuperate—although it seems to me that no matter where they would have brought us, we would see beauty everywhere. From now on we will always see and feel the value of every beautiful thing that we come across. I lay down on a mound of grass and stretched out my body to its full length, with my arms thrown over my head. I had the feeling that I was covering the whole earth. Above me a thick clump of trees formed a circle, their branches entwined with clasped hands as if they were dancing beneath the blue festive sky. Nothing else happened, but this was enough. The world and life. I turned with my face to the earth and buried my head deep in the grass. The sweet smell of earth permeated my body and intoxicated my limbs. I bit off a blade of grass with my teeth and started to chew it. At this very moment, in distant towns and countries people are drinking wine. Poor fools. They will never know the taste of grass.

June 28

Two girls from our barrack did not come back to sleep last night. They arrived in time for lunch, bringing with them cigarettes and chocolates. They are not yet twenty years old. The Englishmen with whom they spent the night are the first men to admire their fresh, newly budding femininity. They are not the only ones in the camp. The forest is full of amorous couples. One meets them strolling along all the roads and pathways. One can hear again the almost-forgotten sound of women's laughter, a laughter meant specifically for men.

Sometimes when I hear this laughter I have the impression that it will suddenly turn into a wild cry, into the painful longing wail of a woman's soul, a woman who tries to find in the eyes, hands, and smiles of a stranger some small trace of the beloved man she once knew. From all the corners of the yard, from all the rooms, I can hear the sounds of gaiety and laughter. "Look, I have forgotten!" the cheerful voices call. But it is enough to look into the women's eyes to know something different.

The eighteen- and nineteen-year-old girls laugh earnestly and un-affectedly. How clever and wonderful life is! As if afraid that the nightmare they have just lived through might destroy their tender, young, newly awoken bodies, Life has taught them to forget. Easy, pleasant forgetfulness. Is it their fault that in their dreams they see the reflections of their parents' faces, or the smiles of their sisters and brothers, or shudder at the horrors they have so recently survived? During the day the girls flutter busily about singing, drawn from every barrack and courtyard to those who will teach them for the first time the language of love. The words may be strange, but they understand the gestures and the kisses. And then there is the sweetness of chocolate to bring back memories of their distant and yet not-so-distant childhoods.

Some women sell themselves to the soldiers simply and knowingly, just for the taste of a slice of white bread.

June 30

We must record and register every detail, even the most insignificant, of what has happened. It is a duty, an obligation, a compulsion. But around me there is sunshine and beauty and the carefree freedom of summer. I do not have the strength to resist it all. This is my first summer. Is it not poisoned to begin with? I postpone the writing from day to day.

I wonder if there will ever be an all-encompassing literary masterpiece that recreates the past. I doubt it. I recall my conversations with Shayevitch in the ghetto, when he was writing his long poem. I told him that such an epic has to be written from a certain perspective. Time has to elapse. He had no way of knowing then how his long poem would end, or that it would remain unfinished. He told me: "Our lives have to be recorded as they are happening. I am letting the story of our daily lives drip off the tip of my pen. We do not need anything else." Today I realize that it could not have been otherwise. The perspective will grow with time; it will stretch out and grow thin. Who then will bring back the terror of those ghetto days? Days like those can only be described as they are happening—with sharp, bated breath. Just as the writers and painters did in the ghetto. When one has distance, one can only remember fragments of the whole. But that memory lacks the pulse of the trembling, feverish present.

How can one construct an artistic history of the ghetto? Would such a work not mask the raw immediacy with which one must approach this topic? Is not the form of the novel too elegant, too peaceful, too comfortable, too quiet? I feel that to write such a novel would be an insult to my dear ones and also to myself.

July 1

I again saw Bunim Shayevitch in my dream. He was radiant with the same light that used to shine so often on his face when he was happy. We communicated with each other without words, just through thoughts alone. "I am very tired," he said. "But I'm happy." He was standing in his wooden shack. From somewhere he produced a big parcel of manuscripts. "Did you save them?" I asked him. He answered with his radiant smile: "I saved enough. Only the long poem, Israel Noble." He started to read the poem.

Suddenly he began to prepare for another journey. I told him: "We have been evacuated already, don't you remember?"

Where are you, Bunim? Where are all our friends? Where are the writers and painters and musicians of the ghetto? We are lonely. We are all together and yet each one of us is alone. What are we going to do with this gift of life? The world is closed to us. Somewhere there is a new beginning. For us time stands still. Long days and nights take us back to the past. The world is rewriting the history of the injustice that has been done to us.

July 5

From everywhere men flood into the camp. They are looking for their women. Every knock on the door makes us tremble with anticipation. With each knock someone new comes into our barrack. They come to ask if we have any news, if we know the whereabouts of their loved ones. They look at us with pleading eyes. "Maybe you know something about...? Please, try to remember. Think hard." They describe their dear ones. Don't they know that the picture they carry in their hearts has long ago been altered, that every day of the many that were spent in the camp changed one's appearance beyond recognition? We too make inquiries. The men answer brusquely, absentmindedly. We tell them what we know, but they have no patience. They jump up and run to another barrack looking for information. From an open door comes the sound of spasmodic sobbing. Bad news! An already forlorn heart has lost its last glimmer of hope. Or perhaps these are the sounds of joy, of a long-cherished dream come true? The sudden emotion has released the pent-up tears so that they gush forth in a stream of joyful relief. For whom does this person cry, for the living or the dead?

We cannot stay still for long. We run downstairs. There is commotion everywhere, as the men move from barrack to barrack. They stand before the open windows and call out long lists of women's names—wives, daughters, sisters. Then they wait to see if the miracle will happen, if from the depths of the rooms there will appear a beloved face. But they are greeted only by the eyes of strangers staring at them from the windows.

—Where do you come from?

—Perhaps you know...?

No, he does not know.

—And you, young lady, perhaps you remember my little daughter?

The camp trembles with expectation. We stop every man we meet. It would be so beautiful if one of these men turned out to be our father. How much strength we would need for such an encounter. When I see from the distance a man resembling my father, my knees give way.

Sometimes a couple walks past us. A man and a woman. They are holding hands, awkwardly caught between pain and joy. They are the lucky ones. We look after them with strange expressions in our eyes.

July 8

Tateh, this very moment I am calling you with all the power of my being. If you are alive somewhere then surely you feel my anguish. Surely you hear my call. Do not lose hope. If you are alive there is no road too far for me to travel. If you are sick, do not give in. Wait. We will come. Our joy will bring you back to life. We will make you well. We are calling you, Tateh!

July 10

We scan the lists of names of survivors of the camps. The long pages are crumpled from passing through too many impatient hands. There are finger marks on every single sheet of paper, like anonymous signatures. My fingers wander over the welter of names, my heart thumping wildly. Behind these names are actual human beings, Jews saved from death. They call to us. "Look, I am alive! I am here! Come find me, brother. Find me sister, friend …" How many of these names will not find an echo in any heart? Strange, solitary, lonely names; hundreds of them.

I have found some familiar names, some of people I knew well, some not so well. I'm glad to know that they are alive. But my fingers do not stop at their names, but continue down the list. I am looking for those who are still closer to me. Very often my heart skips a beat. The same name as…! No, it is another man with the same name. I continue the search.

July 16
We are losing our peace of mind. The uncertainty is destroying us. It is painful to catch the eye of the strange men moving about our camp. They are healthy, with strong, tanned, half-naked bodies. I see them and I cannot keep from thinking about the men dearest to me.

July 19, Wednesday
We have news of Father! By chance we stopped a man in the camp and asked him if he knew anything about Father. Yes, he knew. He was with Father until two days before the liberation.

July 20, Thursday
Henia and I are going to look for Father. We left the camp this morning.

August 28
We are back in the camp. Why am I telling all this anyway?

For four long weeks we trudged all over Germany. We got lifts on coal wagons, hitched rides with lorries packed with horses. We walked for miles, tired, frightened, with an uneasy feeling in our hearts. We were not the only ones on the road. We met hundreds of lonely children just like us. Hundreds of wandering fathers, hundreds of solitary wives.

It was all for nothing. Somewhere, perhaps in a forest or in a field lies the mutilated body of our father. Perhaps we passed the very spot, and did not hear the mute call of his body. He did not live long enough to feel our arms around his neck; we never even had the chance to kiss his wounds.

We looked for Simkha-Buniun Shayevitch, but that too was a fruitless search. Perhaps somewhere a breeze blew past us carrying the breath of his burned body. But we did not feel it. When we returned to the camp the bad news was waiting for us, brought by a friend who has survived. We have recovered a friend—but we have lost our father. Joy and sorrow. Why does the poor heart not break in agony? Our friend found our names on the lists. He told us that Father perished a day before the liberation, killed when an American bomb landed on the train that the Germans were using to transport Dachau prisoners deeper into Germany. Shayevitch was taken on the very last transport to the gas chambers. There is nobody left any more for whom to wait.

September 1

I do not read the names on the lists any more. I do not go anywhere. I know that I shall never see my father again. Actually I have known this for a long time. I felt it in Auschwitz the day we parted for the last time.

Now I must find all kinds of refined means to deaden my pain. I am going to make a lot of noise. I am going to run, laugh, busy myself with work, do everything I can to stifle the constant longing in my heart. But where does one get the strength for joy? How does one poison longing? Even Nature has lost its charm for me. I am empty of all desires.

I cannot get away from thoughts of my father's death. I experience it over and over again. I lose myself in thoughts of his lonely suffering—and yet, I am not dying of sorrow. I suppose that there must be still greater depth of pain that I cannot reach.

Last night I had a dream. I saw myself in the concentration camp with Henia. Every day fifty women were taken out of the camp to be shot. Henia and I tried every ruse we could think of to postpone being taken. When it was no longer possible to avoid our deaths, we begged the SS women guards to postpone our execution for just one day, because it was the Sabbath. We knew that we had to die, but could it not be one day later? That one extra day we pleaded for seemed to us to be more beautiful and enticing than our entire lifetimes. We pleaded with the guards and begged for that single day, but they did not want to grant it to us.

They were already preparing the execution grounds, when suddenly Father appeared with a burning staff in his hand. The SS women disappeared and Father told us that he would fight with us. It was true, he said, that we would have to die, but in fighting one does not feel one's death. We were so afraid for our father. He was talking so loudly, somebody might betray him to the guards. Later I saw us fighting. All the camps rose in one great uprising, Hamburg, Dachau, Buchenwald, and Bergen-Belsen. I saw a wave of flame sweeping over all of Germany. And we, the fighters, glowed victorious in that flame. It was a night of fire and everywhere I looked I saw my father with the burning staff in his hand. That staff emitted such fierce flames that the Germans sent airplanes to bomb us and we had to run to the fields in order to escape. It was then that Father suddenly appeared next to us, saying that he wanted to die together with us.

Never before had death seemed so attractive as it was in my dream. Later I saw us all in a cellar, but Father was no longer with us. Somebody opened the door. Our eyes were blinded by a grey shaft of light and I felt a great sorrow in my heart. It was the beginning of a new day.

1948 (in Yiddish); 2014 (in English translation)

Goldie Morgentaler, "My Mother's Very Special Relationship"

My mother, Chava Rosenfarb, was liberated at Bergen-Belsen by the British army on April 15, 1945. At the time, she did not know that she was free because, like many of the inmates, she had typhus. The British took her to a makeshift hospital on the grounds of the Bergen-Belsen displaced persons camp and there she slowly recovered.

The British encouraged a return to normality after the horrific conditions they found in the camp by providing venues for concerts to be staged by the former camp inmates. Once recovered, my mother, her sister, and their mother—my grandmother was one of the few older women who survived the war—went to one of these concerts. Waiting for the show to begin, my mother noticed a British soldier sitting alone in the row in front of her. She wondered how he would understand what was going on, as the concert was in Yiddish and she assumed—correctly as it turned out—that he was not Jewish. She tapped him on the shoulder and offered her services as translator. Her English was rudimentary, but good enough to start and maintain a conversation because by the end of the concert she and the soldier had become friends.

Where my mother learned enough English to communicate with the British soldier is a mystery I will never solve now that she is gone. She was born in Lodz, Poland and educated in Yiddish, Polish, and German, but not in English.

Who was this out-of-place soldier who decided to spend his free evening attending a Yiddish variety concert, despite knowing that he would not understand the language? His name was Douglas Jensen and he was the youngest son of a baker from Sheffield. Before being drafted he had trained as a graphic artist, an occupation to which he would return after the war. Douglas was a shy man of moderate height, athletic and good looking with a snub nose and pale blue eyes, but re-served—very English, my mother would say. Despite his shyness, he had an eye for pretty women and my mother, even with her hair shorn, was a beauty.

"I remember that a year ago I was still in the ghetto. A cold and dreary day. We have no coal for fire to warm our bodies. We are hungry and we have not to eat. We are so weary, so tired of our hopeless, senseless life. I am lying in the bed and with stiff fingers I am writing my poem. I'm no more in prison, I am no more a girl of a poor, humiliated, insulted nation. I am a victorious free soul. Happy moments!

"Now I am alone. My good friends—they remained in Auschwitz. It was the longest and darkest year of my life. Now is that terrible year past. The English army has freed us from the murderer's hand. In this time I met you. You have offered me the door to the world. Thank you. You often asked me why I am smiling. It was because I was remembering the good old time, when I walked with my friends, hand in hand. Then it was good to be. Now I have nobody.

"But the darkness has not completely returned. I walk each evening in our wood near the camp. And when it rains I stand under the trees and smile. I have the sun in my heart, the wind in my hair, and the rain in my eyes."

In another letter, dated October 28, 1945, she tells him that she has learned of the death of her father, one day before the liberation, when an American bomb struck the train on which he and other Dachau inmates were being transported by the Nazis deeper into Germany. She writes: "I cannot find freedom for my weeping soul."

Occasionally, a note of exasperation enters her letters that illustrates the distance between the survivors, struggling to return to normality, and the rest of the world. She feels that Douglas, despite having seen the conditions in Bergen-Belsen with its starving, diseased inmates and ubiquitous mounds of dead bodies, does not fully grasp what she has just lived through, nor the sense of displacement and homelessness that she feels. "How can you expect me to go back to Poland, where even now we have heard of a massacre of Polish Jews? I am a Jew and I am proud that I belong to this unlucky but intelligent nation. I don't want to go to a country where I am a citizen of the second category."

My mother's early letters to Douglas hint at a failed romance. She is flirtatious at first, but that tone changes when my father appears in the camp. My parents grew up together, sat on the same bench at school, won the same prizes, were high school sweethearts and hid together with their families in a secret room when the Nazis liquidated the Lodz ghetto in August 1944. The entire group was caught and transported to Auschwitz, where the men were separated from the women; my father and grandfather were sent to Dachau. Until my father arrived at Bergen-Belsen looking for her, my mother had no idea that he was alive. It was he who brought the news of her father's death.

Time passed. The romance may have cooled, but the friendship did not. Douglas had a gift for friendship, especially for friendship with women. During all my mother's postwar wanderings, until she made Canada her home in 1950, Douglas sent her newspapers and books. He sent her a gilt-edged copy of Shakespeare's plays, which she cherished her entire life and which I still have. He sent her his drawings, usually illustrations of poems, including a lovely watercolour illustration of William Blake's "The Sick Rose" that she kept in her workroom until the day she died. In 1948, after she published her first book of poetry, she was invited to London to give a reading at a Yiddish literary soiree. Douglas accompanied her, although he did not understand a word of what was said. Every year, he sent flowers on her birthday including her last birthday, eleven months before she died in 2011.

Not all my mother's letters are as dramatic as the ones she wrote right after the war. But they all trace the lineaments of her life, and taken together they form an autobiography in letters. Unfortunately, I have only her side of the exchange. I have not found Douglas's letters to her.

For sixty-five years, my mother and Douglas kept up their correspondence; she in Canada, he in England. She announced the birth of her daughter, then her son; he announced his marriage to a fellow artist. She sent him all her Yiddish publications and he advertised in the British press for someone who could translate so that he could read them.

Then, strangely, their marriages fell apart at the same time and for the same reason—the infidelity of their respective spouses. One day my mother impulsively bought a ticket to England and stayed with Douglas for several weeks. She made him chicken soup, tended his house, and wrote poetry. They wandered around London when he was not working, went to plays and flower shows. I would like to think that they became intimate, but I doubt it. They were both bitter about relationships then; and romance can poison friendship. But what do children ever know of their parents' sexual lives? What I do know is that my mother returned to Canada, to her children and her home, but not to her husband.

A few months after that encounter, she wrote to Douglas: "How good that we can cry on each other's shoulders! Douglas, tell me what is in your heart. In England you let me glimpse your frightening loneliness, which you are trying to deepen still further, because, you said, animals hide when they are wounded. But we animals are also human. I too feel like hiding, but there is nothing more meaningful for me than contact with people close to my heart."

When I was old enough to travel on my own, my mother insisted that I look Douglas up when I visited England and she wrote to tell him that I was coming. I was twenty-one and newly graduated from college. I was sitting on a wall outside my London B&B when I first laid eyes on this man about whom I had heard so much. He was white-haired by then, still spry, very polite, very reserved, and very witty in an understated English way. He showed me around London. He took me to the theatre. He let me watch as he drew his animated cartoons, a labour-intensive process in the days before computers. He apologized for not offering to let me stay at his house, but he lived there alone and it wouldn't be proper. This was in the early '70s, and with the smug superiority of youth, I found his anxious respectability very quaint.

After that, whenever I went to England, I visited Douglas, and, in the end, I did often stay at his house. My mother too visited Douglas, sometimes with her second husband, an Australian travel agent.

Douglas never remarried, not even after the premature death of his exwife, whom he always hoped would return to him. All his life, he was a recluse, a man of deep feeling and profound reserve, who mistrusted people in general, but relaxed in the company of women. He was athletic and, until the age of eighty when back problems made it difficult, he liked to go for day-long hikes in the Yorkshire Dales, where he had moved after he retired. But my mother's worries about him cutting himself off from human contact were not unfounded. After he retired, he lived alone in a cottage in a tiny village in Yorkshire, far from the nearest town. He was, he claimed, a contented recluse, surrounded by his books and paintings.

He died alone in hospital, not far from his cottage. He had just turned ninety-five. He had no children and as he was the youngest of his siblings, they had all predeceased him. I learned this from the solicitor who called me, in November 2012, to tell me that Douglas had left everything—his money, his paintings, his house, and its contents—to me. In Douglas's house, after his death, I found all the letters that my mother had written to him over the years, as well as copies of her books in Yiddish and in English translation. He appears never to have thrown out a word she wrote.

So I come back to the letters and the iridescent line they trace between the past and the present. In those letters I can hear the voice of my mother as a young woman, full of pain at the loss of all the people she had loved in her youth and of the irretrievable life that she had known before the war. And I can hear her as a new immigrant to Canada, feeling her way through the maze of the alien world in which she found herself, apologizing for her poor English. I can hear her as a middle-aged matron boasting about her children's accomplishments. And I can hear her as a wronged wife in despair over the breakup of her marriage. Most of all, I can hear her as the writer, discussing her books, proudly proclaiming, "I love to write!" and ending her letters to Douglas with the peremptory, "Jensen, write to me!"

As for Douglas, he is everywhere in my house. His self-portrait hangs over my fireplace, his hand-drawn birthday cards decorate all my bookshelves, his paintings hang on my wall.

I was born in Canada and have lived a comfortable life there. I have never been poor, gone hungry, lost friends to war, experienced persecution, seen people murdered before my eyes. Yet the dark shadow of the Holocaust has hovered over all of my life. Sometimes, however, that shadow lets through a ray of sunshine.

My mother's friendship with Douglas, immortalized in the form of letters, has been passed on to me as a gift from the past to the future. From youth to middle age to old age, they moved through life together, separated by an ocean, by different countries, backgrounds, faiths, and political outlooks, but always in sympathy. I am on the periphery of their story and yet I am its beneficiary, the heir to a life-long friendship that arose out of the ashes of genocide and devastation long before I was born.

2015

Ron Charach, "The Only Man in the World His Size"

You start off your morning
at the all-purpose store,
a confabulation of lottery tickets,
toiletries and adult magazines,
mainly to observe The Man.
A Yiddish Caruso at his register,
when you ask him how much the Clorets are
he chants the latest, like a cantor, *"Forty-Eight!"*
The only man in the world his size,
he goes to "The Bank" each day at 2 PM
and when he gets there, walks straight past the line
and heads for the glass booth at the back,
where *he tells them.*
He parks his wife at the lotteries desk,
won her after a kind of numbers game
of tattooed forearms
and odds of surviving
only a numbers man would go for.
His accidental escape,
had anyone noticed,
might have made fools of sadists.

He keeps registering fools,
fools who buy cigarettes instead of Havanas,
nervous souls who need a dirty picture
in the middle of a work day
(though The Man goes easy
with these types,
and says he "*understands ... Some people ...*")
Once, when I tried rushing him
on a rainy day of streetcars worth chasing
he froze me in place with the words, "*You too.*"
But all he needs is to make a few sales
and he pulls in his thickly bruised horns.

Once I heard him brag
that he and three other inmates kept their *Lager* so clean
that for two days the Nazis killed *Nobody*.
He only suffers to kill with a nasty look,
even takes the streetcar to work
though he could pick up an Audi or a Porsche
and still have change.
But by the end of the day
whatever his machine
it would turn into the same
Babylonian wheel.
Behind explosive laughs
and uncanny smiles
he hides his special powers: in dreams
he works a folksy version of this streetwise store,
one where Jews and Germans buy sausages together
without a second thought,
where the *Jude!* sign means welcome
in any language, and the hours he keeps
are humane.

Late at night
he floods his spotless house
with so many lights
that the Hydro keeps sending him
inappropriate Christmas cards.

But the only thing he cannot downplay
is his uncontrollable growth:
his wife already blended into his right arm
though moody, and too quick
to reach for a hanky;
and his son long ago became his right leg.
With his laboratory hours piling up like his Dad's
already he may have a kick
at the Nobel Prize.

He spends the early morning hours
after the wife is cottoned out,
binging on baked goods much too tempting to carry.

But the blender he uses
to reduce the separate chunks of life
to a custard of gain
by now has grown the kind of blade
that can make even sponge cake and heavy cream
bleed —

2007

Judith Kalman, "The County of Birches"

My mother, Sári, met my father, Gábor in a schoolhouse in September 1945. She sat with the women at the back of the schoolroom that smelled of dust and dry leaves and a trace of chalk, like ash. The evocation of ash was almost sensual. Powdery and soft as child's hair, and that unreal. Murmuring was subdued, because of those who weren't there.

The young men improvising the Rosh Hashanah service sat up front behind a lectern. One by one they stood to read the prayers they knew by heart, avoiding the eyes of those who had gathered.

"And this one?" Sári whispered. "Who is the one pulling his ear like a sidelock? Kramer, you say, from Nyirbátor? And the one with red hair...?"

She had drifted to her first husband's county when she had found no one of her own in Beregszász. In any event, the conference in Yalta had traded her hometown to the Soviets. She left while the boundaries were just dotted and pencilled in, as empty-handed as she'd arrived. What could she have taken that would have survived the war, a bolt of cloth from her mother's shop?

"What about this one, the big one? Weisz? Weisz, you say? What Weisz? Which Weisz? From where—Vaja? The Vaja Weiszes? No." No, János had never mentioned any relations from that village.

Sári Friedlander Weisz shared Gábor's name by marriage. She would have passed him over like the rest had she not learned from the other women that he was head of local JOINT, where those who came back sought assistance. Gábor Weisz was the man to see about finding János.

Sári observed him reading. The voice tuneless but proficient, round head nodding to an age-old cadence, thick fingers turning the page ahead of his words, just like any old-fashioned davening Jew. He couldn't have been more different from her János. Weisz. The same name, and from the same county. It was a cruel coincidence that another Weisz, but of no shared blood, belonged to this sad scrap of earth.

The town of Nyiregyháza where Sári met Gábor is named for the birch tree, like many of the cities and hamlets of the plain in northeastern Hungary. This flatland is actually more distinguished by the acacias that grow profusely in its sandy soil than by anything we North Americans would recognize as birch. Nonetheless, my father's region abounds in tributes to the white-barked tree. The Nyirség, it is called— the state of being birch—and its towns reflect this birchness in name if nothing else: Nyirmada, Nyirgyulaj, Nyirbátor, Nyirvásvári, Nyirmegges, Nyirjákó, Nyirvaja. The birch names are as ubiquitous as they are unpronounceable in English.

I begin here, when, after the service, Gábor passed through the congregation clasping hands. Round-faced Gábor, his nose long and sorrowful, his brown eyes initially shrinking from something so lovely as this woman with hair she threw back like a mare tossing its mane, accepted the hand Sári held out first. Sári Friedlander Weisz deliberately flaunted her hair as though it had grown thick and rich, long and dark, out of defiance. Her inborn vanity had not been expunged by near death from gas and starvation. She was a woman, who had grown back hardier and harder, like a rosebush pruned close to the quick. Her hair had been fair before it was shaved.

I imagine myself conceived when my mother, tossing back her hair, felt my father's eyes upon her. Light-sensitive eyes that had sworn off joy. Deeply impressionable, they drank in her hair, brown and un-fettered like his first wife Miri's had been only in the privacy of their bedroom, and her legs like a doe's slim and long, and her hand out-stretched like a man's.

I begin at this point when my father's heart rekindles, though theo-retically I go back further, before the great conflagration that reduced the numbers of his family from over a hundred to fewer than twenty, to the very beginning in fact of what we know of his ancestry, the pious vagabond without a surname called Itzig the Jew, which may have been a name generic to every Jew in the countryside. Itzig the Jew dragging his caftan in the dust of the Hungarian countryside at the end of the eighteenth century. I also hark back to the vineyards where my mother grew up and she and her six siblings played hide and seek, though it was forbidden to touch or trample the valuable fruit. (Among seven children, there are always a few young and small enough to wriggle belly down along the furrows, and fast enough to flee the raised fists of the field hands when they are discovered.) The story really starts with them, because who my parents once were and where they came from is a sum I repeatedly figure, trying to calculate how it adds up to me and my sister.

Like any child, most of all I care about the *I*. The I that clamours to speak for itself. This I owes less to the piety of generations of orthodox Jews or to the mercantile candour that characterized my mother's fam-ily than it does—its very inception—to the war that wedded them and to which it became reluctant heir.

I knew this war like I knew the pale hand that held the spoon to my mouth. A hand moderately proportioned, distinguished by its smooth-ness and the incipient arthritic swell of its knuckles. I felt these joints when I played with her wedding band, working the ring up and over the first knuckle. Even the second one arched slightly, causing the ring to skin its surface. I have always known the war like I knew the impa-tient withdrawal of that hand if food was not taken quickly enough or if the ring slipped and fell from my stubby fingers. I have never not known of the war, though I don't recall hearing about it for the first time any more than I remember the first chime of my mother's voice or kiss of fresh air.

The war came to me with all that is good. It dawned on me like my own sweet flesh and buds of toes and the bright gold band that lay on the soft pads of my palm.

My mother's marriage, the one before Gábor, was hardly more than a courtship. Promenading arm-in-arm along the *korzo*, she in her smart suit and box hat, her military man uniformed, they made a decorative couple. People mated during the disastrous decade. People stepped out and showed off. They would wake up one day and the nightmare would be over. A beautiful girl like Sári, her parents reasoned, would need to be married. My mother dwelt on that, the promenading, the handsome figure they cut as a pair. It was all she had to tell us, all there was to that match.

And that on her wedding night she was slipped under the wire of the labour camp. She'd say that matter-of-factly. On her three-week honeymoon she was smuggled into the camp nightly. *Under the wire of the labour camp.*

Sári, my mother, who would squirm away impatiently whenever Gábor gave her fanny a friendly pat. Sári who, kissing me goodnight, would pull both my arms from under the bedclothes and press them firmly over the blankets, admonishing me to keep them that way. Sári who educated me early in the decorum of intimacy with the cryptic warning, "Remember, it's always the man who takes and the woman who gives." Her stance was prudish and ingenuous, as though she had never been touched by men's hands.

Yet every night for three weeks, she had allowed herself to be smuggled onto János's pallet. Risking military discipline, they made a love that must have been memorable. Love, among the coughs and groans and gases of male strangers. He waited for her in the dark beside the wire fence he and his friends had clipped and disguised, then pulled her through the dark into the barracks that smelled of boots and sweat. This young woman who had accepted his kisses coquettishly, always drawing back, who had lived sheltered in her parents' home, never exposed to danger. In that animal kingdom of men and their fear of death, I assume he used humour to disarm her. *Humour.* Because what we knew about my mother's first husband, we had heard from Gábor.

My father described János Weisz as a professional soldier, an officer in fact, who had served as captain in the Magyar army. Stripped by the so-called "Jewish Laws" of his rank and career, János Weisz was conscripted into the labour service in the fall of 1941, just like Gábor and his brother Bandi, agronomists by profession, and their lawyer-brother Miklós. They were thrown together with village boys so poor and unschooled my father and his brothers had to take them in hand, show them what part of the boot to polish, simple village Jews whose main skill was the practice of Jewish tradition. János Weisz became their natural leader. When the actual sergeant turned out to be a Hungarian peasant much like themselves, pulled from his hut and put in charge of a regiment, no one questioned the authority of János Weisz over the ragtail band. The military officer was relieved to lie low in the local café.

The first labour service bore little resemblance to what would follow. As the war progressed, licence with life was taken increasingly. But when the labour service was first established, Hungarian Jews were emboldened to believe that if this was all that was going to happen—this and their restriction from professions and owning land—if what was to be taken from them fell short of breath, they could bear it. Labour service would kill Bandi in the copper mines of Bor and abandon János Weisz on the Russian front, but it saved my father from Buchenwald.

Gábor respected János Weisz. János was not a big man, but his military bearing gave him stature. He was younger than Gábor but, Gábor said, you could see that he was a man of the world, not easily intimidated. My father was impressed by the distance János Weisz kept from the rest of them, for the sake of authority.

Enlistment took place a few weeks before Jewish New Year. For many of the men in the troop this would be their first Rosh Hashanah away from home. Business and education had led Jews of the monied class out into the world, but it was usual for poor Jews of the countryside to live their lives in one village. Observance of the High Holy Days was through prayer and strict abstention from work. The village Jews assumed that the Lord would see to it that His Law, as intrinsic as the laws of nature, would prevail. Tension mounted as the High Holy Days approached and the Lord had not indicated what they should do.

János Weisz became aware that the poor Jews in his company had started looking on him as the unlikely instrument of the Lord. They were fearful and uncertain, bowed beneath centuries of religious tradition and cowed by secular authority. János Weisz knew the ways of their military and Christian masters. They didn't accept him as a real Jew; he was too worldly, too tainted by outside influences. But in his own way he was enough like them to understand their dilemma. János Weisz grew aloof. He withdrew and ate alone, giving no indication of how he would direct them on upcoming Rosh Hashanah.

Gábor and his brothers were orthodox Jews, but their God appreciated extenuating circumstances. They would risk His wrath before that of their taskmasters. Gábor sympathized with János Weisz, whose authority was unofficial at best. The slightest leniency on János Weisz's part, or suggestion that he was sparing the Jews, might unleash upon them all some devil sent to teach them a lesson, and on himself a personal penalty. But when a delegation begged Gábor to appeal to János Weisz to permit them to observe the Holy Day with respect, Gábor could not bring himself to refuse. He saw their beardless faces and heads shaved in military fashion, so incongruous with the pious stoop of their shoulders and bends of their noses and melancholy eyes, and he felt for them a deep pity. These people were helpless without their customs.

On *erev* Rosh Hashanah, the eve of the holiday, Gábor approached János Weisz. The mood in the barracks was heavy with dread. János Weisz was losing his patience. Had someone died here? Which one of them had been beaten recently, or received a bullet in the head? Which one of them had passed a day without eating? What were these fools mooning about? Did they not realize? Did they not know that Jews elsewhere in Europe were dying? Now here was Gábor Weisz, a man of good sense who should know better; what did Weisz expect of him?

"János," Gábor began, "the men are deeply distressed at having to work and desecrate this Holy Day."

"Is that so?" The reply was curt and impassive. "Let them make their apologies to the Lord then."

Gábor was surprised and offended. He was a man of social standing, accustomed to respect in the Jewish community. Shrugging, he returned to the others.

Rosh Hashanah dawned, a day like any other. And as on any other day, János Weisz marched his men into the woods.

Ten days later, on Yom Kippur, no one appealed to the Jew in János Weisz. True, Gábor recalled, the mood among the company was funereal. But no one suggested observing the Day of Days. Those who chose would fast and pray while they worked. János Weisz called up his company on Yom Kippur and marched them out. Each man carried his axe and his pack. At home, they would have walked the shortest distance to *shul.* They would have spent the day in prayer neither drinking nor eating until the first star appeared in the heavens. This Yom Kippur morning was cold and clear. The sun rose in a cloudless sky, brightening the firmament. Ordinarily it would have been the kind of fall day they might have liked being outside. The trees would wear long shadows; the men would take in the cold air, and watch clouds of breath affirm that they were alive. But because it was Yom Kippur, the boots marched into the forest bearing them like husks.

The discontent, unvoiced, was nonetheless pronounced. Day after day their company of Jews had felled timber to meet a daily quota. The military officer had come out once or twice to keep up a semblance of command, but regularly he was more than content to leave the company's direction to Weisz. Far from the front, and performing menial back-up services, their company had received only tertiary attention from the authorities. All Rosh Hashanah day they had wielded their axes. And if János Weisz had called just a fifteen-minute break for them to respectfully say a few prayers, there would have been none to know the difference. When his men looked at János Weisz, they did not see his military training. That meant nothing to them. What they saw was an apostate Jew, and he affected them with horror.

At noon of the holiest day of the year, János Weisz gave the order to stop. The axes ceased swinging. The men looked up. No one pulled bread from his pack. János Weisz barked, "Quota met! Company, dismissed!" The men stood irresolutely, unsure of what was meant by the command. Clearly they had not achieved the day's requirement. "Dismissed!" János Weisz shouted again.

Gábor summoned his two younger brothers. Arms around each other, they turned to face east to the Holy Land, as did each member of the company. Then, not daring to murmur their prayers aloud, they began to sway to an ingrained measure. Some had hats; others tore leaves from the trees to cover their heads, not to appear bareheaded before the Lord.

Outside, under the sun and among the trees, they celebrated the Holy One, praised be He. Gábor said later that the sun's rays had poured over them. In all his life, he never had—and never would again—feel so tangibly the presence of God. As a boy in the synagogue of his paternal grandfather he had not felt so near to the Deity. Nagyapa Weisz with his prophet's face and passion had awed the boy with the force of his faith. Yet here in the woods, in the open air, Gábor felt the Creator in His element. Gábor felt loved by God.

"What do you mean, Apu?" I asked, hearing this story for the third or fourth time. "What do you mean, 'loved by God'? How did He love you different from the others? Why you, Apu, why did God love you and not János Weisz or Bandi-bácsi or Miklós-bácsi, or your wife Miri-néni or your baby Clárika?"

"I don't say God loved only me, where do you get that?" he answered testily. "I say that I felt at that moment that indeed God loved me. He loved us all to pour His glory over us. To let us worship Him so purely out in the open amid His creations. He could only love us to create for us such a wonderful moment. Terror and sorrow and loss transformed into the glory of God. He must have loved us to create for us such a moment. And I felt He loved me. That He was there with me, beside me, warming me with the breath of His love."

While the company of Jews prayed, János Weisz struck his axe. Throughout the afternoon, he maintained a steady rhythm. That is how the sergeant found them. From a distance, a single axe stroke did not sound thin. But as the sergeant neared it would have become evident that not everyone could be working. Even so, he was taken by surprise at the sight awaiting him when he came through the trees. Men scattered in the woods, swaying silently, lost in their own private worlds like inmates in an asylum for lunatics. One madman swinging an axe. A company of mindless mutes, facing east, swaying on its heels.

The sergeant was a thick-armed peasant. Having neither money nor education nor aristocratic name, he would never have reached the rank of officer in normal times. Some officers with little experience compensated with excessive brutality.

"Weisz! What's the meaning of this?" he demanded.

János Weisz had laid down his axe, Gábor said. He stood smartly at attention to answer his commanding officer.

"Sir," he said distinctly and without hesitation, "the men are overworked, Sir. They need to rest."

"And who decided this? Who said they are tired? Who gave them permission to rest?"

"I did, Sir."

Stalled by the authority in his subordinate's response, the sergeant wavered indecisively until he was struck by a baffling observation.

"On their feet! They rest on their feet?"

"Yes, Sir," said János Weisz without blinking or expression. "That's how they rest, Sir—Jews. Like horses."

"*Like horses*," Gábor said. "János Weisz said 'like horses.'" And Gábor would chuckle slyly. He was not a man given to laughter. When he did laugh, it was always with some guilt. "*Like horses.* Do you see?" Not one of us enjoyed the joke more than Gábor. It was always fresh for him.

No one had laughed in the woods. No one moved for some moments. The silence was complete, palpable with the sense of impending reprisal. But the sergeant retreated without comment.

My mother listened quietly whenever Gábor told us the story of the Yom Kippur woods. She never said impatiently, as she did to so many of my father's anecdotes, "We know that one already." The rapt way in which I followed Gábor's tales usually made her fidget or get up to make a phone call. But she would listen to this story, told always the same way, ending always with Gábor's chuckle, "Like horses." My mother recognized the humour. She knew the man who wooed a young bride inside a barracks that was a portico to death, the man who could find something funny in these circumstances. At the time she had understood János's recklessness as ardour, but Gábor's story showed a man who defied the inexorable march of history by slowing it down a few paces. As Gábor wove the scene of the Erdelyi Woods, Sári listened. So this was the man who had pleasured her in the dark. This was the man with whom she might have spent her life.

Gábor survived four labour services altogether. It was during a discharge, as he was about to board the train that would take him home to where his wife, Miri, and their child had moved to be with his parents, that his path literally crossed that of his fellow serviceman. János Weisz was disembarking. He had been called up to re-enlist. The two men greeted each other warmly, hands clasping in the steaming stench and roar of the station.

And how have you fared in these lousy times?

They had not been close, not friends. After the Yom Kippur episode, János Weisz had maintained his reserve. But when they met in the Nagyvárad train station, János and Gábor felt a warmth for each other that might have blossomed into friendship in another clime. They shook hands, and Gábor clapped the other man's shoulder.

"So, you're on your way then. Do you know where they're sending you?"

"Who knows anything?" János replied. "But you're going home. That's what matters. Look, I'm not doing so bad. Let me show you."

Gábor was anxious to board. At home they were waiting for him. Miri had written that the child, Clárika, had started to read since he'd last seen her. She had taught herself her letters, and not yet four years old. They would be waiting in the carriage sent to meet his train.

János Weisz pulled something from his breast pocket. Grinning, he handed it to Gábor.

"She's a beauty, isn't she? We've just been engaged."

Gábor said he didn't take much notice of the photograph. It was a studio shot that revealed little more than a pretty face.

He glanced at the photograph of Sári Friedlander courteously. He was glad for János Weisz. You had to go on living, believing that one day the world would turn itself right side up.

"I wish you one hundred and twenty years of happiness," Gábor said, using a Yiddish expression.

They had parted, one going home and the other away, one east and the other west. But they didn't end up at different destinations. Inscrutable the ways of the Lord that bestowed and denied, filled a moment with meaning and discarded human life. Their paths eventually met rather than crossed. They joined at the woman who would bear their name.

János Weisz returned to Hungary from the Soviet Union in June of 1948, when my sister, Lili, was seven months old. Sári and Gábor had known of his whereabouts for a short while. They were lovers at the time János was traced to a camp for prisoners of war, as the first prisoners were released by the Russians and began to trickle home, bringing with them the names of others.

Sári lost her bearings when János wrote to say he was coming home. She had given him up with the others for dead. How could he be alive if everyone else who had belonged to her was done for or gone? She had been deserted by everyone. Mamuka. Apuka. Her sisters, too: Toni, Netti, Erzsike, all her older sisters dead. Her brother Laci had escaped to England to avoid the labour service draft. Izi, her other brother, was pioneering in Palestine. Only Sári and her youngest sister, Cimi, remained. The dead were all dead. They were a vast collective. She was numb at the thought of them. Them, the solid crowd of them. When János broke from the ranks of the dead, the whole company crumpled into separate, excruciating parts.

Gábor and Sári weren't married. Without death certificates for their spouses, they could not legally marry for seven years. This allowed for the lost to be found, the departed to return, for time to sort the living from the dead. They were not officially joined, and now János was said to be alive when Sári considered someone else in every way her husband.

She had no idea what her parents would have had her do. No one had taught her the rules for this contingency. Where were Mamuka and Apuka when she needed their guidance most? How could they have left her? What would they tell her was right? Right for her. Right for János, and right for this man they had never met but who looked to her as a plant looks up at the sun and drinks the rain. She was distracted by rage and loss. Cimi was no help. Cimi was starving somewhere in the south of the country, with a Chassidic boy she had picked up like a stray cat. Sári screamed at Gábor to keep away.

Gábor found a rabbi—most likely a reasonable proxy, a young man who was once a rabbinical student, perhaps—and they built a *chupah*, the ceremonial canopy used in Jewish weddings. He told Sári: What did the state matter? They would be joined as Jews, they would become man and wife in the eyes of the Lord.

"And János?"

Gábor, essentially a conservative man, did not even attempt to overlook the affront to decency posed by his displacement of János. János was his burden, another twist of fate to Gábor's right arm.

"János will know it couldn't be helped," he sighed.

Sári married Gábor, older than her by thirteen years, the same age difference there had been between Sári and her eldest sister, Toni, in whose house she used to set the table and rock the baby. She would care for her own children as she had learned to nurse that baby who had been in Sári's girlhood the best of toys. Gábor had lost a child too, also a little girl. Sári saw in Gábor someone who might span the chasm between her parents and her present. He was the bridge she crossed to bind the broken pieces of her life.

János had written for the first time from the Soviet Union. He wrote three identical letters, sending them in care of the JOINT offices in Budapest, in Munkács and in Nyiregyháza, the places Sári would most likely have gone back to. Sári responded, telling him of her new circumstances. She asked for his forgiveness.

No further news came from János until just before his return journey. Lili was a newborn. Sári wrote back that it was no use. But János persisted. He wrote that in the black pit of his deprivations he had thought of her and the darkness that had woven them together. He was coming home to her and to the baby, it didn't matter whose. He wanted her and he wanted the baby and he wanted them to begin. They had never had the chance to even start their life together. They'd never known what it was like to live as man and wife.

She answered that she was now the wife of another.

He wrote a last time once he was back in the country. János said he bore Sári no ill. The man she had favoured was a decent man, János recognized that. He wished them well.

As children Lili and I knew of our parents' first spouses as we knew of all their lost relatives. The card came every holiday season from another world, somewhere called Argentina: "Best wishes, János." It was Gábor who responded, not Sári, signing on behalf of us all.

It puzzled me, the Nyirség, the county where my parents met. Why was it named for birches? When I asked him, Gábor would shrug. No, he would say, birches could never have grown there. Acacias were indigenous. Acacias in the Nyirség, the county of birches. The Nyirség became for me a place of mind against which our real acacia world would never measure up.

Gábor and Sári were plain people, something belied in the storybook concurrence of their encounter. They worked, raised their children, tended their garden, socialized little. They cared about family, tradition, and security. But their story was heroic. This discrepancy irked me. The circumstances of their past imbued them with a grandeur that didn't fit. They were ennobled by tragic events, and elevated further when these events were shaped through telling. Gábor's stories grafted meaning to their lives. There was a point always to his anecdotes, as though history has form we have only to uncover. Caught up in the story, I learned to expect meaning that makes sense of time.

Gábor often said that the finger of God pointed him the way out of each brush with death—the finger of God, because he was not an intuitive man, nor one given to notions beyond reason, and because he would never attribute to himself any special good sense that was not shared by other members of his family. Gábor believed in the finger of God, because he had to explain somehow the chance of his survival. And I believed in it too; otherwise why was I here? What I figured was that for some reason or other *I* had to happen. Those people and their world must have been misconceived. God had made a mistake, brushed off the chalkboard, and begun again. Otherwise the tally didn't add up. My father depicted an earlier world that was a golden era of wealth and community and insoluble family bonds. The glory, and most of the happiness, predated me. Only cataclysm could have brought about my parents' union. And whatever for? Why would that have been?

There's a photograph of me before we left Hungary. I am standing in a field, on unsteady legs wrapped in ribbed leggings. I am hatless, and my few wisps of hair have been gathered in a spout on top of my head. My expression wavers between a frown and a smile. I have been crying, says my mother, because I don't want to be photographed. The long grasses of the field bend in the breeze. I still have it in my hand, she says, the gold wedding band she has given me to distract me from my tears. It is there in the picture, although we can't see it clutched in my plump paw. It is our last unglimpsed knowledge of its whereabouts. I know it, feel it pressed into the soft folds of my skin. It brings the tentative smile to my face. The gold in my hand is the sun emerging from my clouded features. I am last to have it, the ring that binds my mother and my father, before I let it slip into the dense wild grasses.

1998

Robyn Sarah, "After the Storm"

The leaf that under
the dripping eaves
receives
rain's overflow,
the darkened leaf, and shiny—
leaf at the end
of the thin branch straying
nearest the wall

has to bow sharply
under the impact
of each drip that falls,
and does so with the
crispness of a
Hasid praying.

2009

Gabriella Goliger, "Maladies of the Inner Ear"

In the Hauptmarktplatz outside Gerda's window all is confusion—the whine of engines, slam of metal doors, footsteps, shouts, murmurs, entreaties, cries. She presses her face into the pillow, but the din continues. Now the noises order themselves into a steady rhythm, a thick *tramp, tramp, tramp* of a thousand boots on flagstones; they approach, recede, approach, recede. Sickening as this is, what follows is worse. For now all is still except for the splash of water from the fountain in the middle of the square. It is a tall, spire-shaped masterpiece of intricate stonework, this fountain—the town's showpiece with its tier upon tier of stone figures from the twelfth century. Cascades of water run down the faces and robes of saints, prophets, popes, and noblemen, bathe their stone eyes. Inches from her ear, it seems, water pummels the ground with merciless *smacks*. She tosses her head sideways. No escape.

∞

In the bedroom of her luxury apartment in Toronto's Forest Hill, Dr. Gerda Levittson is finally fully awake and staring at a familiar trapezoid of reflected light on the ceiling. The cacophony of the Hauptmarktplatz is over, replaced by a shapeless, nameless roaring. Something like a sea is in her head. It thrashes against the walls of her skull with dizzying, deafening force. It is what Gerda calls her demon and she senses its laughter as she drowns and drowns in noise, is sucked under by foul despair.

With effort, she pushes herself into sitting position. She fumbles in the drawer for her hearing aid and pushes the cool moulded plastic into her ear. As she raps with her knuckles, testing, on the bedside table, this blessed sound from the outer world penetrates. *Tap, tap.* A message of hope, calm and real. She switches on the radio. Late-night jazz. Muffled trumpet notes above the waves.

Outside, the night is black beyond the glow of the streetlamp. It is 2:16 a.m. The sleeping pills that were supposed to deliver her into morning haven't worked. Time, perhaps, to administer a higher dosage. Insomnia is the worst part of the affliction that has tormented her for the past two months. Same for everyone. This fact is confirmed not only by the medical journals and textbooks, but by the sighs and moans of fellow group members. Those like herself, who are new to the misery, have the pale, strained faces and nervous tics of insomniacs.

Each one hears something different. Mr. Somerville, self-appointed chairperson of the group, hears the distant but persistent drone of an airplane. Lucy hears crickets and sometimes, on a very bad day, the sound of smashing china. Bob hears the crackle of radio static, as if his head were caught between channels. "I keep wanting to adjust the dial," he says with a wry grin, while his fingers twitch.

Gerda switches on the bedside table lamp and attempts to read more of her novel, but the words swim on the page and the clamour worsens. Learn to live with it, they say in her group. Learn to relax and accept the rushing, roaring wind in the cave as if it were as normal and natural as the ticking of a clock. So it abates, becomes background noise and you can hear yourself think. Interesting phrase. Never, until now, has she realized what it meant, or what its *opposite* might mean. The steady inner voice that has kept her company for seventy-five years is now gone, roughly expelled. She won't find it again until the dawn spreads its calm, grey light through her apartment and solid edges re-appear—top of the dresser, silver frame around the family portrait cir-ca 1932—father, mother, Ludwig, and herself, a plump, bespectacled adolescent.

∞

Friday nights back in Germany. The dinner table laden with gilt-edged serving dishes that offered up smells of roast chicken, dumplings, challah, and wine. The family kept the commandments, but in mod-eration, according to their liberal faith, and in the time-honoured, decorum-loving way of the German Jewish bourgeoisie. On Saturday, although Gerda's father closed the store, he went in to do accounts in the shuttered gloom or to sort through order forms and samples of material—tweeds from England, silks from Japan. On Friday evening, they all gathered around the dining-room table, lit candles, murmured blessings in Hebrew and German, and tucked into the courses that the maid put before them. Her father with his stern bulldog face sat dis-tracted, stealing glances at the neatly folded newspaper at his elbow. Her mother, thin and wan in the light of the Sabbath candles, was al-ready showing the signs of illness. The family was able to see her safely to her grave shortly after the first volley of boycotts and decrees and be-fore the Law for the Protection of German Blood and German Honour.

Her brother, Ludwig, was twenty-six, a teacher at the leading pro-gressive, secular school. He was remote and handsome with a neat moustache and wavy hair trained back to show off his high, noble fore-head. With his confident laugh, he teased her about her lessons, what she didn't remember or hadn't yet learned. He recited Heine: "'Oh Germany, distant love of mine ...' Well, what comes next?" Her cheeks flushed with indignation. She could have told him about the stages of photosynthesis, but he asked the wrong questions.

Her father mumbled his abbreviated version of *Birkat Hamazon*, "Grace after Meals." "Lord our God ... sustains the whole world ... food to all creatures ... may the Merciful One reign...."

Before the amen, and despite entreaties from their mother, Ludwig was up from his chair and dashing toward the hall.

"What a way to behave. You'll spoil your digestion."

He sat his fedora on his head, blew a kiss, and was gone. They knew he was off to the Hauptmarktplatz where young people gathered on Friday and Saturday nights to exchange news and argue politics. But mostly they went to flirt and to court or be courted. Arm in arm, newly matched couples paraded around the perimeter of the square, while those still single clustered in small groups by the fountain. Ludwig was in great demand.

∞

It is dark. It is the middle of the night. Outside, beyond Forest Hill's stately homes, the woods of the ravine lie still in the heavy air. The sweet, rotting smell of late August wafts through the window. She would like to walk outside right now, in her nightgown, into the embrace of the bathwater-warm air but … muggers and maniacs. This too is new, this timidity. A few months ago, Dr. Gerda Levittson, despite her age, her deafness, her cane, walked the most secluded paths of the park whenever she pleased. Former patients, whose faces she always remembered although she forgot their names, greeted her with delight. "It's just not the same since you retired," an old-timer would say. "The young ones these days don't know how to listen."

She went once a month to Rinaldo's Hair Design to have her favourite colour, Sunset Glow, reapplied by Rinaldo's deft hands. Afterward, as she stumped along through the crowds in Yorkville, she chuckled to herself at a passerby's occasional startled glance or indulgent smile. This wonderful parade of fashionable young people in their leathers and silks and studied indifference.

But her heart is no longer in Rinaldo's and Yorkville. The hairdryer bothers her, the smells and most of all being confined in the chair with the hot, sticky plastic apron tied tight around her neck. She wonders whether, beneath the cooing encouragement, Rinaldo has been laughing at her all these years. Her real colour, yellowish grey, has grown back in, pushing the band of orange-red away from her head and looking, for the first few weeks, like a gaudy, badly arranged bandanna.

She reaches under the bed for her notepad and pen to work on the little talk on medications she is preparing for her group.

"*Tinnitus,*" she has written. "From the Latin, meaning to toll or ring like a bell. It can be almost any kind of noise—a hissing, whistling, crackling, grinding, roaring, thrumming, clicking, chirping, pulsing, rattling, booming (or any combination of these), or even a tune, endlessly, distractingly repeated. It is a symptom, not a disease. Some possible causes: an increase of fluid in the inner ear, pressure on nerve fibres due to infections, tumours, multiple sclerosis, muscular spasms, circulation problems, reactions to drugs, caffeine, alcohol, loud noises, hormonal changes, anxiety, depression, shock."

Two-thirty a.m. The endless night creeps on its belly.

She reaches for the telephone, longs to hear her name spoken by a friend, words to anchor her, but who at this hour...? Although Hannah Birnbaum in Montreal might be willing to talk, it would be Ernst who would answer the phone, dazed, worried, then somewhat annoyed by her assurances that everything was all right, that she just wanted to chat. And Hannah would be distressed beyond all proportion because her Gerda had always been the strong one. Months ago, Hannah had phoned, depressed and lonely. Gerda, setting out for her afternoon ramble, had suggested joining a group, though she knew full well Hannah was incapable of reaching out to strangers. Later she called back and apologized for her curtness and they reminisced about old times, the youth group in Germany—the outings, flirtations, misadventures. "Remember," Hannah said, "the day I knocked over the bench during the talk on kibbutz life? I almost howled with laughter!"

Hannah had been lovely then, innocent and bumbling as a calf, driven by a restless yearning for nature. On outings in the country she trembled with rapture at the sight of a tumbled-down wall overgrown with wildflowers, while Gerda collected botanical specimens.

Before Hitler, and for many months afterward, the youth group had been about camaraderie, purpose, and fun, an escape from cold shoulders and outbreaks of violence on the streets. Serious business, yes, but only to a point. Anyway, who took the Zionist rhetoric literally? Not even the leaders who wrote the manifestos. Ludwig, of course, had always scoffed at the "little ghetto in Palestine" and at propaganda that stressed divisions between Germans and Jews. One learned to shut out ugliness, to make much of small triumphs, to bear insults—a complaint about the garlicky smell of Jews in the tram—with head held high.

As the noose tightened, friends, one by one, departed for Palestine and America, but Gerda resisted the temptation to join them. Despite the strict quotas, she still hoped for a place at the university and, besides, she was needed at home to help care for her mother, suffering through the last stages of tuberculosis. When everyone, not just the young folks, began talking of emigration, havens had become harder to find.

∞

At what point did she forget to think about Ludwig? Was it when she and her father walked in a daze down the platform at Union Station? It had been sheer luck that they got out when they did. They had been like all the other lost souls without papers, scurrying along the streets, ducking their heads when a Brownshirt appeared. Then, a miracle: a visitor's permit to England and, later, boat tickets to Canada from a cousin, Sheldon, in Toronto.

The last time they saw Ludwig, he was in his cellar flat in Berlin, chain-smoking at the kitchen table, his blue eyes confused and sad. A brief, proud light flared in him when her father tried to persuade him to leave. He could not face more grovelling in the anterooms of consulates. He was determined to wait the Nazis out.

Somehow Ludwig slipped from her mind and, at that moment, it would seem, a cattle car slammed shut. Insane thought, outrageous and utterly symptomatic, according to the psychologists. She cannot bring herself to think beyond the slamming of the door. It shuts and her mind retreats and she is relieved by her lack of morbidity and she is aghast at her cowardice and it goes around and around. A textbook case. Still, she searches for the exact moment she forgot him. She recalls the old apartment on Bathurst Street, her father's bedroom and her own next door, where the radiators in winter gave off too much heat and she sat near an open window letting gusts of wind keep her awake.

She loved the lonely night hours. In those days Gerda Levittson, the medical student living in her father's house, itched for eleven o'clock, for the dreary Friday-evening Sabbath ritual to be over and for her father to plod down the corridor to his bed. Then, laying a towel along the bottom of the door to prevent light from spilling into the hall and arousing her father's peevish anger, she switched on the desk lamp. That fine, intense glare on the printed page. She tunnelled into the text, noted, memorized, added knowledge, brick by brick, to her solid foundations. The late-night stillness, immense and calm, buoyed her. She lifted her head from her books and felt it press against her. Solitude was a muscular embrace.

∞

Friday nights in the Bathurst Street apartment. She and her father sat crowded amid the serving dishes in the dining room, which was cluttered with unnecessary sideboards and chairs. When did her father go back to the strict orthodoxy of his childhood? After the Red Cross telegram, or before? One day, when she had come back from a lab, a gleaming set of crockery, uncontaminated and ready for the new kosher regime, stood on the kitchen counter. A long list of injunctions went with it. On the Sabbath she was not to turn on a light, not to tear a page, not to put pen to paper, not to ride, not to carry any object—not even a book—outside the house. A prayer for rising and for lying down to sleep. A benediction for hearing good tidings and for hearing bad. A chain-link fence of rituals and commandments that invested the minutiae of daily life with enormous significance and kept everything outside at bay. The quaver in her father's voice as he laid down the law made her go along with it, while she planned her respites and escapes. How Ludwig might have teased and waggled a forefinger. She could hear his voice: "Have you said the benediction for slicing into a cadaver?"

Her father cooked and cleaned while Gerda went to her classes at the university. On Fridays she had to be home in time for the lighting of the candles. When she arrived he was wearing a velvet skullcap—special for *Shabbas*—on his bald, liver-spotted head and it made his jowly face look more withered and pathetic than ever.

He fussed, he shuffled between dining room and kitchen preparing the table—the two challah loaves and their cloth covers, the saltcellar, prayer book, dishes, and cutlery. His aged hand held the *kiddush* cup in the air, the dark wine trembling at the brim as he recited the blessing in a gravelly voice. He did the *motzi*, blessing over bread. Slowly his stiff fingers tore off a piece of challah for her, sprinkled salt, and placed it by her plate.

When she opened her mouth to say something, his hand flew to his face in an alarmed gesture. No talking between *kiddush* and *motzi*, she remembered. As she ate her salted bread, he hurried to the kitchen to bring out the meal. A pale chicken broth with bits of parsley and droplets of fat, just as his own mother used to make. Roast chicken, potato dumplings, peas, and beets. The same dinner repeated itself every Friday, down to the canned dessert peaches and vanilla wafers, imported from Israel. He munched in silence, methodically, without a sign of pleasure or appetite. After sopping the last bit of gravy from his plate with his bread, he launched into a rambling monologue about arcane family customs.

"In your aunt's house they took their salt from a little crystal dish. Do you remember? No, you were too young. A silver-and-crystal dish, part of a set she had. They took a pinch between forefinger and thumb and sprinkled it on the challah. Like this, see? My mother thought it uncivilized, everyone dipping their fingers in the same dish. The thing is, now I don't know what is right...." His voice trailed off, thin and plaintive.

"Ask a rabbi," Gerda said, her eye on the clock.

"*Ach*, the rabbis here. Pollacks and Russians. They know things, of course. But it's not the same as a rabbi from home."

Finally, "Grace after Meals": "... for your covenant, which you sealed in our flesh; for your Torah ... for your laws ... for life, grace, and kindness...." His voice was a flat monotone. He couldn't carry the tune at the singing parts, but did not seem to expect her to join in. At the last words he rapped on the table. "*Pflicht getan.*" Duty done.

∞

"Insomnia," she writes in her notebook, "is the most troublesome side effect. Medications: anti-spasmodic clonazepan (brand name Rivotril) ... the tricyclic amitriptyline ... a specialist from New Zealand prescribes an anti-convulsive...."

The group members are proud to have her in their midst. They look to her for answers. "I know nothing more than you do. There is little substantial research...." No matter. They describe symptoms and wait for her answers. Often she walks out of the meeting more dazed and battered than when she entered. Still she regards the meetings every second Thursday as a necessity. They are fellow shipwrecked travellers. They know, they hear. In their strained smiles and anxious eyes she sees the reflection of her own pain. It is as necessary to be in contact with them as to locate familiar objects in her room after troubled sleep. She envies them their simple-minded faith. They are eager to try herbal remedies, sound-masking devices, reflexology, colour therapy, acupuncture, although, from what Gerda can tell, the results of these treatments are highly inconclusive.

"Chronic *tinnitus* is chronic pain. Our nervous systems are not adapted to absorb the impact of a constant stimulus. Internally generated sound, from which there is no escape, creates an abnormal situation that can call forth the production of noradrenaline, a neuro-chemical that primes our responses...."

The nerve endings in the inner ear quiver. They cannot stop. The liquid around them is in perpetual motion.

∞

One of the more bizarre theories to float out of the pages of the *Volkischer Beobachter* maintained that you could distinguish Jew from Aryan by the shape of the left ear. Ludwig snorted with delight when he read this. He had his photo taken in left profile and sent it, under the pseudonym Reiner Deutschmann, to the editor. An example of an impeccable Aryan ear. They printed it, with thanks. Ludwig was on top of the world.

∞

The telegram from the British Red Cross was as brief and final as words on a tombstone. "Ludwig Levittson: last seen Berlin February 1943 boarding transport. Destination eastern territories. Regret no further information at this time." A scrap of newsprint paper with three badly typed lines, large "X"s over the mistakes and the date on top—September 5, 1946. The end of almost eight years of anxious inquiries, nightmarish rumours, a clutching at hopeful signs and growing certainty of doom. She put it in the file folder marked "Red Cross," which she slipped to the back of the drawer.

Her father had sat hunched at the end of his bed, his hands limp in his lap, tears dripping from his nose and chin. First he'd waved the brutal truth away. The telegram was vague, so sparse in detail. What kind of transport and which part of the East, could the Red Cross not find out, could it not have been possible...? Gerda shook her head, grim, determined to end this futile hanging on, this water torture of letters to officials and their carefully worded replies. Finally, he crumpled up and wept, resigned, helpless, exhausted, unrestrained. While horrified at their abundance, Gerda envied him his simple flood of tears. It seemed he would cry the life out of himself. She stroked his shoulders and head, rocked him in her arms, averting her face from his wet, loose cheeks, his odour of age and despair.

As he wept, she planned the days ahead. Her first term of medical school was about to begin. She could not afford to miss a lecture, but could put off long study sessions for a couple of weeks while she kept him company until the worst was over. Then she must drive on with her own life's course. During the months that followed, she prepared for midterm exams. She ignored the silence that fell and the burst of chatter that rose up again like a wall when she walked into the med school cafeteria. All those male voices linked in camaraderie and common disdain. She bent her head, cheeks burning, toward her books.

At night, when her overcharged brain would not shut down, she would pick up the anatomy text at her bedside table. She'd trace the course of blood through the body, recite the soothing names of the heart's chambers: superior vena cava, inferior vena cava, atrium, atrioventricular valve. Aorta to arteries to minute capillaries where the blood cells push through, one by one by one, transform themselves through intricate chemical reactions, then carry on their timeless, perfect journey back to the heart.

∞

Words roll and buckle on the page. Metal gates *crash, smash* against tender membranes already whipped raw. Noise is pain is noise and she is buried in it, six feet under, mouth, nose, ears stuffed with *smash, crash,* and the *yowl* of the dead. This is not madness, it's a condition, it's all the same. "Enough now. Stop." Her frail, cracked voice takes aim at the bedlam. "Enough of this nonsense."

She reads aloud. She recites: *"Yitgadal v'yitkadash sh'mei raba.... Im eshkachekh Yerushalayim* ... If I forget you, O Jerusalem...." Whatever words come to hand until she stands solid again above the waves. *"Tinnitus,* from the Latin, meaning to ring or toll like a bell...."

The young ones these days don't know how to listen. Was she a good listener? Was she, really? She certainly knew how to translate the anguished, but vague, complaints into precise symptoms. The files on Mr. X grew fat. Symptoms noted, tests ordered, results collected, medications prescribed, side effects noted, medications changed.

∞

Another scorcher, the radio announcer promises. The sky, glimpsed through the curtains of the kitchen window, has gone from black to milky grey. Streetlights wink, bring the daytime world into faint but unmistakable relief. Later on, the street will lie in dusty, yellow heat, but for now a pleasant breeze parts the kitchen curtains and caresses her face. The ocean roar is beginning to subside. Gerda sips scalding hot chamomile tea to soothe her stomach, which threatens to heave bile. Every bodily function now—a stubborn bowel movement, a fit of tears—can start up the tidal wave in her head. She takes small, wary sips. The stomach above all is a capricious beast that must be treated with respect.

Across the hall, she hears the soft click of a neighbour's door. Gerda opens her own door to greet Mrs. Paulsen, a pink-cheeked woman about Gerda's age, but younger looking, who is on her way to the garbage chute. Mrs. Paulsen's eyes, limpid and innocent, show that she takes the calm around her for granted. Her movements cause no reverberations. She could not imagine the shroud of echoes Gerda is buried beneath, although she has clicked her tongue and shaken her head over Gerda's ailments.

Back in the apartment, Gerda listens to the radio announcers, a man and a woman, who chatter about tie-ups on the 401 and a stalled truck that's spilled its load of hamburger buns onto the Don Valley Parkway. Morning sounds. A miracle of solid ground through the waves.

Who is she to deserve miracles?

She closes her eyes for just one instant, her attention wanders and look what happens. A row of naked, emaciated men totter above a

ditch, topple down into the cold ooze, their mouths open but sound-
less, their eyes crying out in unspeakable horror. If she had kept that
fine-tooled mind more alert, if she had listened for the clanging of the
gate....

She continues writing: "Some people find relief through various
treatments ... masking devices that generate white noise ... cassette
tapes with the sounds of nature, ocean waves breaking on a shore."

There is no cure. Slowly, the mind flattens itself, adjusts, yields to
the pounding wash. Slowly, sound and silence are one. A firmament
appears in the midst of the waters.

2000

Sharon Nelson, "On Tasting Any Fruit for the First Time in the Season"

Taste the early strawberries,
sun-warmed and sweet,
the tiny wild fruit we pick,
each one a perfect treat,
the first *real* fruit of the season.

And here, now, alive,
glorying in summer heat,
we eat fat peas and slender beans,
each the first of its kind, the first of its season,
and new potatoes, small and round,
speckled in their pale skins.

My grandmother cooked,
then skinned each one,
quickly, scalding her fingers.

She served them in the pot to keep them hot,
with dill, freshly cut, green, and clinging.

Dill on new potatoes
carries the flavour
of the Old World from which we've come,
the stories from another time,
the telling we live out.

2002

Susan Glickman, "Between God and Evil"

Is the title of the book review in the Saturday paper
which I am trying, ineffectually, to read
with Rachel on my lap, coffee cooling just out of reach.
She grabs a blue pencil *(turquoise,* she corrects me,
turquoise and violet being her two favourite colours)
and methodically circles all the words she recognizes:

> *to, the, and, in,*
> *look, little, one,*
> *me, you, or,*
> *love, lost,* and *garden.*

She skips over *Nazis* and *Hildegard of Bingen;* ignores *destiny*
and *hallucinations;* turns her pyjama-clad back righteously
on *fundamentalism.* And maybe she's right.
None of those words have brought you and me any closer
to love, or to the little one lost
in the garden.

2012

Eva Hoffman, "Exile"

We are in Montreal, in an echoing, dark train station, and we are huddled on a bench waiting for someone to give us some guidance. Timidly, I walk a few steps away from my parents to explore this *terra incognita*, and I come back with snippets of amazing news. There is this young girl, maybe my age, in high-heeled shoes and lipstick! She looks so vulgar, I complain. Or maybe this is just some sort of costume? There is also a black man at whom I stare for a while; he's as handsome as Harry Belafonte, the only black man whose face I know from pictures in Polish magazines, except here he is, big as life. Are all black men this handsome, I wonder?

Eventually, a man speaking broken Polish approaches us, takes us to the ticket window, and then helps us board our train. And so begins yet another segment of this longest journey—all the longer because we don't exactly know when it will end, when we'll reach our destination. We only know that Vancouver is very far away.

The people on the train look at us askance, and avoid sitting close to us. This may be because we've brought suitcases full of dried cake, canned sardines, and sausages, which would keep during the long transatlantic journey. We don't know about dining cars, and when we discover that this train has such a thing, we can hardly afford to go there once a day on the few dollars that my father has brought with him. Two dollars could buy a bicycle, or several pairs of shoes in Poland. It seems like a great deal to pay for four bowls of soup.

The train cuts through endless expanses of terrain, most of it flat and monotonous, and it seems to me that the relentless rhythm of the wheels is like scissors cutting a three-thousand-mile rip through my life. From now on, my life will be divided into two parts, with the line drawn by that train. After a while, I subside into a silent indifference, and I don't want to look at the landscape anymore; these are not the friendly fields, the farmyards of Polish countryside; this is vast, dull, and formless. By the time we reach the Rockies, my parents try to pull me out of my stupor and make me look at the spectacular landscapes we're passing by. But I don't want to. These peaks and ravines, these mountain streams and enormous boulders hurt my eyes—they hurt my soul. They're too big, too forbidding, and I can't imagine feeling that I'm part of them, that I'm in them. I recede into sleep; I sleep through the day and the night, and my parents can't shake me out of it. My sister, perhaps recoiling even more deeply from all this strangeness, is in a state of feverish illness and can hardly raise her head.

On the second day, we briefly meet a passenger who speaks Yiddish. My father enters into an animated conversation with him and learns some thrilling tales. For example, there's the story of a Polish Jew who came to Canada and made a fortune—he's now a millionaire!—on producing Polish pickles. Pickles! If one can make a fortune on that, well—it shouldn't be hard to get rich in this country. My father is energized, excited by this story, but I subside into an even more determined sullenness. "Millionaire" is one of those fairy-tale words that has no meaning to me whatsoever—a word like "emigration" or "Canada." In spite of my parents' protestations, I go back to sleep, and I miss some of the most prized sights on the North American continent.

∞

By the time we've reached Vancouver, there are very few people left on the train. My mother has dressed my sister and me in our best outfits—

identical navy blue dresses with sailor collars and grey coats handmade of good gabardine. My parents' faces reflect anticipation and anxiety. "Get off the train on the right foot," my mother tells us. "For luck in the new life."

I look out of the train window with a heavy heart. Where have I been brought to? As the train approaches the station, I see what is indeed a bit of nowhere. It's a drizzly day, and the platform is nearly empty. Everything is the colour of slate. From this bleakness, two figures approach us—a nondescript middle-aged man and woman—and after making sure that we are the right people, the arrivals from the other side of the world, they hug us; but I don't feel much warmth in their half-embarrassed embrace. "You should kneel down and kiss the ground," the man tells my parents. "You're lucky to be here." My parents' faces fill with a kind of naïve hope. Perhaps everything will be well after all. They need signs, portents, at this hour.

Then we all get into an enormous car—yes, this is America—and drive into the city that is to be our home.

The Rosenbergs' house is a matter of utter bafflement to me. This one-storey structure surrounded by a large garden surely doesn't belong in a city—but neither can it be imagined in the country. The garden itself is of such pruned and trimmed neatness that I'm half afraid to walk in it. Its lawn is improbably smooth and velvety (Ah, the time and worry spent on the shaving of these lawns! But I will only learn of that later), and the rows of marigolds, the circles of geraniums seem almost artificial in their perfect symmetries, in their subordination to orderliness.

Still, I much prefer sitting out here in the sun to being inside. The house is larger than any apartment I have seen in Poland, with enormous "picture" windows, a separate room for every member of the family, and soft pastel-coloured rugs covering all the floors. These are all features that, I know, are intended to signify good taste and wealth—but there's an incongruity between the message I'm supposed to get and my secret perceptions of these surroundings. To me, these interiors seem oddly flat, devoid of imagination, ingenuous. The spaces are so plain, low-ceilinged, obvious; there are no curves, niches, odd angles, nooks, or crannies—nothing that gathers a house into itself, giving it a sense of privacy, or of depth—of interiority. There's no solid wood here, no accretion either of age or dust. There is only the open sincerity of the simple spaces, open right out to the street. (No peering out the window here, to catch glimpses of exchanges on the street; the picture windows are designed to give everyone full view of everyone else, to declare there's no mystery, nothing to hide. Not true, of course, but that's the statement.) There is also the disingenuousness of the furniture, all of it whitish with gold trimming. The whole thing is too revealing of an aspiration to good taste, but the unintended effect is thin and insubstantial—as if it was planned and put up just yesterday, and could just as well be dismantled tomorrow. The only rooms that really impress me are the bathroom and the kitchen—both of them so shiny, polished, and full of unfamiliar, fabulously functional appliances that they remind me of interiors which we occasionally glimpsed in French or American movies, and which, in our bedraggled Poland, we couldn't distinguish from fantasy. "Do you think people really live like this?" we would ask after one of these films, neglecting all the drama of the plot for the interest of these incidental features. Here is something worth describing to my friends in Krakow, down to such mind-boggling details as a shaggy rug in the bathroom and toilet paper that comes in different colours.

For the few days we stay at the Rosenbergs', we are relegated to the basement, where there's an extra apartment usually rented out to lodgers. My father looks up to Mr. Rosenberg with the respect, even a touch of awe due to someone who is a certified millionaire. Mr. Rosenberg is a big man in the small Duddy Kravitz community of Polish Jews, most of whom came to Canada shortly after the war, and most of whom have made good in junk peddling and real estate—but none as good as he. Mr. Rosenberg, who is now almost seventy, had the combined chutzpah and good luck to ride on Vancouver's real-estate boom—and now he's the richest of them all. This hardly makes him the most popular, but it automatically makes him the wisest. People from the community come to him for business advice, which he dispenses, in Yiddish, as if it were precious currency given away for free only through his grandiose generosity.

In the uncompromising vehemence of adolescence and injured pride, I begin to see Mr. Rosenberg not as our benefactor but as a Dickensian figure of personal tyranny, and my feeling toward him quickly rises to something that can only be called hate. He has made stinginess into principle; I feel it as a nonhuman hardness, a conversion of flesh and feeling into stone. His face never lights up with humour or affection or wit. But then, he takes himself very seriously; to him too his wealth is the proof of his righteousness. In accordance with his principles, he demands money for our train tickets from Montreal as soon as we arrive. I never forgive him. We've brought gifts we thought handsome, but in addition, my father gives him all the dollars he accumulated in Poland—something that would start us off in Canada, we thought, but is now all gone. We'll have to scratch out our living somehow, starting from zero: my father begins to pinch the flesh of his arms nervously.

Mrs. Rosenberg, a worn-faced, nearly inarticulate, diffident woman, would probably show us more generosity were she not so intimidated by her husband. As it is, she and her daughter, Diane, feed us white bread with sliced cheese and bologna for lunch, and laugh at our incredulity at the mushy textures, the plastic wrapping, the pre-sliced convenience of the various items. Privately, we comment that this is not real food: it has no taste, it smells of plastic. The two women also give us clothing they can no longer use. I can't imagine a state of affairs in which one would want to discard the delicate, transparent bathrobes and the angora sweaters they pass on to us, but luscious though these items seem—beyond anything I ever hoped to own—the show of gratitude required from me on receiving them sours the pleasure of new ownership. "Say thank you," my mother prompts me in preparation for receiving a batch of clothing. "People like to be appreciated." I coo and murmur ingratiatingly; I'm beginning to master the trick of saying thank you with just the right turn of the head, just the right balance between modesty and obsequiousness. In the next few years, this is a skill I'll have to use often. But in my heart I feel no real gratitude at being the recipient of so much mercy.

On about the third night at the Rosenbergs' house, I have a nightmare in which I'm drowning in the ocean while my mother and father swim farther and farther away from me. I know, in this dream, what it is to be cast adrift in incomprehensible space; I know what it is to lose one's mooring. I wake up in the middle of a prolonged scream. The fear is stronger than anything I've ever known. My parents wake up and hush me up quickly; they don't want the Rosenbergs to hear this disturbing sound. I try to calm myself and go back to sleep, but I feel as though I've stepped through a door into a dark place. Psychoanalysts talk about "mutative insights," through which the patient gains an entirely new perspective and discards some part of a cherished neurosis. The primal scream of my birth into the New World is a mutative insight of a negative kind—and I know that I can never lose the knowledge it brings me. The black, bituminous terror of the dream solders itself to the chemical base of my being—and from then on, fragments of the fear lodge themselves in my consciousness, thorn and pinpricks of anxiety, loose electricity floating in a psyche that has been forcibly pried from its structures. Eventually I become accustomed to it; I know that it comes, and that it also goes; but when it hits with full force, in its pure form, I call it the Big Fear.

After about a week of lodging us in his house, Mr. Rosenberg decides that he has done enough for us, and, using some acquired American wisdom, explains that it isn't good for us to be dependent on his charity: there is of course no question of kindness. There is no question, either, of Mrs. Rosenberg intervening on our behalf, as she might like to do. We have no place to go, no way to pay for a meal. And so we begin.

1989

Malca Litovitz, "Provincial Olive"

In Muskoka, the furniture creaks
and the lake hangs dull green.
Loons and seagulls haunt the painting.
I am that provincial olive born in Ontario
yet somehow exotic:
not fully of this soil yet rooted in it.

1998

Elana Wolff, "Snow Bolls"

Driving back on Bathurst Street,
I see a sudden cotton tree and understand
they also grow in cold. Formed from slim deciduous
limbs whose lingering leaves get masked to bolls
that won't become designer clothes or batting,
but little fists that ferry me to Israel and Egypt
where the cotton boils on bushes.

There's an image I have of stomping in a bin
near En Haród. Alone in the heat for long enough,
I dare to take my T-shirt off. I stand there sweating,
gaping at my naked cotton bra.
The bolls beneath my feet are pliant fibre:
I'm pariah-white,
strafed with blood from scrapes with bracts and burrs.

2006

Naïm Kattan, "Cities of Birth"

I want to tell you my city's tale. I'm on the top floor of a new building downtown. From my balcony, I survey the city. Here is the river, here the Jacques Cartier bridge. In the distance, the hills of Mt Saint-Bruno. At the other end, curved like a question mark, the Olympic Stadium.

I want to tell you my city's tale. Neither hymn nor celebration. A city that encompasses all others.

I had just turned nineteen when I first saw the streets and roofs of Paris, a city only just emerging from war, from the occupation, from everything that had stripped it of its essence. In the effervescence of universally rediscovered youth, people were beginning to savour the taste of freedom. Nevertheless, rationing was in effect. Coupons for bread. No butter, and cheese a rare luxury. Electricity was cut off during the day, and was weak and miserable in the evenings. The City of Light had lost its lustre. Before lectures began, I had a week to play tourist.

Climbing on foot to the top of the Arc de Triomphe, I saw the city stretched out before me. In my most extravagant dreams I had never imagined such splendour. Over the months and years, I ambled down avenues and streets. For half a century, every time I crossed the Pont Neuf, I would feel a surge of pleasure, a thrill that has never diminished. This beauty would never be equalled.

I will tell you Montreal's tale. To take in the spread of the city, we are at the top of the mountain. We get out of the car. Inexhaustible landscape. In Paris, the world was revealed to me. First evening at the theatre, first concert, first kiss in the street. Expansive memory with its light and shadow. There I knew times of exaltation and despair, dazzling hours and days of distress and anguish. The streets are signs, enchanting evocations, sometimes nightmares that I always bury without ever managing to erase. At every visit I cry to myself "here I am, I remain." In those moments I don't know which hymn of thanks to sing, which celebration of life I should mark. A city within memory's reach, unleashed in an imagination as material as the lights of my current city. There is no superimposition, and thus no nostalgia. It was the city of arrival, and will remain so even if the arrival now doubles as a return. A city that I carry even while elsewhere is within me and while I anchor it, tie it to the city of return.

I will tell you the city's tale in its twists and mysteries, its deserted paths and public places. Let's take the road by the river. We're in front of the Verdun swimming pool. Let's walk on, to Promenade Marquette in Lachine. On my arrival in Rio de Janeiro, the sands of the coastline snatched me. I barely noticed the mountains that circle the sea like a crown. At that time, in 1961, Brazil was living in an explosion of hope. Everything was possible, even the wildest promises. Along the foam of the waves, women danced on the beach while boys celebrated their bodies and their youth in a game where a kick at the ball seemed more a message of affection than a strategy for scoring points and winning the match. The match was won before it began, since there was the sea, open to infinity, and the women, too, abandoned themselves to the joys of the body every time they set a foot in the sand.

Rio was a city of celebration, and the party lasted till dawn. In the glow of the streetlamps and the moon, little groups would congregate, men and women, each playing an instrument, and the music tore through the night. Passers-by stopped to sing and dance.

I have returned to Rio a number of times, but over the course of my more recent visits, the city's face has changed. The mountains are still there, and the beaches, hills, and sea, but fear has taken root. Everyone is afraid of street kids, attackers feared at every hour of the day and night. People may still sing and dance, but they are taking a chance, as though at the foot of a volcano. Fear, mistrust, and suspicion seize us. Everything seems buried in a misery that invades the streets and the mind. Dancing, like the body, puts up some resistance, and voices still sing, but now I can only see splendour in an ever-living past, alive like the foam of the waves and the sand on the beach.

Look at the river. Long ago, very long ago, a Dutch friend of mine had rented a cottage on Dorval Island. I remember our day by the water. And yes, I also swam in the Saint Lawrence River. I know its water and its sand, and I watch the little waves, like shivers of the sea.

I want to tell you my city's tale. It's the sidewalk sale on Boulevard Saint-Laurent. I don't want to buy anything. Perhaps, to mark our presence in the crowd, I'll give you an ear of corn. Produce of Asia and America, Europe and Africa. The merchants sell goods that are becoming more and more common at a discount. Here we are, and we watch the movement of humanity which, in this two-bit market, is searching out a hope of riches to come, built in the street, day after day.

I am in the Grand Bazaar in Istanbul. The smells quickly tear us from the dazzling colours. We wander through the well-organized maze where build-ups of diversity are planned, past stacks of some object's multiplicity, perpetually similar to itself, like a ghost whose image changes with the direction of a look and the brightness of the light. Unlike North Africa's *souks* and India's emporia, here you are left alone, abandoned to yourself. You slow your pace; you wait. Still, selling is not despised, and not neglected.

Here's a seller of spices who hails from Casablanca. The jeweller is a Jewish Turk, a son of the city. He complains that his children aren't following him into the business, that they are wandering to far-off places, sometimes to distant countries and, which is worse, into activities that they deem better paid and more profitable.

I walk down the alley of spices and back, enter a shop, lean over the stalls, capture the odours, breathe the perfume. I double back in search of a lost feeling, and memory throws me back to childhood where, leaving the Rue de Torate (the Street of the Torah) in the Kamber Ali quarter, I turn toward the Alliance school in the depths of the Chorjasouk, a covered market whose bazaar-like stalls awoke me every morning to the reality of the city. Jewish spice merchants beside Muslim fruit sellers, not far from the *alawis*, the rice and wheat warehouses across from the house where I was born beside the Méir synagogue. The Heskel (Ezekiel) synagogue is on a street corner. Nestled in the folds of memory, the Chorja *souk*, the Alliance school, and the Khan Merjan leading to Al-Rachid Street evoke an absence of light. In the summertime, we had to protect ourselves from the burning rays of the sun, a persistent enemy; in winter, we took care to avoid streets without asphalt that the rain would turn into expanses of mud. On torrid summer days, the beneficent opacity would sap the strength of a sun that we never dared confront. From the sesame oil to the rosewater, from the *hel* (cardamom) to the *zaater*, the smells sank into me.

I move along through Istanbul's two bazaars, the Grand and the Egyptian, toward my childhood, not to recover lost happiness but to tease out a guiding thread, something continuous that crosses lines and knows no borders. Childhood grips me with its profusion of light, and at the same time the colours that had been denied me are miraculously restored.

In the shade of that distant alley, I must have dreamt of a bazaar with tortuous paths and many passageways where colour and light finally allow the smells to blossom. Is it the West, longed for and reviled in turn, that attributes to a bazaar the expansiveness of a life of its own, where smells flourish instead of fading? Is it the passing of the years, proof against nostalgia, that incites me to give thanks to life triumphant over the opacity of forgetfulness? Is it the memory of perfumes that turns the alley into an enchanted world?

I will tell you Montreal's tale. Just after I arrived, I lived very close to the mountain. During the summer, the symphony orchestra played free concerts outdoors at the Chalet. Once, as I went home, it was raining hard, and I had the feeling that my body was drenched with music. A strange and unique feeling, this impression that you are being watered with music and that the water is sinking right to the bone. Sometimes, sitting in the warmth of Place des Arts or the National Arts Centre, I feel the strains of the orchestra pierce through my skin and reach the bone.

During my last visit to Berlin, I deliberately avoided the concert hall that had so impressed me on my first visit, when the city was still chopped in half by the wall. The orchestra played in a pit, surrounded by an attentive audience. I have never seen so many attentive listeners anywhere else, many with the score lying in their laps. I waited for the sounds to trickle into me, but self-possession got the upper hand. The music was triumphal, but it was still just music.

This time around, the previously truncated part of Berlin has been recovered, and my visit becomes a pilgrimage. I go to the building which, before Hitler, had been a posh synagogue and today has become a museum. Documents from a period that had been lost in the mists of time have been recovered. Announcements of weddings, conferences, communal celebrations. Vanished, erased humanity. A reminder that time exists, that the years pass, but that men and women ripped from the core of their lives, torn from their loves, have left names, letters, traces of their existence behind.

The next day, in front of the reinstated Reichstag, I walk along the pit, the immense hole carved in the city's gut where a monument is to be erected in memory of the Shoah.

I plunge into the subway, heading for the Jewish Museum. Brand new. Hallways, alleyways, storeys, and then a door that I open before diving into the cold. The unusually high walls close in toward the top, but don't completely manage to hide the sky. It's a concentration camp, as imagined by the architect. These walls, I'm told, will remain brutally bare. On the way out we move through a maze that unsettles us and deliberately makes us lose our balance. Empty rooms. I'm assured that they will be filled with objects and documents that will evoke Jewish history, not only in its years of agony but as the expression of a civilization that has infused so many others.

I wait until Saturday morning to attend the sabbath service. On the ground floor is a building to house the Jewish communal services, set up as an oratory, a prayer hall. In the crowded space, I'm handed the *talith* and the *siddour* as though I were a regular. The *hazan* has a stentorian voice, similar to those that gave New York's Metropolitan Opera so many great tenors. His incantation of the *paracha* goes by the book. When he recites the prayers, he gives himself up to the joy of blanketing the hall with the convolutions of his voice. A *shamash*, in Russian, demands silence from overly talkative worshippers.

I'm in the heart of Berlin, I think to myself. Here are the remains, the ones that Jeremiah spoke of. As though, through bones given breath by Ezekiel, I could hear the ancient words come alive over Hitler's coffin.

I had visited the Pergamum Museum when it was still in East Berlin, on a tour under the watchful eye of an official guide. I barely had time to look at the reconstruction of Ishtar's temple at Babylon, which had naturally taken me in my mind to Baghdad. German archaeologists had brought back from their digs at Babylon the stones that made the magisterial reconstruction of the temple possible. Objects of the period—bowls, amulets, jewels—conspired to give me a tremendous surprise. In a corner, a bowl with Hebrew inscriptions. Blessings, calligraphic words from the *chema*, placed in a ring in several sizes. I shook with emotion. There I was, in the heart of Berlin, standing before an extraordinary artefact. Much more than a relic, it bore living witness to the sojourn of my ancestors in the place where Nebuchadnezzar had led them as prisoners. I was motionless before an object that had survived twenty-five centuries, survived empires and caliphates. Imagining myself in front of an invisible crowd, I murmured: *we are still here.* As slaves, we have inscribed our word, in our language, defying time and transcending the centuries. We are still here to take up that word and repeat it. We have changed places, crossed deserts and oceans, and we are still present when the hour comes, and we utter praise and lamentations, gratitude and confidence, syllable for syllable and word for word.

We have outlived empires, and the word subsists and will outlive us. Again and again, I will tell you my city's tale. I start the day by swimming lengths in my building's pool. I'm there by myself most of the time. Water is ever my companion, and in my effort to keep afloat it is both my ally and my adversary. My body moves, stops, registers the rhythm of the water, that element that receives the light and reflects the image wedded to my intangible desire in the midst of a subterranean life, and that I rediscover day after day ... In the summertime, a lake, at Magog or Saint-Adolphe, I see its lines in a space. My body marks its trace, a border deliberately drawn in a marvel of stillness at the centre of motion.

In Tel-Aviv we choose a hotel facing the sea at Rehov Hayarkon. Every morning before breakfast I walk along the sand, and the waves, gentle and friendly, make me welcome. My body is wet. I move slowly forward, relishing the moments of encounter and, my arms raised, I let myself slide into the water. Weightless, my body moves along, freed from all control. I am light, so very light. Head underwater, I leave space behind: the earth moves away and escapes from beneath my feet. I lie on my back, float and watch the sand and street drift off. I am in the throes of a festival whose celebration I will only interrupt to preserve its feel. One would have to bring the celebration to an end soon, so that it could begin again, start over the next day and, slowly, without losing energy, be reborn day after day. I recognize the stopping point as though I were obeying the tolling of an hour, and I let my body command the rhythm.

At the late afternoon sunset I wander down the long avenue along the sea, where the whole universe seems to meet. Men, women, and children, grandparents and young lovers. I settle on a bench and watch the balloon, jewel, and pistachio sellers go by. The city is celebrating, and the citizens enjoy the gentle evening. My eyes follow the strolling faces, the laughter, and the children's shouts. Is this joy? Is this happiness? Or is it just the act of living?

Saturday night is the *Havdala* celebration, the passage from one week to the next, from one time to another. After sabbath rest comes the working week. An evening of expectation and gratitude. The week has ended, and we are living still. We're about to embark on the grand adventure of a new week. Orchestras invite passers-by to join in the songs and dance. We come from everywhere, from East and West. The party is open, and all are invited. I join in the dance and let my body impose its own movements. It is released, and evolves to the beat of the music, unified in this big circle of strangers I have joined to mark the passage from one week to the next, I am travelling in time.

Another week of life for me, and I bless the moment when, in charge of my body, I blend into a close and unknown humanity where I am part of a body that is an extension of my own, stretching out to reach the common rhythm. I strike the earth with my feet as though to say, "I'm here too." Another week and, seven days hence, another yet.

I grip the life I carry and share with strangers. They are near to me, because they too strike the ground with their feet and feel themselves take flight. And they stretch their arms out to their neighbours as though to make sure they are still on the ground. And the dance goes on.

I want to tell you my city's tale, and never stop the telling. It is all cities that magically emerge from the shadows, not to suck me in and draw me down a road to elsewhere, but to anchor me in a city that has become all others, without the one negating the other or taking umbrage at the other's presence, like one love combining with another, with all others.

All the cities that I visit and revisit are facets of the one where I have chosen to live because it brings this multiplicity together. Together, each of us, man and woman, strolls through its streets as we recreate them, tinker with them, bringing landscapes, scenes from other houses, streets, and gardens to the heart of the city.

The walls crumble, and we are here and elsewhere, elsewhere and here.

2005

PART III · PRACTICE

Malca Litovitz, "The Welcoming"

Into our house on a twilit night
comes Avraham,
with Kabbalah for the layman.
Tales of astrology, reincarnation,
and God pour into our house,
echoes from an ancient land.

I show Avraham the camel on our mantel
and the two spice boxes of earth.
We talk of the transmigration of souls
and the desert, a place for revelations.

God, grace, breath:
my mind reaches out
like the three stars of evening.

1998

Merle Nudelman, "The Sabbath Queen"

1
Roasting smells of the Sabbath meal
warm the night, wet our mouths
as we wait dressed in finery.
You crown black waves with creamy lace

then, like a bride, approach the linen cloth,
near the brilliance of the silver candelabra.
You flame the wicks of stocky white candles,
circle silvery branches thrice, beckon

the Sabbath Queen. Eyes finger-veiled,
you drift in a moment golden and eternal
intone the blessing, your prayer
spilling hope.

2
On the counter, translucent bowls—
cream edged in gold washed peach at dusk.
Mother stirs a pot of chicken soup and I

bounce at her side, eyes level with the burners.

She ladles bountiful servings and into broth
plops triangular *kreplach.* Plump
with beef and liver, pungent with garlic and onions.
We ease the bowls onto the dining room table

pristine in crocheted lace. Father pours
sacramental wine. Blessings sung, I bend close
to *kreplach* floating in a soupy haze. My china bowl
rings when silver-touched as I section *kreplach*

into mouth-size bites, capture a sliver with broth, carrot.
Spoon pressed to lips, I puff cooling breath, inhale
perfume of chicken stock mingled with spiced meat.
Taste. Dough firm, filling rough on my tongue.
The bowl shines empty.

2003

Ronna Bloom, "Yom Kippur, 1998"

This year on Yom Kippur
I have a big breakfast
(eggs, home fries, toast).
I come home, have sex
with my husband (not Jewish),
get undressed in front of the window,
take enormous pleasure
in my body and his. I have starved
for eighteen years to keep the family
rules intact: Stay small.
Be good. Dress nice.
I hope I have days
and days of atonement
like this one.

2000

Janis Rapoport, "Pesach 5735"

Earlier than April
the sun speckles
albino filaments of caviar
along the horizons of the windshield.
Jeremy wonders
why the moon's roundness spins as
proportionately westward as we travel east,
trailing translucent strands across
the twilight. Estayr sleeps
but Sara says,
with the Cartesian wisdom of a two-year-old:
because I am,
therefore you are.
When we arrive
at the long Seder table,
the crystal goblets already
brimming with Dali's rubies,
prism aural rainbows
while we wait, patient, in Egypt,
for Elijah.

1979

Gina Roitman, "Pesach en Provence"

In 1989, I was in a business meeting with some Francophones in Montreal. As the meeting wrapped up, someone made a cutting comment that could be misconstrued as unkind to Anglophones. This was at the peak of the debate about whether Quebec should separate from Canada. Everyone laughed and then, I was remembered. All eyes turned my way. The man who had commented shrugged his shoulders and said he was sorry, that he had meant no offence. I said none was taken but he continued, explaining that I couldn't possibly understand what it is like to be afraid that your language will be lost to your children and that your culture will one day disappear. In fact, I said, I understood perfectly. My mother tongue was Yiddish and it had already been designated a dead language. More to the point, as my parents were Holocaust survivors, I had been raised with the values and mores of a culture that was gone before I was born, leaving me lonely, and hungering for something I never had.

In the Alpes-Martimes, the mountain range lurking behind the Riviera, I rent a cozy and uncluttered apartment from a Danish couple I have never met. I have been coming to Grasse since 1997, at first because I have a second cousin living here but now mostly because it is a place where, with a cliff wall rising at my back and a panoramic view plunging to the sea, I can effectively empty myself to make room for the stories I want to write. I come in spring when the air is redolent with thyme, jasmine, and wisteria, Grasse being world famous for its perfumes.

My mother wears Evening in Paris but only on special occasions like Pesach. The midnight blue bottle is the one bright spot on her otherwise drab dresser.

The idea of making a Passover Seder first comes to me soon after I arrive in Grasse. I am going through the kitchen cupboards, taking inventory when I suddenly come across a box of matzo. Two years earlier I had left a half empty box. I know it's not the same package but I wonder whether the Danish couple discovered and somehow grew fond of this tasteless, constipating cracker all because of me.

I am not planning a *real* Seder, that would be impossible, just something to help me through the holiday period, to keep me connected to Montreal despite all the trouble I have gone to in removing myself from there. So I plan a *faux* Seder, but for whom? My cousin and her husband will be away, visiting their children in California. Undaunted, I invite my friend Julie, a woman raised by nuns in a Montreal convent and the widow of a real Cossack. The irony is not lost on me. My life is like that, a constant sliding backwards and forwards along some slippery groove carved out long before I got here. Wherever I am, a part of me is sliding for a home somewhere else.

What I know of Seders is not informed so much by religious teachings but by the force of family dynamics, the tailoring of the event to various players. That is what now remains of this holiday for me. Before I was even born, World War II consumed most of my family, leaving my brother and me suffering from a deficit of relatives. The few we did have were far-flung; vaguely familiar faces in photographs that arrived in a letter once a year. This deficit was never more obvious than during the holidays, especially Passover. It was just the four of us, five if you count the ghost of the Prophet Elijah.

The kitchen table is moved into the living room because you don't eat dinner in the kitchen on "yontif." We are all dressed in our finest and, despite the lack of company, the table is set with linen, china and a silver candelabrum.

"Bennick," my mother says to my father who is revelling in the Passover rituals, "do we have to do the whole Hagaddah? The children are hungry."

Because it is a holiday and my mother exhausted from the effort of preparation, my father is able to negotiate for the recounting of one more story. This is the part he is good at, reading out loud to us the story of how we came out of bondage.

My mother was a woman of enormous energy. A week before Passover, there was a frenzy of activity, scrubbing kitchen cupboards to make way for the Passover things. The holidays always caused my mother to become even more highly-strung than usual, more likely to snap at my father or brother or me. I remember offering to help once but my mother took this as an opportunity to remind me what a talent I had for breaking things. Not that we had anything precious, no heirlooms salvaged from previous generations, no treasured pieces passed on with interesting family histories. Our Passover dishes were purchased second hand in a refugee camp in Germany. And like our family, the set was incomplete.

When I am twelve, I return home from a friend's house to see my mother preparing to store the chometz in our apartment locker.

"Bella's mother says we are supposed to throw out the chometz," I say innocently.

"Bella's mother never buried a child who died from hunger," my mother replies, sharply. "Bella's mother was born here in Canada and never had a hungry day in her life. It's a sin against God to throw away food," she says in that tone that suggests the discussion is over.

This is how our family is bound together, as if by the barbed wire from the fences of Auschwitz, a name more familiar to me than Toronto. Growing up, Toronto is the far side of the moon while Auschwitz could be right outside our door.

For my *faux* Seder, some innovation is required. To make matzo meal, I crush the boxed matzo in the coffee grinder and get the Manischewitz recipe for matzo balls off the Internet. I think about my mother as I make *charoses* using Canada apples grown in France, although I've never seen them at home. I guess if we did grow them in Canada, they'd be called something else just like French fries are just frites in France. In Grasse, I am a Canada apple but I'm not so sure what I am back in Montreal.

"Bring me the copper 'pesedikeh' plate," my mother calls from the kitchen. "I will give you a job, if you want to help." I am to grate apples for the charoses while my mother cracks and empties walnuts shells. "You are doing Baileh's job. I always cracked the nuts, Malka mixed it all together with the honey; Ruchmeh would be helping der Mameh and Shaindel would be singing." With a few words, my mother conjures up the one-room "shteibel" in Chnanow where she lived with her parents and four sisters before The War.

I am much loved in my family for the turkey and matzo ball soup I make. It's a recipe given to me by my mother while she was in the hospital with the cancer that would kill her at the age of sixty-three. I make the soup every holiday for family gatherings; my family, for the most part, being the one I married into. At twenty, I acquired a pair of sisters-in-law, brothers-in-law, numerous nieces and nephews, three sets of aunts and uncles, and a bonanza of first cousins. When I left the marriage, I kept my dowry of relatives and my position as the best maker of matzo ball soup, that being the part I'm good at.

The Seders were invariably held at my brother-in-law's house because, being wealthy, he had the room. The length of the table set for as many as fourteen, and all of them immediate family, filled me with happy anticipation. But not having children of my own, the only thing brought along was the soup. These Seders were family gatherings but without any of the decipherable traditions from my childhood, only a few grudging prayers, laboriously squeaked out by my brother-in-law once the grandfathers had died. I missed the storytelling although I had complained about it so bitterly as a young girl. So as much as I treasured the coming together of family, stripped of ceremony, these Seders were often laced with a bittersweet loneliness.

For my *faux* Seder in Provence, I roast a whole chicken stuffed with vegetables and smothered in garlic, a recipe I also find on the Internet. It's too much food and, though Julie asks for seconds, I can see I'll have enough for at least three more meals. Too much food is a Passover tradition, I tell her. My mother would lade the table as if all her sisters were coming to dine. It's as if having survived hunger, she had to find ways to reassure herself that we had more than we needed. As a result, I have inherited an abhorrence of half-filled fridges and sparse meals. I wonder if it's because I am Jewish or because I was raised with a refugee's mentality, or both.

At supper, Julie will ask me if I consider myself a Canadian or a Jew and I tell her that my nationality is Canadian but my soul is Jewish. That satisfies her but leaves me uneasy, knowing I had not really answered the question.

"When we're gone," my mother repeats like a daily prayer, "you and Marvin will only have each other. You are the only ones left of all our family. Remember that. Remember."

In my sleep, sodden with too much food and rosé, I discern a jangling sound that, with a start, I identify as the telephone. I run down the darkened hall.

Hello? It's Nancy, my brother's wife calling from Toronto where it is only a quarter to six. They're waiting for their Seder guests to arrive and I am instantly nostalgic, regretful of being here and not there, in that foreign land called Toronto where Marvin, Nancy, and the boys shower me with love when I visit. Nancy, so full of the same kind of energy my mother had but without the angst and anguish, gives me a rundown of her menu. My mother would have loved her (although I am convinced Nancy would have been nagged into converting). Nancy speaks of having prepared the *charoses* and having the hard-boiled eggs standing by with the pitcher of salted water, "...the salted tears of the Israelites," she reminds me, jokingly. I had forgotten about that.

Nancy is a wonder with her love of puns and loopy lyrics that she makes up, and an ability to invent new traditions when she cannot draw on the old. One Seder when the boys were young, she held a matzo board to her face and created Matzo Man. She sang it to the tune of the Village People's "Macho Man." It became a tradition for a while.

Now I crawl back into my narrow Provençal bed, groggy with half-formed thoughts and the weight of too much food and drink. Throughout the day, my mother had been shadowing me as I washed the floors of the apartment and prepared the *faux* Seder. She is back now, hovering on the edge of my consciousness, intruding on my attempts to retrieve sleep. I wonder what she's trying to tell me, what I was thinking to have made so much food, why I found it important to cook all day for just Julie and me. I could easily have done something simple. But then, I think while drifting off, it would not have been a Passover Seder; it would have just been a friend coming over for dinner. Where's the memory in that?

2008

Merle Nudelman, "The Finding"

1

The policeman squints through the gauzy windowpane,
says, "There, on the floor. His legs."
He shatters the silence with his nightstick, reaches
into the tidiness of the house, pries open the door.
They enter, he first—uncle, aunt trailing,
then goes forward alone, bends,
lays his hand on stillness.
He guides them, docile, into the kitchen,
tenders water, words of waiting.
The blackness unfurls, enfolds.

2

The cottage phone rings. A stranger's voice.
"Stay calm," he says. "Bad news."
I blink dry-eyed, fall from my skin
into the hollow of a woman
that wears my face, my shape.
She stumbles to the door, pours into the car,
crawls home through the gloom of a July night.

3

There is an aesthetic to symmetry,
a lightness to balance,
but where's the beauty when her trauma
flames in him short years later, to the day?
Silent offerings to the heart's misstep
in the flowering moment of summer.

4

My midnight eyes, ringed in red, watch
his house ablaze with yellow lights,
the front door gaping wide.
Uncle, aunt huddle in shadows.
The doorway darkens—my brother's silhouette,
no one else.

"I want to see Dad."

But I am moments late and he, hours dead,
delivered to funeral home arms.

5

      We push against air,
stumble into the grey light of the waiting room.
Brick wall, fireplace, deep sofa and chairs
of mute leather,
an open staircase falling down
to the panelled offices,
the morgue.

      A shelf of broken dolls
we sit, attend to the hum
of the director sliding down his list

questions asked, answered
monies paid after we stroll
around the casket room pointing
to oak, to traditional white shroud.

We caress navy velvet,
the pouch holding his prayer shawl—
fringes I braided with childhood fingers—
and drop our molten eyes as we leave
his mantle in the director's care.

6
We arc around the director,
heads bowed, eyes streaming,
and he pins a black ribbon
over our hearts.
He intones a brief prayer,
tells us, "Tear the fabric."
We are ripped asunder.

I wear that mourning-badge
seven days,
then bury it
within my darkness.

7
David piles his bags into the car,
slips on mellow jazz,
pulls out of the Chicago morning
north to Toronto.
His mind sifts memories
back, forth like sand
through an hourglass.

That evening he says
he wants to speak
at his Zaidie's funeral.

He steps to the podium in sailor-navy
exhales crystal bubbles—
his Zaidie's taste for herring and cheesecake,
their mania for the Leafs.
He holds out his voice
clear, steady and we float
in his reverie.

8
Seven days I crouch,
rise early, rush to prayers,
press bread to my lips.
The days are stones, heavy, the same.
I pour water down my throat,
water to fill emptiness.
Low on the naked sofa frame,
cushions stacked to the side,
I cling to coiled tissues.

Visitors come, and come,
touch my hand, my cheek
say, "Such a shock,"
and move to a chair,
to the table of cakes,
the counter of sticky schnapps.
They nod, tongues thickened.
Father, the shadow dancing
through my rooms.

9

His legion of friends stumble before me.
Their lips tremble as they murmur
about his cheering calls, his errand-boy ways.
Kalman—everyone's *gut Freund.*
Bruised, their love for him
salves my skin.

10

Lisa takes my hand, says,
"I'd like to move in for the shiva."
She cradles my pieces in her arms,
her black hair a prayer on my cheek.
In the morning kitchen she sets out
plates, soft drinks, cakes
and fresh in afternoon light
returns to warm dinner, ready the table.
At night, callers leave and she sits
at my side, reads my eyes,
shepherds me as I tumble
into my sorrow.

11

I listen to the fluttering of the walls.
The house breathes.
The doors quiet.
My granite heart bears down
on sodden lungs,
throat knotted like a hangman's noose.
I hear the hiss of my serpentine mind
and know
I am alone.

2003

Janis Rapoport, "From This Time Forth and Forever"

Remembrance is the only paradise out of which we cannot be driven away.
—Jean Paul Richter

The glow of the sun and the moon and the stars
disappeared with the unravelling
of celestial harpstrings into shadow.
Then darkness sheltered in the umbra of your eyes

And death was your interpreter,
from this time forth and forever.
Your life was a tapestry, threaded with hope
and happiness and the colours of pain, and desire.

Our lamentations—mixed with laughter—
slowly gather into the fibres
of remembrance. Yet laughter is always heard
further than weeping.

With us are family and friends
who stood parallel, in rows,
as we left your grave,

plucking our few knots of grass.

We pour water over our hands, each one
setting down the pitcher, just as
we shovelled the earth, disconnected:
may the loss that began with your death there end.

We sit next to the ground, dust
on our feet and in our hair. We have ripped
our clothes instead of gashing ourselves,
counting your good deeds by our tears.

During the meal of condolence we are silent
as boiled eggs sealed inside their shells. Mouths
close around lentils that turn over in throats:
small, endless wheels of joy and of sorrow.

Our grief ripples into the concentric circles
formed by a stone flung onto water.
In the flame of the candle nearby: illumination
your wisdom brought to our lives.

Do not look for your body's reflection
in these mirrors, so recently covered.
Perhaps it is only such glass
that separates our worlds.

Let us offer a prayer brought by angels,
as the weave of your life is now spun
into the memory of children, bearers of your dreams,
from this time forth and forever.

1996

Libby Scheier, "Elat Chayyim"
for Shefa Gold

August 1

the Catskill mountains
daven under the grey sky
hills rolling and unrolling before me
their tallis of summer trees swaying,
dizzy

a bright yellow bird with black wings
swoops by
angelically

        my father is ill

I am trying on the techniques
of spiritual experience

chance favours the prepared mind
as does grace

I eat an apple with equanimity
and pleasure

(yes, they can go together)
under the grey-white skies of morning prayer

my father is ill

birdcalls reverberate in rounds
like sacred chanting
each bird different each the same

my father is ill

I see inside myself two seeds, one black
and tiny and shiny and hard
one yellow and soft
shaped like an almost-half moon
or heavenly canoe

enigmatic pod

yud of my heart

if you open will I find you?

I am praying for my father
praying for myself
and others
those who have hurt me
those I have hurt
those I know and
those I don't
I am praying for the prayer

will you open open to me?

1999

Rhea Tregebov, "Some Notes on the Story of Esther"

To look at the parallels between the position of women in male culture and Jews in Christian culture, replace for the moment the word "Jew" with "woman":

"So you're a woman! My mother was a woman but my sisters and I were all raised as men."

"I didn't find out my mother was a woman until I was fourteen. It just wasn't important to her, so she didn't mention it."

"My parents gave me a female education, but I'm not any gender now."

"Are you a woman? That's funny, you don't look female!"

I could go on. What becomes apparent is the shared ambiguity to our role: not until we explicitly identify ourselves as different are we perceived as such.

Women are visibly women; Jews may or may not be visibly Jews. We are, however, mutually expected to be one of the guys or, more specifically, one with the guys. Not until we declare ourselves as outside the norm are we perceived as standing in opposition to things-as-they-are.

It is a vexed question, this question of our visibility or invisibility as Jews. We can, in many cases, "pass" in a way Blacks or Natives or Asians cannot. At a recent Passover dinner, in reply to my remark that "This is the one day I get to be Jewish" (I am very sporadically observant), a Black friend said, "And lucky me—I get to be Black every day."

The parallel, however, may well extend to people whose background is mixed, or whose "racial" identity, because it does not match the stereotype (be it because of appearance or of class), may be uncertain. This uncertainty does carry its own pain, and I would suggest that, precisely because of the possibility of "passing," the risk of internalization is perhaps greater for those of us who are ambiguously what we are.

Our invisibility requires that we declare ourselves as standing in opposition. Women are generally expected to be sympathetic with, if not proponents of, male culture. Jews in turn are expected to be sympathetic toward and supportive of Christian culture. This includes the expectation of sympathy with the anti-woman and anti-Semitic aspects of the culture: the woman/Jew who is the target of the sexist/anti-Semitic joke is expected to laugh along.

The assumption demands a basic denial of one's identity. The conversations begin, "Oh, you're not like other women/Jews!" (you aren't who you are) and then inevitably continue with a litany of the ills and evils women/Jews embody—a litany with which the listener is expected to agree.

We have learned to respond by refusing any ground of agreement; by openly expressing our anger, our refusal of complicity. By insisting on having our differences, our difference defined; and thus, even in this minimal way, insisting on being acknowledged.

I (along with many others) use the two terms, "other" and "different," in very specific ways. Women are genuinely *different* from men in terms of our biology, our historical position, and many of the facts of our lives. Jews are genuinely *different* from Christians in our religious beliefs, our historical position, and many of our cultural values.

Both groups, however, have suffered from the *otherness* imposed upon us by the dominant culture. Our difference is not, however, regarded as a positive attribute. We are instead viewed as *other*, as "unmen" or "not-men"; as "un-Christians" or "not-Christians"; shadowy beings whose otherness defines and describes the dominant group, not ourselves. Since we are continually battling external definitions—definitions which are more than merely negative: they are an annihilation of our selves—our lives come to take on an artificiality which never really leaves us. The word which kept coming to mind again and again, with a peculiar resonance, was "imposter." As false men, false Christians,[1] until the point at which we declare our difference, at which we explicitly eliminate the ambiguity of our role, we act as imposters, deceivers.

Within the patriarchy, femaleness is perceived in so distorted a fashion that we cannot act simply as women, but are compelled to act as female impersonators. We so contort ourselves, either in acquiescing to the distortions or in constantly reacting in opposition to them, that a "naturalness," an ease, a sense of sitting *bien dans sa peau*, is rare if not impossible.

The same may be said of the Jew. Say "Jew." I flinch. It is painful for me to admit it, but so deeply, so ineradicably have I internalized the anti-Semitism I grew up with, that I cannot hear, cannot say the word "Jew" without experiencing it as an epithet, without sensing the negative resonance it has acquired over millennia of attack.

There does exist for writers the possibility of "passing" and all the dangers inherent in such a move. Writers can, up to a point, remain anonymous. (This is of course a possibility for Black and other "visible" writers as well.) In the past we adopted male pen names. It was also not uncommon to adopt British pseudonyms, or to change one's name. I still see young women writers hiding their identifying first names under initials, at least until they get that first book accepted for publication. But there is also the more subtle and more destructive attempt to "pass" in terms of content, in terms of not acknowledging or not fully acknowledging who we are, or whom we're writing for.

So how do we, as writers, women, Jews, integrate into our work what we really are, as opposed to these refutations or denials, these shadows of otherness, these acquiescences? What it all means to me as a writer is, first of all, that if I spent the first five years of my writing career writing as a man, I certainly spent the first ten years writing as a Christian. And then, of course, there are the fifteen years I spent reading as a man. As a young woman raised and educated without access to an articulated feminism, I identified with men, I identified with the male authors I read. A kind of literary tomboyism. I would certainly feel some sort of discomfort when I came across sexism in my reading, but I had no word for it, I had no way of placing it. My primary response was "*I* am not a woman like that," not "Women are not like that." And as a young writer, while I began to experience a sense of exclusion, while the strain of identifying with male authors and teachers and any accompanying sexual bias increased, the wish, unexpressed, to be one of the boys continued. I had my "us" and "them" confused.

And so I did not begin writing authentically until that point at which an articulated feminism made it possible for me to identify myself—not so much merely as a *feminist*, but at the primary level as *female*. This may all sound incredible to younger women, but I don't think at the time it was an uncommon experience. Much of it was the struggle, still ongoing, against the prevalent notion that the male (and the Christian) are universal. If you speak as man and Christian, you address everyone. The words "male" and "Christian" are not necessary as qualifiers: it's not the Oxford (Norton, Penguin, etc.) anthology of male, Christian literature, it's the Oxford anthology of literature. Whereas, when we speak as women, as Jews, the assumption is that this is a specialty literature, that we are speaking only to a select (read insignificant) group.

The eruption of feminist consciousness in my writing was followed years later by a less well-defined consciousness of my Jewishness. Although I had been writing for a decade, only in 1982 did I first begin work on a piece which dealt specifically and at length with Jewish content. "I'm talking from my time" was a performance piece/slide show which juxtaposed the images and words of my husband's ninety-six-year-old Russian Jewish grandmother with my own poetry.

Any writer's reasons for writing a given piece are, necessarily, multiple. But I do feel I was impelled to work on it, from a reactive position, in response to the feeling of being invisible. I remember the shock when a Québécoise writer talked to me about "you Anglos." (In North End Winnipeg, anyone whose first language was English was called English, even if they were of Scottish, Irish, Welsh, or Brazilian origin. No Jew was an Anglo.) There was some kind of pervasive filter in the Toronto milieu in which I wrote that could not see or wished to eradicate the differences that began, increasingly, to define me for myself: my Western roots, my un-bourgeois, left-wing background, my Jewishness. I felt myself becoming vague, bleached. Ambiguous.

I was, in addition, responding to the mainstream (mostly American) writing about Jewish experience; its sexism (the castrating Jewish mother); its painful pandering to stereotypes (the grasping, materialistic, bourgeois Jew); its eye on the Christian audience. In summary, its assertion of our otherness.

As women and Jews we share a common posture; a tenuous, ambiguous position in a social structure which is emphatically not our own and yet which we know and understand intimately, profoundly. The parallels are not, of course, exact, but they can act in powerfully similar ways in our lives, and in our lives as writers in particular. Our writing, once it is conscious, can grow to be an assertion of our difference, and a refutation of the otherness imposed upon us.

1990

---

1 The scope of this essay does not permit a consideration of those "false Americans," the Canadians, much as I wish it did.

Robyn Sarah, "Vidui"

Poetry is my firepan. In it
I offer up my smoking heart
in words that burn and give off
a sweet savour.

If this my only service
be unacceptable unto the One
Who heareth prayer, alas! what
will become of me?

2003

Susan Glickman, "(The) Others"
for Rhea Tregebov

who we fear and grieve for, children
unloved or broken against the world's business
whose eyes accuse us, and not only their eyes
but ours
of pure dumb luck—

them, the others, whose wounds leave our children's skin
unscarred, whose hunger spares our bellies,
let us bless them

    for carrying away a little of the danger
    in their empty hands

    for being innumerable as the stars of heaven
    and as invisible in daylight

    for being statistics, the modern kabbalah
    in which we read our fate

and therefore let us bless our fear of them,
which is the last vestige of religious awe
as it was the first

    O spare us, Evil Eye

    Let the universe right itself and the meek
    inherit the earth
    but spare us too

Spare us to our proper work
and let us yet rejoice in righteousness
spare us to our children

or if not us
just spare our children

1990

Elana Wolff, "Tikva"

We're on the down-side of summer.

This year the mulberries
didn't even ripen in my absence.
You didn't get to eat any
before they fell green on the junipers.

That's the way it is sometimes:
Up and down. In Hebrew the four-
letter word for hope comes from
the two-letter word for line.

Up and down.

The direction of the line is clear
from the other two letters in the word—
from the last letter in the alphabet,
to the letter that stands for God.

2001

BIOGRAPHICAL NOTES

Ronna Bloom (1961–) was born in Montreal. She is the author of six collections of poetry. Her writing has aired on CBC Radio and has been shortlisted for several prestigious awards, including the Gerald Lampert Award for *Fear of the Ride* (1996), the Pat Lowther Award for *Public Works* (2004) and *Permiso* (2009), and the ReLit Award for *Cloudy with a Fire in the Basement* (2012). For twelve years, Bloom was a psychotherapist at the University of Toronto where she developed and continues to lead the Poet in the Community program. She is currently poet-in-residence at Mount Sinai Hospital. Bloom also runs Poetry Goes to Work, where she offers workshops and talks on effecting personal and organizational change through poetry.

Ron Charach (1951–) was born in Winnipeg. He now lives in Toronto, where he is a practicing psychiatrist. The author of nine volumes of poetry, his verse regularly appears in literary journals and medical publications. His sixth collection, *Dungenessque* (2002), won the Canadian Jewish Book Award for Poetry. Charach is the editor of *The Naked Physician: Poems about the Lives of Patients and Doctors* (1990), the only anthology of Canadian physician poetry, and the author of *Cowboys and Bleeding Hearts: Essays on Violence, Health and Identity* (2009). His debut novel, *cabana the big*, appeared in 2016. Charach is a frequent contributor to the *Globe and Mail*, the *National Post*, and the *Toronto Star*.

Matt Cohen (1942–1999) was born in Kingston, Ontario, and grew up in Ottawa. In the late 1960s, he taught political philosophy and religion at McMaster University. Cohen was a founding member of the Writers' Union of Canada and served both on its executive board and as president for several years. He was a prolific writer, the author of fourteen novels, eleven short story collections, two volumes of poetry, and ten books for children published under the pseudonym Teddy Jam. Cohen wrote the screenplay for the 2007 film adaptation of his novel *Emotional Arithmetic* (1990). His novel, *Elizabeth and After* (1999), won the Governor General's Literary Award. His memoir, *Typing: A Life in 26 Keys*, was published posthumously in 2000. Cohen died in Toronto.

Susan Glickman (1953–) was born in Baltimore, Maryland and grew up in Montreal. She completed a BA in English at Oxford University and a PhD at the University of Toronto. Glickman is the author of a scholarly monograph, six books of poetry, three novels, and a trilogy of children's books. *The Picturesque and the Sublime: A Poetics of the Canadian Landscape* (1998) won the Raymond Klibansky Prize for the best English book in the humanities, as well as the Gabrielle Roy Prize for the best work of Canadian literary criticism written in English. *Running in Prospect Cemetery: New and Selected Poems* appeared in 2004. Her first novel, *The Violin Lover* (2006), was named one of the *National Post*'s Best Novels of the Year and won the Canadian Jewish Book Award for Fiction. Glickman lives in Toronto, where she teaches at Ryerson University's Chang School and the University of Toronto's School of Continuing Studies. She also works as a freelance editor with a focus on academic books.

Nora Gold (1952–) was born in Montreal. She is a writer, editor, and activist. Her collection of short stories, *Marrow and Other Stories* (1998), won the Canadian Jewish Book Award for Fiction. Her first novel, *Fields of Exile* (2014), won the Canadian Jewish Literary Award and her second novel, *The Dead Man*, was published in 2016. Gold is the founder and editor of the online literary journal Jewish Fiction. net. Currently, she is writer-in-residence and Associate Scholar in the Centre for Women's Studies in Education at the Ontario Institute for Studies in Education, University of Toronto, where she coordinates the Wonderful Women Writers reading series. Gold is also the co-founder of multiple progressive organizations in support of Israel, including Canadian Friends of Givat Haviva, JSpaceCanada, and the New Israel Fund of Canada. She divides her time between Toronto and Israel.

Gabriella Goliger (1949–) was born in Italy, but grew up in Montreal. She completed a BA in English at McGill University and an MA at the Hebrew University of Jerusalem. Her work has appeared in a variety of magazines and journals, such as *Canadian Forum* and *Parchment: Contemporary Canadian Jewish Writing*, and has been anthologized in *Coming Attractions 98* and *Best New American Voices 2000*. Goliger received the Prism International Award in 1993 and the Journey Prize in 1997 for her short story "Maladies of the Inner Ear." Her collection of short stories, *Song of Ascent* (2000), won the Upper Canada Writer's Craft Award, and her novel, *Girl Unwrapped* (2010), won the Ottawa Book Award. Goliger lives in Ottawa.

Eva Hoffman (1945–) was born in Krakow, Poland to Holocaust survivors. When she was thirteen, she and her family immigrated to Vancouver. Hoffman holds a PhD in English from Harvard University and is the author of a memoir, two novels, and five works of non-fiction. Her memoir, *Lost in Translation: A Life in a New Language* (1989), has been translated into several languages. From 1979 to 1990,

Hoffman worked as an editor and writer for the *New York Times*. She was a visiting professor at MIT, a visiting fellow at the University of California, Berkeley in 2000 and at Cambridge University in 2001, and the Amnesty Lecturer at Oxford University in 2001. Hoffman has received a Guggenheim Fellowship, the Jean Stein Award from the Academy of Arts and Letters, the Prix Italia for radio, and the Whiting Award. She lives in London, England, where she teaches at Kingston University London.

Judith Kalman (1954–) was born in Budapest, Hungary and immigrated to Montreal with her family in 1959. She completed an MA in English and Creative Writing at the University of Windsor. Her writing has been published in numerous literary journals, including *Descant*, *Fiddlehead*, *Grain*, and *Prairie Fire*. She won the Tilden Canadian Literary Award in 1995, and received both the Gold Award and the President's Medal from the National Magazine Awards in 1996. Kalman is the author of the short story collection *The County of Birches* (1998), which was a finalist for the Danuta Gleed Literary Award and the National Jewish Book Award (US). She lives in Toronto.

Naïm Kattan (1928–) was born in Baghdad, Iraq and immigrated to Montreal in 1954, where he lives today. Although Arabic is his first language, Kattan writes in French. His semi-autobiographical trilogy *Adieu, Babylon* (1975; translated into English as *Farewell, Babylon*), *Les fruits arrachés* (1977; translated into English as *Paris Interlude*), and *La fiancée promise* (1983) describes a Jewish man's childhood in Baghdad, university education in Paris, and establishment in Ottawa and Montreal following his arrival in Canada in 1954. Kattan has been awarded the Prix Athanase-David, the Prix France-Canada, and the Prix Hervé Deluen by the Académie française. He is an Officer of the Order of Canada, a Knight of the National Order of Quebec, and a Chevalier of the Légion d'honneur.

Malca Litovitz (1952–2005) was born in Hamilton, Ontario. She completed an MA in English at McMaster University and a BEd at the University of Toronto. In 1988, she joined Seneca College, where she taught English Studies. Litovitz was published in numerous magazines and released five volumes of poetry, including *To Light, To Water* (1998), which won the Canadian Jewish Book Award for Poetry, *At The Moonbean Café* (2003), and *First Day* (2008). She was a member of the editorial board of *Parchment: Contemporary Canadian Jewish Writing*. In 2008, she collaborated with Elana Wolff to write *Slow Dancing: Creativity and Illness: Duologue and Rengas*, a poetry collection that explores her own battle with illness in the final months of her life. Litovitz died in Toronto.

Seymour Mayne (1944–) was born and raised in Montreal. He is Professor of English at the University of Ottawa, where he is also the coordinator of the Vered Jewish Canadian Studies program. Mayne is the prolific author, editor, or translator of more than seventy works, including anthologies and critical texts. He has won the Canadian Jewish Book Award four times for *Killing Time* (1994), *Jerusalem: An Anthology of Jewish Canadian Poetry* (1997), *A Rich Garland: Poems for A. M. Klein* (2000), and *September Rain* (2007). He is also the recipient of the J. I. Segal Prize and the ALTA (American Literary Translators Association) Poetry Translation Award for his renditions from the Yiddish. In 2009, Mayne received the Louis Rosenberg Canadian Jewish Studies Distinguished Service Award in recognition of his significant contribution to the field.

Goldie Morgentaler (1950–) was born in Montreal. She is Professor of English at the University of Lethbridge, where she specializes in nineteenth-century British and American Literature. Morgentaler is the daughter of the Yiddish writer Chava Rosenfarb and has translated much of Rosenfarb's work into English. Her translation of Rosenfarb's collection of short stories, *Survivors: Seven Short Stories* (2004), was awarded the Canadian Jewish Book Award for Yiddish Translation and the Modern Language Association's Fenia and Yaakov Memorial Prize in Yiddish Studies. She also translated Michel Tremblay's play *Les Belles-Soeurs* into Yiddish for performance at Montreal's Saidye Bronfman Centre (now the Segal Centre) in May 1992 and revived in 2012.

Sharon Nelson (1948–2016) spent her life in Montreal. A poet and essayist, she published multiple poetry chapbooks and eight volumes of poetry. Her collection, *The Work of Our Hands* (1992), was shortlisted for the A. M. Klein Prize for Poetry. She was the founding coordinator of the Feminist Caucus of the League of Canadian Poets, and a founding member, first executive member, and first advisory board chair of the Quebec Writers' Federation. Nelson managed Metonymy Productions, a company that produced technical literature and provided editorial services.

Merle Nudelman (1949–) was born and raised in Toronto, where she lives today. She is a poet, editor, teacher, and retired lawyer. Her verse has appeared in numerous publications, including the *Literary Review of Canada*, *Quills Canadian Poetry Magazine*, and the *White Wall Review*. Nudelman is the author of *Borrowed Light* (2003), which won the Canadian Jewish Book Award for Poetry, *We the Women* (2006), *The He We Knew* (2010), and *True as Moonlight* (2014). Her writing has also received several honorable mentions from the Scarborough Arts Council and the Arizona Authors Association. Nudelman conducts workshops on poetry and memoir writing and gives lectures on healing through creative expression.

Janis Rapoport (1946–) was born and raised in Toronto. She is an editor, poet, playwright, and creative writing instructor. Rapoport was associate editor of *Tamarack Review* from 1970 to 1982 and editor of *Ethos* from 1983 to 1986. She is the author of six volumes of poetry, including *Upon Her Fluent Route* (1991) and *After Paradise* (1996), and has held multiple writing residencies in both poetry and playwriting. Rapoport was the recipient of the New York Art Directors Club Award of Merit in 1983, an American Poetry Association Award in 1986, and a Canada Council for the Arts Award in 1991. She taught creative writing through the University of Toronto's School of Continuing Studies. Rapoport has lived in the United Kingdom and Peru.

Gina Roitman (1948–) was born in Passau, Germany to Holocaust survivors. Before immigrating to Montreal with her family, she lived in the Pocking-Waldstadt Displaced Persons Camp. Roitman has worked as a travel media consultant and as the head of her own communications agency. Her work has appeared in *carte-blanche*, the *Globe and Mail*, *Quills Canadian Poetry Magazine*, and has aired on CBC Radio. Roitman is the author of a collection of short stories, *Tell Me a Story, Tell Me the Truth* (2008), and a biography, *Midway to China and Beyond* (with Gary Bromberg, 2015). With Jane Hawtin, she co-produced the film *My Mother, the Nazi Midwife and Me*, a documentary about her search to uncover the horrifying truth about Jewish infant deaths in the Pocking-Waldstadt Displaced Persons Camp. The film aired on CBC's documentary channel in 2013 and was the recipient of a MADA (Making a Difference Award). Roitman lives in Saint-Colomban, Quebec.

Chava Rosenfarb (1923–2011) was born and raised in Lodz, Poland. She was incarcerated in the Lodz Ghetto from 1939 until it was liquidated in 1944, at which point she and her family were moved to Auschwitz. She survived with her mother and sister, and in 1950 they immigrated to Canada, settling in Montreal. Rosenfarb was a renowned and prolific Yiddish writer. The widely acclaimed *The Tree of Life: A Trilogy of Life in the Lodz Ghetto* (1972) was awarded the Manger Prize (one of Israel's most prestigious literary awards) in 1979. Her collection of short stories, *Survivors: Seven Short Stories* (2004), translated into English by her daughter Goldie Morgentaler, won the Canadian Jewish Book Award for Yiddish Translation and the Modern Language Association's Fenia and Yaakov Leviant Memorial Prize in Yiddish Studies. Rosenfarb died in Lethbridge, Alberta.

Robyn Sarah (1949–) was born in New York City but grew up in Montreal, where she lives today. She is the author of several volumes of poetry, two short story collections, and a book of essays on poetry. She won the CBC Poetry Prize in 1990 and her short story, "Accept My Story," was the recipient of a National Magazine Award in 1994. Her short story collection, *Promise of Shelter* (1997), was shortlisted for the Quebec Writers' Federation Award and *My Shoes Are Killing Me* (2015) won the Governor General's Literary Award for Poetry and the Canadian Jewish Literary Award. Sarah is the editor of *Undercurrents: New Voices in Canadian Poetry* (2011). She edited several volumes in the Essential Poets series issued by Porcupine's Quill, and is currently the poetry editor for Cormorant Books.

Libby Scheier (1946–2000) was born in Brooklyn and moved to Toronto in 1975. She was a member of the League of Canadian Poets, the Modern Language Association, and the Canadian Union of Educational Workers. She held various offices in the Writers' Union of Canada, including a term as chair of its Rights and Freedoms Committee. Scheier published four volumes of poetry, including *Second Nature* (1986) and *Kaddish for My Father* (1999), as well as a book of short stories, *Saints and Runners: Stories and a Novella* (1993). She was poetry editor for the *Toronto Star*, taught creative writing at York University from 1988 to 1994, and founded the Toronto Writing Workshop in 1994. Scheier died in Toronto.

Karen Shenfeld (1956–) was born and raised in Toronto. She is the author of three volumes of poetry: *The Law of Return* (1999), which won the Canadian Jewish Book Award for Poetry, *The Fertile Crescent*

(2005), and *My Father's Hands Spoke in Yiddish* (2010). Her work has appeared in numerous literary journals, both nationally and internationally, and has been featured on CBC Radio. Her personal documentary, *Il Giardino, The Gardens of Little Italy*, screened in 2007 at Planet in Focus, an annual environmental film festival. Shenfeld is also a peace activist and a member of Shalom Salaam Toronto. She divides her time between Toronto and Huntsville, Ontario.

Kenneth Sherman (1950–) was born and raised in Toronto, where he lives today. He is a poet, essayist, and educator. Sherman is the author of ten books of poetry, two collections of essays, and the memoir *Wait Time: A Memoir of Cancer* (2016). His essay collection, *What the Furies Bring* (2009), won a Canadian Jewish Book Award, an IPPY (an Independent Publisher Book Award), and was runner-up for the Foreword INDIES Book of the Year Award. Sherman was co-founder of the literary journal *Waves*. He taught humanities and communications at Sheridan College, creative writing at York University, and currently conducts poetry workshops.

David Solway (1941–) was born in northern Quebec. He has published numerous collections of poetry, including *Franklin's Passage* (2003), which won the Grand Prix du livre de Montréal. He was the recipient of the A. M. Klein Prize for Poetry for his translation, *Reaching for the Clear: The Poetry of Rhys Savarin* (2007). He is also the author of *The Big Lie: On Terror, Antisemitism, and Identity* (2007). Solway has worked as a scriptwriter for the CBC and has taught at various institutions, including Dawson College, John Abbott College, McGill University, and Brigham Young University. In 1999, he was writer-in-residence at Concordia University. He lives in Gananoque, Ontario.

J. J. Steinfeld (1946–) was born in a displaced persons camp in Germany to Polish Jewish Holocaust survivors. After living in several North American cities, he settled in Toronto and then moved steadily east, from Peterborough, where he received his master's degree in history from Trent University, to Ottawa and a PhD program at the University of Ottawa. He abandoned that program after two years and moved in 1980 to Charlottetown to write full time. Steinfeld is a fiction writer, poet, and playwright who has published two novels, *Our Hero in the Cradle of Confederation* (1987) and *Word Burials* (2009), and twelve short story collections, most recently *Identity Dreams and Memory Sounds* (2014) and *Absurdity, Woe Is Me, Glory Be* (2017). His poems have appeared in numerous anthologies and periodicals internationally, and over fifty of his one-act plays and a handful of his full-length plays have been performed in Canada and the United States.

Rhea Tregebov (1953–) was born in Saskatoon and raised in Winnipeg. She now lives in Vancouver, where she is Associate Professor in the Creative Writing Program at the University of British Columbia. Tregebov is the author of seven books of poetry, one novel, and five children's books. She is also the editor of the anthology *Arguing with the Storm: Stories by Yiddish Women Writers* (2007). She has been the recipient of a Pat Lowther Award, a *Prairie Schooner* Readers' Choice Award, and the *Malahat Review*'s Long Poem Prize. Her novel, *The Knife Sharpener's Bell* (2009), won the J. I. Segal Award for Fiction.

S. Weilbach (1931–) (a pseudonym; as a child known as Suzanne Weil) was born in Germany. During the Holocaust, she escaped with her family aboard the refugee ship *St. Louis*. She is a retired psychologist, therapist, teacher, and social activist. At the age of eighty, Weilbach published her first work, *Singing from the Darktime: A Childhood Memoir in Poetry and Prose* (2011), about her childhood in Germany and her experiences during World War II. It was awarded the Canadian Jewish Book Award for Poetry. She lives in British Columbia, where she is completing her first novel.

Helen Weinzweig (1915–2010) was born in Radom, Poland and immigrated to Canada in 1924 with her divorced mother. She published two novels and a short story collection. Her first short story, "Surprise," appeared in the *Canadian Forum* in 1967. Weinzweig's debut novel, *Passing Ceremony* (1973), was hailed as an important feminist work and her second novel, *Basic Black with Pearls* (1980), won the Toronto Book Award. *A View from the Room* (1989), her collection of short stories, was nominated for the Governor General's Literary Award. Three stories were adapted for the stage and C B C Radio by playwright Dave Carley as *A View from the Roof*. Weinzweig died in Toronto.

Elana Wolff is the author of four collections of poetry. Her third collection, *You Speak to Me in Trees* (2006), won the F. G. Bressani Prize for Poetry and her fourth collection, *Startled Night* (2011), was shortlisted for the ReLit Award. She is also the co-author with Malca Litovitz of *Slow Dancing: Creativity and Illness: Duologue and Rengas* (2008), and author of *Implicate Me: Short Essays on Reading Contemporary Poems* (2010). *Helleborous et Alchémille* (2013), a bilingual edition of her selected poems translated by Stéphanie Roesler, won the John Glassco Translation Prize. Wolff has taught English for Academic Purposes at York University and the Hebrew University of Jerusalem and is currently an editor at Guernica Editions. She lives in Toronto.

Shulamis Yelin (1913–2002) was born and raised in Montreal. She graduated from Macdonald College as a teacher in 1930 and moved to New York to study at Columbia University. Returning to Montreal, she completed an MA in English at Université de Montréal. Yelin had a distinguished teaching career and eventually was named a master teacher by the Protestant School Board of Greater Montreal. In 1963, she was the recipient of the LaMed Award from the National Foundation for Jewish Culture (US). Yelin published a volume of poetry, *Seeded in Sinai* (1975), and a collection of short stories, *Shulamis: Stories from a Montreal Childhood* (1983).

PERMISSIONS

Helen Weinzweig, "My Mother's Luck" reprinted from *A View from the Roof* (Goose Lane, 2001) with the permission of Daniel and Paul Weinzweig.

Shulamis Yelin, "Shekspir Was Jewis" reprinted from *Shulamis: Stories from a Montreal Childhood* (Véhicule Press, 1984) with the permission of Gilah Yelin Hirsch.

Sharon Nelson, "The Liberation" reprinted from *Blood Poems* (Fiddlehead Press, 1978) with permission of Peter Grogono, literary executor.

S. Weilbach, "The Linoleum-Floored Room" reprinted from *Singing from the Dark Time: A Childhood Memoir in Poetry and Prose* (McGill-Queen's University Press, 2011) with the permission of the publisher.

Libby Scheier, "Cut Flowers" reprinted from *Second Nature* (Coach House Press, 1986) with the permission of ECW Press.

Seymour Mayne, "The Story of My Aunt's Comforter" reprinted from *The Old Blue Couch and Other Stories* (Ronald P. Frye & Company, 2012) with the permission of the author.

Ron Charach, "One Laughing Uncle" reprinted from *Selected Portraits* (Wolsak & Wynn, 2007) with the permission of the author.

Matt Cohen, "Trotsky's First Confessions." Copyright Stickland Limited 2016. First published in *Lives of the Mind Slaves* (Porcupine's Quill, 1994).

David Solway, "Acid Blues" reprinted from *Selected Poems*, (Signal Editions, 1982) with the permission of the author.

J. J. Steinfeld, "The Idea of Assassination, Toronto, 1973" reprinted from *The Miraculous Hand and Other Stories* (Ragweed Press, 1991) with the permission of the author.

Karen Shenfeld, "Theatre Doctor" reprinted from *The Law of Return* (Guernica Editions, 1999) with the permission of the author.

Karen Shenfeld, "My Father's Hands Spoke in Yiddish" reprinted from *My Father's Hands Spoke in Yiddish* (Guernica Editions, 2010) with the permission of the author.

Kenneth Sherman, "Who Knows You Here?" reprinted from *What the Furies Bring* (Porcupine's Quill, 2009) with permission of the publisher.

David Solway, "After the Flood" reprinted from *Selected Poems* (Signal Editions, 1998) with the permission of the author.

Nora Gold, "Yosepha" reprinted from *Marrow and Other Stories* (Warwick, 1998) with the permission of the author. First published in *Lilith Magazine*.

Ronna Bloom, "Personal Effects" reprinted from *Personal Effects* (Pedlar Press, 2000) with the permission of the author.

Chava Rosenfarb, "Bergen Belsen Diary, 1945" reprinted from *Tablet Magazine* (January 27, 2014) with the permission of Goldie Morgentaler, translator and literary executor.

Goldie Morgentaler, "My Mother's Very Special Relationship" reprinted from the *Guardian* (14 November 2015) with the permission of the author.

Ron Charach, "The Only Man in the World His Size" reprinted from *Selected Portraits* (Wolsak & Wynn, 2007) with the permission of the author.

Judith Kalman, "The County of Birches" reprinted from *The County of Birches* (Douglas & McIntyre, 1998) with the permission of the author.

Robyn Sarah, "After the Storm" reprinted from *Pause for Breath* (Biblioasis 2009) with the permission of the publisher and the author.

Gabriella Goliger, "Maladies of the Inner Ear" reprinted from *Song of Ascent: Stories* (Raincoast Books, 2000) with the permission of the author.

Sharon Nelson, "On Tasting Any Fruit for the First Time in the Season" reprinted from *This Flesh, These Words* (Ekstasis Editions, 2002) with permission of Peter Grogono, literary executor.

Susan Glickman, "Between God and Evil" reprinted from *Running in Prospect Cemetery: New and Selected Poems* (Signal Editions, 2004) with the permission of the author.

Eva Hoffman, "Exile" reprinted from *Lost in Translation* (Penguin, 1990) with the permission of the author.

Malca Litovitz, "Provincial Olive" reprinted from *To Light, To Water* (Lugus, 1998) with permission of the Malca Litovitz Estate.

Elana Wolff, "Snow Bolls" reprinted from *You Speak to Me in Trees* (Guernica Editions, 2006) with the permission of the publisher.

Naïm Kattan, "Cities of Birth" reprinted from *Queen's Quarterly* 112.4 (Winter 2005) with the permission of the author.

Malca Litovitz, "The Welcoming" reprinted from *To Light, To Water* (Lugus, 1998) with permission of the Malca Litovitz Estate.

Merle Nudelman, "The Sabbath Queen" reprinted from *Borrowed Light* (Guernica Editions, 2003) with the permission of the publisher.

Ronna Bloom, "Yom Kippur, 1998" reprinted from *Personal Effects* (Pedlar Press, 2000) with the permission of the author.

Janis Rapoport, "Pesach 5735" reprinted from *Winter Flowers* (Hounslow Press, 1979) with permission of the author.

Gina Roitman, "Pesach en Provence" reprinted from *Tell Me a Story, Tell Me the Truth* (Second Story Press, 2008) with the permission of the publisher.

Merle Nudelman, "The Finding" reprinted from *Borrowed Light* (Guernica Editions, 2003) with the permission of the publisher.

Janis Rapoport, "From This Time Forth and Forever" reprinted from *After Paradise* (Simon and Pierre, 1996) with the permission of the author.

Libby Scheier, "Elat Chayyim" reprinted from *Kaddish for My Father* (ECW Press, 1999) with the permission of Jacob Scheier.

Rhea Tregebov, "Some Notes on the Story of Esther" reprinted from *Language in Her Eye*. Eds. Libby Scheier, Sarah Sheard, Eleanor Wachtel (Coach House Press, 1990) with the permission of the author.

Robyn Sarah, "Vidiu" reprinted from *A Day's Grace* (Porcupine's Quill, 2003) with the permission of the publisher.

Susan Glickman, "(The) Others" reprinted from *Henry Moore's Sheep* (Signal Editions, 1990) with the permission of the author.

Elana Wolff, "Tikva" reprinted from *Birdheart* (Guernica Editions, 2001), with the permission of the publisher.

17 18 19 20 21 · 5 4 3 2 1